"Blake's writing is graceful, often elegiac, and her characters hum with humanity. Her examination of the divisive issues facing an influential religious organization in a fast-changing society gives a rich background to an entertaining mystery." —*Publishers Weekly*

"This well-put-together . . . mystery offers an in-depth look at the Episcopalian world and is sure to appeal to crime-fiction fans with an interest in the religion." —*Booklist*

"[An] assured and satisfying debut novel. Ms. Blake has pulled off quite a coup . . . and her creation of a protagonist . . . is both human and humane. Readers are not only entertained but enlightened, and left eagerly awaiting the next Lily Connor adventure." —*Denton Record-Chronicle*

"Like Father Andrew Greeley, Michelle Blake manages to pull us not only into a good twisting mystery, but into the fascinating tensions and politics of a troubled congregation. She wields a fine double-edged sword."
—Craig Holden, author of the highly acclaimed thriller *Four Corners of the Night*

"*The Tentmaker* is a fabulous amateur sleuth tale that centers on individuals questioning their beliefs. Though the story line is entertaining, this novel clearly focuses on Lily, an intrepid, complex character who hopefully will take her 'tentmaking' skills to future parishes and mysteries."
—*Midwest Book Review*

"Like Chesterton's Father Brown, Lily is a pretty good priest for a detective." —*Boston Magazine*

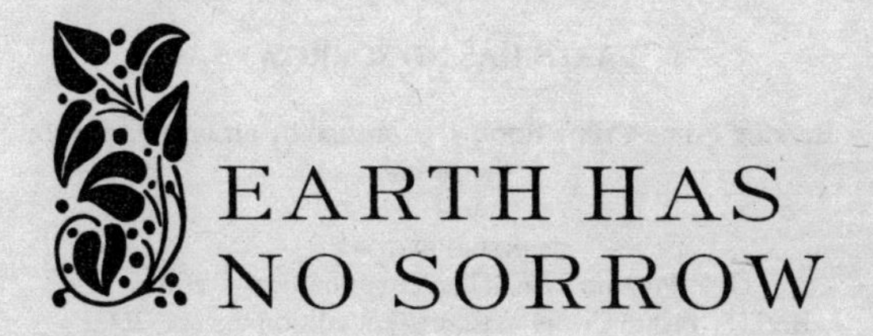

EARTH HAS NO SORROW

MICHELLE BLAKE

BERKLEY PRIME CRIME, NEW YORK

EARTH HAS NO SORROW

A Berkley Prime Crime Book / published by arrangement with the author

PRINTING HISTORY
G. P. Putnam's Sons hardcover edition / 2001
Berkley Prime Crime mass-market edition / June 2002

Cover art by Greg Harlin/Wood Ronsavill Harlin Inc.

For information address: G. P. Putnam's Sons,
a division of Penguin Putnam Inc.,
375 Hudson Street, New York, New York 10014.

Visit our website at
www.penguinputnam.com

ISBN: 0-425-18523-0

Berkley Prime Crime books are published
by The Berkley Publishing Group,
a division of Penguin Putnam Inc.,
375 Hudson Street, New York, New York 10014.
The name BERKLEY PRIME CRIME and
the BERKLEY PRIME CRIME design
are trademarks belonging to Penguin Putnam Inc.

PRINTED IN THE UNITED STATES OF AMERICA

10 9 8 7 6 5 4 3 2 1

TO SAM, KATHARINE, AND DENNIS

WITH ALL MY LOVE

Earth has no sorrow
that heaven cannot cure.

"Come, Ye Disconsolate," words by

THOMAS MOORE

CHAPTER 1

The six glass columns glowed in the muted light. A cold mist had lifted earlier, leaving a gray cloud cover, appropriate for the ceremony and the day. Lily pulled her red gloves out of the pocket of her coat and put them on, then wrapped a red wool scarf more closely around her neck. Her braid got caught in the scarf; she freed it and took a step forward, toward the Holocaust Memorial, where a man in a black fedora stood reading out loud from the inscription on the third column, the one representing Sobibor.

The columns rose out of a concrete walkway surrounded by a small park. A few hundred yards away, tourists in Faneuil Hall sipped microbrew and wore Mickey Mouse hats with BOSTON printed across the front. From the nearby streets came the noise of traffic and the distant strains of construction work behind high wooden fences. But an air of quiet surrounded the memorial, as if it were set apart by the dense reality of its purpose. Lily could hear perfectly.

". . . a childhood friend of mine once found a raspberry in the camp and carried it in her pocket all day to present to me that night on a leaf," the man read. "Imagine a world in which your entire possession is one raspberry and you give it to your friend."

Lily felt surprised to find herself near tears. Over the years she had heard so many testimonies, read so many descriptions of the camps, that she had begun to fear she was beyond feeling. She quickly wiped her eyes and stood straighter. At moments like this, her height served her well (she was usually the tallest woman in a group and often one of the taller people): though the crowd was dense, she could see the reader, and she was spared any threat from the lurking claustrophobia that sometimes jumped her in close spaces.

In front of her, Anna Banieka stood next to Charlie Cooper. The top of Anna's head just reached Charlie's shoulder; Lily noticed the woman's scalp showing through her black hair—dyed and permed, vampish, from another era. Anna's narrow shoulders looked lopsided from the back, but her bearing was erect. Lily couldn't see Anna's face. But her own tears suddenly felt sentimental.

A gust of wind blew grit and sand over the fence of the construction site. Lily turned away, and when she turned back, she saw that Anna had taken Charlie's arm. He leaned down and whispered to his companion, then they both moved quietly to the side of the crowd, where Anna sat on a low stone wall near the entrance to the memorial. Charlie stood next to her, watching the ceremony. Anna closed her eyes, and her slight smile seemed distant, almost ironic.

Lily turned again to face the memorial. After the reading, there were a few moments for silent prayer and reflection, then the crowd moved on to the next column, the one representing Majdanek. Lily felt a tap on her shoulder and turned to see Charlie behind her. He was a couple of inches taller than she was, with the same coloring—thick brown hair, brown eyes, pale skin. But Charlie's face was long, shadowed, Goya-like, and his eyes were dark brown. Her own face was rounder, much less dramatic, and her eyes light brown, sometimes hazel, sometimes almost green.

"Anna wants to start for the cathedral now," he whispered. "It's going to take her a while to walk there. She's not feeling so great."

"Okay," said Lily, softly, then asked, "Can I come, too?"

"Yes," he said. "That's why I told you. Let's go."

Lily wondered if it was all right for her to leave with Anna and Charlie; the three of them had planned the ceremony and the church service that would follow. But they'd had the foresight to put Bishop Spencer in charge of the day's proceedings, and he was reliable. Besides, Lily felt cold and a little bored. She followed Charlie without looking back.

Anna walked slowly up the steps to Government Center, her arm linked through Charlie's. She appeared to be leaning on him now, and her face looked almost gray.

"What did you think?" Charlie asked Anna as they crossed the plaza, moonlike with its empty stretches of white concrete platforms and plateaus.

"Of that?" asked Anna. She inclined her head back and to the right, in the direction of the memorial.

"Yes," said Charlie. "Of that."

She smiled. "It's a good thing to do," she said. "I appreciate the effort. And I appreciate the sentiment behind it."

Sentimental, thought Lily, like my tears.

Anna put her other hand on Lily's arm. "May I?" she asked. "I can't seem to get my breath today."

"Of course," said Lily, then she consciously slowed her pace.

"I've always liked the fact that they put Niemöller—that quotation from him—at the entrance, or is it the exit?," said Anna. "He was an anti-Semite, you know. He preached very ardent sermons on the subject of Jewish conversion. Then he saw the light, as they say, when Hitler tried to take over his church."

"It says on the inscription he was anti-Semitic," said Charlie.

"I know," said Anna. "It's the most interesting thing about him."

Charlie laughed. "What's the most interesting thing," he asked, "that he was an anti-Semite?"

"No," said Anna. "That he changed. So few people are capable of that."

"Do you think?" asked Lily. "I know most people don't change much in their lives. But I believe almost everyone *can* change."

Anna was silent for a moment, then she said, "Yes. Of course you're right. Although, it's very hard."

Lily felt pleased, as if she had just gotten an "A" from a favorite teacher. In fact, Lily had been a student of Anna Banieka's writing for a long time, long before she had met the woman herself. Years ago, at the end of their first term in seminary, Lily had given Charlie the book *Work Makes Freedom.*

He had considered it the most depressing Christmas gift he'd ever received. But he'd gone on to read the rest of Anna's work: the two studies of anti-Jewish imagery and language in the early church; the book of interviews with rescuers; the book of interviews with perpetrators; and the three volumes of poems.

Anna lived and taught in a college town in western Massachusetts. When she came to Boston, she stayed with the brothers at the monastery on Brattle, The Society of St. Peter, where Charlie now lived. Anna and Charlie had gotten to know each other over time. Then Charlie had introduced Lily to Anna, and the circle had been completed—or so it felt to Lily.

Especially over the last year, since she had joined the Ecumenical Council, Lily had come to rely on Anna as a source of advice and even comfort. That hadn't been a conscious decision, but from time to time, and increasingly,

Lily found herself calling Anna at home to ask her opinion. Whenever she called, Anna seemed more than just glad to hear from her; the older woman sounded thrilled, even grateful. Over the past couple of months, with the planning for the service, they had talked at least once a week.

After a short walk down Tremont, the three of them reached the Episcopal Cathedral of St. Michael's and All Angels. Anna paused and glanced up toward the building entrance.

"Do you want to go in through the bookstore, around the side?" asked Lily. "There aren't as many stairs that way."

"No, no," said Anna. "I just need to catch my breath."

Her hold on Lily's arm tightened as they started the climb. Lily began to feel concerned; Anna's skin was still pale, despite the cold wind. With her dark hair, large, dark eyes, and broad mouth, she looked like a twentieth-century Madonna—an aging Audrey Hepburn as the Holy Mother. Anna moved steadily toward the top, and soon they stood inside, at the north end of the narthex.

Charlie reached out and pulled on one of the smaller doors leading to the north aisle. It didn't open.

"Great," he said. "I knew there'd be some kind of foul-up."

"They probably haven't unlocked everything yet," said Lily. "I'll check the ones at the other end."

But when she tried the doors at the opposite end, she found those locked, too.

"Weird," she said. "Try the main doors."

"Those are never open," said Charlie, but he pulled the large wooden handle and the door swung out silently. "Cool," he said, then bowed to Anna, who stood in the same spot at which they had first entered. Her color looked better, thought Lily, as she walked back to her friends.

Lily reached the central door just ahead of Anna. Courtesy told her to wait and go second, but something else told her to go first. As she walked into the huge empty space, she heard a crashing sound, something heavy being dropped nearby. Where are the lights, she wondered. And then, as her eyes adjusted, she saw the brilliant red swath of color draped over the main altar, the black and white swastika centered across the front, and, finally, the body of a child, dressed in the striped uniform of the camps, swinging by a rope from a crossbeam above the nave.

CHAPTER 2

Lily couldn't take her eyes off the small feet of the hanging body. They were bare and white, a pure white, unreal.

"It's a doll," said Anna. She had slipped in and sat down in the last pew.

Charlie walked up behind Anna and placed his right hand on her shoulder.

"Yes," he said. "It must be."

"It is," Anna said. "And quite a good one. At Beth Shalom, they had one crucified—nailed on a cross. I never understood the significance."

"What do you mean?" he asked.

"I just didn't understand—did the child somehow represent Jesus? It was supposed to be a Jewish child—probably—it was dressed the same as this one. But surely they weren't making some profound theological connection between the suffering of Jesus and the suffering of the Jewish children in the camps."

Lily listened to this exchange through a veil of confusion. She found that she had sat down, two pews in front of Anna.

"You're giving a group of crackpots an awful lot of credit," said Charlie. "You want these shenanigans to mean something, but I doubt they ever think about what it means. This is just visceral hatred pouring out. There's no statement here."

"Don't underestimate them," said Anna.

"Who's 'them'?" Lily finally asked. She felt surprised to hear her own voice.

"Who knows?" said Charlie. "After Beth Shalom, the police questioned a group of skinheads who had spray-painted a Jewish cemetery nearby. But this stuff obviously isn't done by kids. There's too much theological content—however whacked-out that content might be."

"They've done it before? How often?"

"Just that once. Right?" he asked Anna.

Anna shrugged. "As far as I know, but it doesn't matter. I hate giving these people attention. It's what they want, it's why they do it."

Charlie walked up to the altar and returned with a Bible. When he held it up, pages facing outward, Lily could see red print in among the black.

"What is it?" she asked.

"One of theirs," he said. "Just like the one at Beth Shalom."

The book had been left open to John 19, the crucifixion. Each time the text cited "the Jews," the two words appeared in red, bold-faced type. All the language spoken by "the Jews" also appeared in red.

After a moment, Charlie handed Anna the book, walked back to the central doors through which they had just entered, and locked them.

"Now," he said, returning to sit in the pew between Lily and Anna, "what do we do?"

Alone in the nave, Lily half-folded, half-wadded the Nazi flag and stuck it under a pew in the far, right-hand corner. Even though no one ever sat back there, she knew this wasn't a very good hiding place, but she was too rattled to come up with anything better. At that moment, she thought of Benton, her hometown in Texas—of the "honor guard," the campers who got to take down the American flag every evening at taps. She remembered how reverently they had faced each other and matched the corners, always keeping the fabric from touching the ground.

Charlie had gone to the cathedral offices in search of a ladder, although the crossbeam was so impossibly high they'd never be able to reach it, ladder or no. The rope must have been flung over the top and pulled back down. For now, they'd have to be satisfied with cutting the rope and leaving a piece still hanging.

Anna had returned to the narthex to stall any early arrivals. Her plan had been to make up a story about the lights being out or the keys being lost—a fixable, meaningless hitch delaying the ceremonies for a few minutes. She had assured Lily that people expected a woman of her age with her background to be vague, even dithering. "This won't be the first time I've used it to my advantage."

Anna, Charlie, and Lily had agreed that the service should go on as planned, so they'd had to act quickly. Now, as Lily turned around from tucking the last of the scarlet fabric under the pew, she saw Charlie struggling through the door to the right of the main altar, the top part of a metal ladder preceding him by a few feet.

"Get the end of this thing, would you?" he called out to her.

She didn't bow to the altar when she crossed before it. Would they have time to consecrate this space before the service? She couldn't see how.

"Where did you find it?" Lily asked. She grasped the top, waited while he locked the side door behind him, then helped him carry the ladder to a spot just below the hanging doll.

"Lying on the floor of the sacristy. I think we heard it hit the ground when we walked in."

"So they left just as we got here?" asked Lily. "Someone must have seen them, right?"

"Not in the bookstore," said Charlie. "I asked. And the diocesan offices are closed already." He adjusted the small grips at the base of each leg of the ladder and made sure the hinged arms were locked. Then he climbed toward the figure dangling above them.

Lily tried to avoid looking at the doll. She had managed to act businesslike, but she felt a disturbing swirl of revulsion, almost nausea, as she glanced up at the small feet turning clockwise then counterclockwise.

She watched Charlie pull a Swiss army knife out of his back pocket and begin to saw away at the rope.

"Get ready to catch the—whatever it is," he said.

"Can't we just let it fall?" She didn't want to hold the thing in her arms.

"I'm not sure," said Charlie. "I think the head is china, or porcelain, or something. It might break and make a big loud mess. Just try to catch it, okay?"

"Okay," she said and positioned herself next to the ladder, holding on to steady it. "Why didn't you tell me about Beth Shalom?"

"Boy, it's a thick one, nylon," he muttered. "I'm not sure it's going to—whoa . . ."

With that Lily saw the figure falling toward her. Instinctively, she raised her arms and caught the doll just above her own head.

At that moment someone entered through the main door. Lily turned and watched Anna walk toward them.

"People are starting to arrive," she said. "I put Jeffrey Tatum in charge. He'll shame them into good behavior, at least." Anna glanced over at Lily and the doll and asked, "Do you want me to take that?"

Lily handed her the limp bundle and stared at its porcelain face. Someone had glued a striped fabric cap to the top of the head. Now that the doll lay in Anna's arms, the eyes were closed and it suddenly looked perversely comical, macabre, a comedian's dummy suited up to look like a child of the death camps.

"Where's the flag?" asked Anna.

"I stuck it under the last pew," said Lily, pointing to the corner.

"Can't we find a better hiding place?" asked Anna. "I don't want anyone to see these things."

"But why?" asked Lily. "Isn't that the reason we're doing this service in the first place?—to expose this kind of insanity."

Anna sat down suddenly in the closest pew and lay the doll next to her. Again, the color had drained from her face; she seemed not to have heard what Lily said. Then she took a deep breath and gave the doll an odd, almost affectionate, pat on the head. "When a child is a certain age," she said, "—four or five, something like that, I can't remember—he does things to get attention. So you learn to give him attention for the things you want him to do, but not for the things you want him to stop doing. These people are like bad little children."

"But ignoring them won't stop them either," said Charlie, who had climbed down from the ladder. "Or it hasn't yet."

"No," said Anna. "But I'm sure it makes them very, very unhappy not to be noticed." She paused and asked, "Is there some way we can make the altar all right again, fit for use?"

"I thought of that," said Lily. "We could do a version of the dedication and consecration—the setting apart of the altar. It's supposed to be the bishop but—"

"No," said Anna. "It should be you. And Charlie. No more people. And someone who saw what this place looked like when we got here."

"Okay," said Lily. "What about the altar?"

"Let's leave it bare," said Charlie.

"Yes," said Anna. "Just like this."

"I'd like to have candles," said Lily, "to light at the end of the dedication."

"Good," said Anna. "That would be good."

"Okay," said Lily. "Charlie and I will get rid of all this stuff and find the candles. You stall them for a few more minutes out front. Then we'll meet back here and do a quick consecration."

Charlie studied her for a couple of seconds. "You sound like someone in an ecclesiastical gangster movie," he said.

The three of them stood behind the altar, Lily in the center, Anna and Charlie on either side of her. At first, Lily felt distracted by the sound of people in the narthex, restless from the wait. And it had been a while since she'd been behind an altar—more than a year, since her last job as an interim priest. But after a moment of silent meditation, she focused on the altar, on the presence of Charlie and Anna, on her task.

"Let us now pray for the setting apart of the Altar," she read from The Book of Common Prayer. They all said the responsive prayers together. Lily ended with the dedication. "Grant that all who eat and drink at this holy Table may be fed and refreshed by his flesh and blood, be forgiven their sins, united with one another, and strengthened for your service." But her mind, and her heart, had been elsewhere throughout the ritual.

They said the blessing, and Charlie lit the candles. There was a moment of calm while they stood in silence. Then a loud pounding on the door to their left made Lily jump.

"Someone's impatient," said Anna. "Shall we see who it is?"

CHAPTER 3

Bishop Spencer stood in the doorway, his black coat buttoned up to his chin.

"An Episcopal visitation," said Charlie.

"What's going on?" asked Spencer, not amused. He was a large man, broad and strong, nearing sixty, with dark brown skin and graceful, long-fingered hands. But with his coat still on and his wool cap pulled down over his ears, he looked like a child, thought Lily, an overgrown child in a pout.

"We're so sorry," said Anna. "For some reason the preparations became muddled. We had asked for—it doesn't matter. In any case, we're ready now."

Lily couldn't help but appreciate Anna's smooth lying. The woman sounded irritated, as if the altar had been draped mistakenly in the green of Pentecost services and not the Nazi flag.

"Can we get started then?" asked Spencer. He took off his hat and began to unbutton his coat.

"Aren't you the celebrant?" asked Charlie.

"In name only," said Spencer, as he turned toward the robing room. "With you three around, in name only."

Lily had an off-key moment of delight at their successful ruse. Then she realized she had no idea why they were lying to begin with, and her delight was replaced by a surge of irritation with Charlie and Anna. They were acting like children themselves, she thought, children with a secret.

The three of them—Lily, Charlie, and Anna—had been planning this service for months, with help from Bishop Spencer. A year ago—after her father's death and a stint as an interim priest for a wealthy parish on Beacon Hill—Spencer had talked Lily into serving on the Ecumenical Council. Though she had been ordained in the Diocese of Eastern Massachusetts, she was a tentmaker, a priest who chose to make her living outside the church. Spencer had made it his mission to be sure Lily stayed connected to the diocese, to her vocation, and to him.

Lily had agreed to join the council because she already had an idea, something she wanted them to do: the Episcopal Church would sponsor a penitential service during Lent in which the larger church—they invited everyone, from Catholic to Quaker—repented for its part in the Holocaust of World War II. She was surprised by the number of people who'd come. The pews were almost full, and the huge room had begun to feel hot and stuffy. Bishop Spencer led them through the opening prayers. Then Anna patted Lily's knee, stood, and walked to the lectern.

Once at the lectern, Anna stood for a few seconds, staring out into the cathedral. People began to shift in their seats, cough. Then Lily looked more closely and saw that Anna was holding herself up, grasping the edge of the lectern for support. Lily felt the beginnings of slow panic; she glanced at Spencer and could tell from his face he was ready to spring, to catch Anna, to give a sermon, whatever was needed. Lily relaxed a fraction.

Finally, Anna nodded to Charlie. He got up and took a folding chair from the nearest corner. He set it up at the top of the three broad steps leading to the chancel. They must have agreed before the service on that arrangement.

Once Anna was settled in the chair, she said, "I have to begin by apologizing for sitting down, I know it's hard to see me, for some of you. I will try to make sure you can hear me."

Anna's words carried out into the cathedral with a sharp clarity. Lily could see color in her cheeks. She could also see what a beautiful woman Anna had once been, with her large, dark eyes and delicate features.

"I had a sermon prepared, of course," Anna continued. "And I'm not fast-thinking enough to abandon it entirely. But I've been very affected by all that's happened today, so I'd like to speak more informally than I had planned. Please be patient with pauses and inconsistencies. I promise to try to tie the threads of my thought together at the end." She shifted in the chair and smiled her distant smile.

Lily was listening, but having trouble hearing. She could hear the words, literally, but her mind was back in the moment when the doll fell into her arms with the rope around its neck. She wanted to concentrate on what Anna was saying—she was talking about understanding, trying to understand the Holocaust. But Lily's mind kept getting drawn to the short piece of rope hanging from the rafter behind her. She couldn't turn around and look. She forced herself to focus on Anna.

". . . I was, of course, one of the lucky ones, in many, many ways. To begin with, I survived. That was in large part because I was there such a short time. Although my brother, my youngest brother, who ended up with me, did not survive.

"But more important, I think, in terms of understanding, is the reason I was sent to the camps. My family—a large, Polish Catholic family—hid Jews. And though I was young—only ten when Germany invaded Poland—I understood what we were doing.

"And I understood that what we did was illegal. And I understood when we were arrested that we were sent to the camps because of something we'd done—something good and right. We were not sent because of something we *were*—that is to say Jewish, or homosexual, or Romany. Although the Nazis didn't think much of Poles—still, that's not why we were arrested . . ."

Lily's throat felt dry, and a little sweat had formed on her forehead. She thought for a moment she might have a fever. She took a quick inventory of her body—there were no aches, pains, no headache. She wished she could see the rope. She wondered if anyone had noticed it yet.

". . . Even so, when I arrived in this country I was deeply confused and embittered. In part, I wanted to blame someone for all that had happened to me and my family," Anna was saying. "But I didn't know whom to blame, and in my blindness, I began by blaming the victims."

Lily found it hard to imagine Anna ever having been confused and embittered. The woman had always struck Lily as a person of such clarity and compassion—even, or especially, Anna's book on the lives of former Nazis showed a kind of breathtaking balance of perception, an innate sense of these criminals as human beings.

"I came to see that I needed more than personal understanding," Anna continued. "So I began to study. How could the Holocaust have happened? Where did it start? Why did everyone do so little to stop it?" As she asked the last two questions, the tone of her voice changed, becoming more certain.

"And the amazing—and horrible—thing that happened was that I kept ending up at the door of the church. The entity that had spawned and shaped contemporary anti-Semitism, which was the force that allowed Hitler to build the camps and carry out his plan for annihilation, was the church . . ."

Lily noticed how quickly the room had grown silent. Before, people had been attentive, polite, but there were the rustlings and throat-clearings that let you know the congregation's comfortable. Someone's out there planning a meal or wondering how he got the spot on his trousers. At that moment, though, it sounded as if no one were moving at all.

". . . There are many examples. I'll give you just one. In 1215, Pope Innocent III convened the Fourth Lateran Council—a huge ecclesiastical event. People traveled for days, and the council lasted for months.

"The business of the Council was to issue decrees—about dress, practice, doctrine, thought. The last four decrees issued by the council all concerned Jews. Jews could not walk out during Easter Week, lest they seem to be mocking the death of Christ. They could not lend money at high rates to Christians. And, most interesting, Jews were required to wear clothes that distinguished them from Christians.

"Distinguishing clothes," Anna repeated. "In some parts of Europe this took the form of round yellow badges, to signify the Jews' supposed love of money and gold. The reason for these badges was to discourage commingling, or intercourse—from the Latin text—between Jewish men and Christian women, and vice versa.

"I remind you, these are edicts issued by the Catholic Church, of which some of us in this room are members. We must know our own histories if we want to do the right thing now, in the present moment. The church has kept too many secrets for too long. It is time for those secrets to be revealed so we can be forgiven. Just as we must reveal the secrets of our own lives in order to be forgiven—"

Lily heard a small sound far behind her, something between a sigh and a groan. Anna seemed to hear it, too. She looked into the congregation, in the direction of the noise. When she spoke again, her voice had softened.

"It's hard to miss the striking parallels between the laws of Nazi Germany and the edicts of the church. Indeed, all of these edicts—except walking out on Easter, I believe—appeared in some form or other in the 1933 Nuremberg Laws . . ."

Again, Lily heard a muffled commotion behind her, as of someone whispering, trying to leave, she wasn't sure. She turned around but couldn't see anything.

"In the epic documentary, *Shoah,* someone asks a Polish man, standing outside the Catholic church in the town, why he thinks the Holocaust happened to the Jews. And the man says it's because they killed Christ. The Shoah happened to them because they killed Christ. How does he know this? asks the interviewer. Because the church says so, the man replies. Because the church says it's so.

"This is the kind of spiritual lie the church has been telling us for centuries. And many of us have believed these lies, indeed, we have taken comfort in them. But the lies need to stop. And the secrets need to be told. Because they harm us all, they harm our families and our children and—"

More noise from behind caused Lily to turn again. This time she saw a tall, pale man—Jeffrey Tatum—standing amid the seated crowd. Then directly in front of him, a gray-haired man fell forward, banged his head against the corner of the pew, and collapsed onto the stone floor of the aisle.

CHAPTER 4

On the square in front of the courthouse in Benton, Texas, stood a large, granite rectangular monument—like a hewn mountain rising out of the grass. On the monument were the names of men who had fought in the war for Texas's independence. Rising from the granite were two flagpoles: one flew the United States flag; the other the Texas flag, a single star on a field of red, white, and blue. For some reason, this was the spot Lily had remembered when she thought of her childhood duties on the honor guard, even though those ceremonies had actually taken place at the old YMCA camp outside of town.

West of the town square was the white section of Benton—rows of clapboard houses, ranging from one-room hovels to large, Victorian-style homes with wraparound porches, leaded glass doors and windows, turrets, and widow's walks. Farther west stood the brick split-levels of the fifties and sixties. And farther still, small farms and cattle ranches spread out across the hill country, with their herds of Angus and Holstein and Hereford. Her father's ranch lay as far west as you could get and still be in the town limits.

If you walked east from the square and on past the first two streets, you came to French Street (named for a former resident, not a nationality). Beyond French was the Mexican-American community, Frenchtown—almost fifty square blocks of houses with four grocerias, two clothing stores, the equivalent of a general store, a dry-cleaning and tailoring service, a smattering of seamstress and laundry services, and a couple of restaurants. Farther east, as the town wandered off into the surrounding hills, lived both the richer and the poorer Mexican-Americans—those who owned working ranches and those who worked subsistence farms.

In the center of Frenchtown stood St. Joseph's Parish and Educational Center—its bell tower rose, solid, resonant, against the span of Texas sky. At one time, St. Joe's had been a mission church, and the courtyard of the original building was still in use. But the church itself had been replaced in the fifties with a flat, square brick building that housed the chapel, the church offices and meeting halls, and the twenty-odd classrooms of the school—attended by the children of most of the Mexican-American families (the Pentecostalists had their own school on the west side of town) and the handful of white Catholic families in Benton, the group to which Lily belonged.

In the summer, a few of the children from St. Joe's—Chicano and white—went to the Y-camp. Every evening, the whole camp would stand at attention, with someone playing the trumpet very badly in the background, and watch the flags being lowered. One August afternoon, with heat radiating off the packed earth of the drill field, a girl had fainted. Lily couldn't remember the girl's name—she was blonde and tiny—but she had been one of the handful of other Anglo girls at St. Joe's.

The whole ordeal with the Nazi banner, the memories of honor guard—and the fact that the anniversary of her father's death was next month—had startled up a flock of details from Lily's childhood. Also, the blonde girl had been the first person Lily had ever seen faint. (She'd seen her mother pass out from drinking, but that was different, slow and big and sloppy.) Lily had thought the girl was dead. She remembered the shock, and then the guilt-ridden thrill that had gone through her body when the girl moaned and dropped.

Lily had seen people faint since then—she'd done two years of field work as a hospital chaplain. But Frank Leslie's collapse in the cathedral counted as the second most exciting fainting spell she'd ever witnessed. There was something about its coming, as it did, near the end of Anna's sermon, that made the event seem like part of the message.

Frank was one of Lily's favorite members of ecumenical circles in Boston, because he didn't pretend to be a Vatican II priest. He was a traditional, even conservative, Catholic who felt called—she'd never been entirely sure why—to engage in dialogue with liberation theologians, gay and lesbian Catholics, Protestants, Jews, Muslims. He would listen and, when asked, say what he believed, which often outraged a good percentage of people in the room.

No one stayed angry at Frank for long. He had a sort of good-hearted, shabby absent-mindedness that seemed to endear him to church types. Once it became clear what had happened in the cathedral, the aisle filled with friends.

Frank woke up immediately, mortified, refusing help, wanting to go home. He claimed this happened when he didn't eat right—he had skipped lunch and meant to pick up something on the way to the service, but never did. Everyone (these were mostly church people, Lily noted, and all seemed to need to be involved in one way or the other) insisted that he go to a hospital or at least get someone to look at the rapidly swelling, deep blue bump on his forehead. He had evidently hit a blood vessel.

But Frank had been adamant. After he had convinced everyone he didn't need to see a brain surgeon, his biggest problem had been fighting off the myriad offers of rides.

Lily had left when the pandemonium of people trying to help had made her begin to feel dizzy herself. When she'd reached the door behind the altar, she could hear Anna taking charge, shooing people back into their seats, insisting they leave Frank alone, give him air.

Lily had stopped on the stairs leading down to the bookstore. She now sat on the top step, sorting through her memories of Benton. She had just conjured the face of her kindergarten teacher when she heard footsteps in the hall behind her. She didn't turn around. She recognized Charlie's "monastery shuffle"—as she had dubbed it—developed over years of walking quietly down echoing corridors.

"Where have you been?" asked Charlie, sounding irritated.

"Benton," said Lily.

"You always escape when this kind of stuff happens."

"You mean when Catholic priests faint in Episcopal cathedrals?"

"You know what I mean," said Charlie.

"And you know I hate group experiences," she said.

"You love group experiences—as long as you're in charge. It's chaos you can't stand."

"How's Frank?" asked Lily.

"He seems fine. He hadn't eaten. And it looks like our earlier guests had cranked the heat all the way up in there. Frank had on that heavy suit he always wears—"

"I know. He's like a caricature of a beloved Father. Do you think he only owns one suit or that he has a closet of them with identical stains and creases?"

"The first. Anyway, he swears he's fine. Jeffrey drove him home."

"I figured Jeffrey would win. Nobody can out-do-good Jeffrey," said Lily. She stood and stretched, then they turned back down the hall to the cathedral. "Has everyone cleared out? Can we go?"

"Let's go," he said. "Anna's out front, shivering in the foyer. She's asked us out for pizza. How does that sound?"

"Pizza? I somehow don't see Anna and pizza in the same establishment."

"It's one of her passions. She's found a new place over in Charlestown. It's that or nothing, she said."

"Do we have to take some form of public transportation?" asked Lily.

"No. We have the station wagon. We can travel in style."

CHAPTER 5

The station wagon was the 1988 wood-paneled Ford owned by the monastery. Lily distrusted the car; she smelled something hot—rubber, oil, electrical wiring—every time she rode in it. But they arrived safely and found the restaurant near the Tobin Bridge.

Having walked up the cracked stoop of an old brownstone, they followed Anna into a tiny hallway, narrow and dim, with an oval mirror and a marble-topped table holding a glass bowl of green and white dinner mints. Lily could smell garlic, of course, but also basil, sage, fresh bread, and, she thought, cloves.

"What is this place?" she whispered to Charlie.

"I think it's run by the Black Hand," he mumbled. "But the food smells great."

"I don't think you're supposed to say Black Hand anymore," said Lily. They followed a woman in a red dress through two small dining rooms, both with faded wallpaper and sconces. In the third room, they were seated at a round table by a window, through which they could see the night sky thick with clouds and a stretch of the lighted bridge. A stocky busboy brought menus, a bottle of sparkling water, a white bowl of olive oil with garlic cloves at the bottom, and focaccia.

"I feel like I'm in another country," said Lily.

"Charlestown *is* another country," said Charlie.

"I think he's very provincial," Anna remarked to Lily. "Don't you?"

"Charlie? Definitely." Lily smiled.

"So what do we do now?" asked Charlie.

"Order," said Anna.

"I mean about what happened today," said Charlie. "About this hate group."

Anna studied the menu and didn't answer.

"Anna?" he said.

She looked at him over the top of the menu. "I may know what's happening. I had this thought after the incident in the temple, but I didn't follow up."

"So what's happening?" Lily asked.

Anna put the menu down on the table. She stared out the window at the lighted bridge as she spoke. "When I first came to this country, I met some people at college. They were members of a Catholic order—sort of a fringe group. I've mentioned this, haven't I?" she asked Charlie.

"Some," he said. "Were they the lay order that broke off from the church for a while and then rejoined years later?"

"Yes," said Anna. "Some of them rejoined. In any case, I still have friends in that group. And I believe they may know something about all this—or at least have an idea of the source. But I don't want my friends involved in any official way. I don't want them to have to deal with the police."

Charlie looked across at Lily. "So?" he asked.

"I'm not sure," said Lily.

"What you don't know about Lily," said Charlie to Anna, "is that her boyfriend is a policeman."

"What a claim," said Lily. "It's like 'Paul's Epistle to the Hebrews.'" She blushed and felt furious at Charlie. She liked Anna to think of her as independent, professional, not caught up in a messy affair with a Catholic police photographer.

"You mean not one noun in it is true?" asked Charlie.

"Virtually," said Lily.

"I'm sorry to hear that," said Anna. "Because if it were true, it could be very useful to us later."

"There's a true version," said Lily. "But it doesn't include the words 'boyfriend' or 'policeman.'"

"He is—"

"Charlie," said Lily. "I don't want to be having this conversation right now. Later, when you and I are speaking again, we can debate the semantics."

A tall, thin, balding man in his sixties arrived to take their orders. Lily hadn't given it a thought, but Anna already had ideas about what they should eat, and, after an efficient consultation with the waiter, she ordered for all of them. As the man scraped the crumbs from the table, collected the menus, and turned away, Lily thought of Jeffrey Tatum, standing alone in his pew at the back of the cathedral.

"I guess he saw him falling," said Lily.

"Who?" asked Charlie. He had just dipped a chunk of focaccia into the bowl of olive oil.

"You're dripping," said Lily.

Charlie quickly put the bread in his mouth.

"Perhaps," said Anna to Lily. "Perhaps he saw him falling, but it was too late."

"Who?" asked Charlie again, his mouth full.

"Aren't they the original odd couple?" asked Lily. "Frank's so rumpled and dumpling-like, and Jeffrey's such a stick."

"I think you and Anna don't like Jeffrey because he's a monk," said Charlie.

"I like him," said Lily. "He's just so—compulsive, neat, punctual—and so aggressively liberal."

"We get the picture," said Charlie. "He's a little sanctimonious, but most monastics are sanctimonious about something. The worst are the ones who are sanctimonious about how worldly they are."

"I have known Jeffrey a long time," said Anna. "Frank as well. Since I first came here. But I have an old prejudice, that has nothing to do with Jeffrey, really. After I left the camps, I was taken to the hospital—"

"Wait," said Lily. "What were you in the hospital for?"

"No one ever told me, of course. But it appears I had some kind of rheumatic fever. They can tell now by looking at my heart, which is not, I'm assured, a thing of beauty. In any case, the hospital terrified me. My brother had died in the camp infirmary, and I must have confused the hospital with the infirmary. The point is that one of the doctors looked so much like Jeffrey—the tall, bony type. Not like you two. More cadaverous. It was years before I could look at Jeffrey without thinking of that man."

There was silence at the table. Finally, Charlie said, "Was he unkind to you, the doctor?"

"I have no idea," said Anna. "It seems to me he was German, so he might have not liked his job very much. But he may have been perfectly nice. In fact, he probably was. My memory is mercurial. When I try to make a whole picture—not just of those years, of a lot of the years following, too—I can't always get the pieces to stay together in one place."

Lily took a sip of water and glanced at Charlie, who was watching Anna. He always seemed relaxed and natural when Anna talked about her past, but Lily sometimes felt self-conscious; what was the right response to someone whose childhood memories included Auschwitz?

"But then," Anna continued, "I'll be doing something else and get a perfect, full-color picture in my mind of a woman, a guard, lifting a child by the back of her shirt, until the child turned red, and then deep blue, sort of purple."

Anna wasn't trying to shock anyone and she wasn't asking for pity, that was clear. She was having a conversation with them; she was talking about her past, a simple privilege most of us take for granted.

"Have you tried using a tape recorder?" asked Charlie.

"Yes, thanks to you, and it helps tremendously," said Anna. "What's most interesting to me is that I don't mind speculating out loud. When I write, I find it hard to write if I'm not sure it's true. But when I record myself trying to remember, it's less—"

"Of a commitment?" asked Lily.

"Yes," said Anna. "Exactly. The written word is such a commitment. The only commitment with this is dragging the damn thing around with me."

"Do you have one of those little ones?" Charlie asked. He indicated a rectangle a couple of inches wide and four or five inches long.

"That small?" asked Anna. "I've never seen one. But I think it may be a good idea."

"I have one at the monastery. I never use it. I'll give it to you when we get back."

"Thank you," said Anna. "I would appreciate it very much."

The waiter reappeared with a plate of crab claws in garlic butter.

"How did you find this place?" asked Charlie.

"That's a secret of mine," said Anna.

"You have so many," said Charlie.

"Yes," said Anna, with her vague smile. "You can imagine, a woman who's been alive as long as I've been. I have a lot of secrets. But I don't want them anymore. And I want you to help me get rid of them—both of you." She reached out and took Lily's left hand and Charlie's right in both her own hands, held them for a moment, then released them, sighed, and said, "Let's eat."

CHAPTER 6

Early the following Monday, Lily sat at her desk at the Women's Center, thinking that, in some ways, she had changed very little since her days at St. Joseph's Catholic School. She was still tall and skinny. She wore her thick, brown hair in one short braid instead of two long ones. Her skin was paler now that she was out of the Texas sun, but most days she still wore the clothes of her childhood—jeans, T-shirts, sweaters, and cowboy boots.

Seven years before, she and five other women had founded the Women's Center, an experiment in practical diversity. They'd begun by offering a discussion group for women of color and white women in a basement room in a Methodist church in Brighton—the first group had started with five people, including Lily; they now offered workshops, courses, and weekend retreats for organizations struggling with all kinds of anti-bias issues—racism, sexism, able-ism. By last year, they'd grown enough to rent spacious—if not elegant—quarters downtown on Mass Ave, between Newbury and Commonwealth, in a building owned by a woman who'd taken workshops and become a supporter.

Morning light from the sun cresting the highrise across the street filled the top panes of the windows. Lily could hear the work crew outside—the occasional grind of the backhoe engine—but inside, the offices were peaceful. She leaned back in the ancient wooden chair, put her feet up on her desk, and watched a plane that had taken off from Logan, heading southwest. Maybe it was time for a trip back to Benton, to see old friends, to visit her father's grave.

She hadn't slept well the past two nights, since the cathedral service on Saturday. She had dreamed a lot, dreams filled with red—red flags, red print, even a jeweled crucifix obscenely studded with rubies. And Anna had been on her mind, waking and sleeping. Lily had meant to call Anna at the monastery on Sunday, but she'd had to do an anti-racism workshop at a Quaker school in Cambridge, so she'd never had a chance to make the call. By now, Anna would be back home in Wharton. Lily would call her later. She put her feet down, opened the right hand drawer of her desk, and took out her prayer book. She had just turned to the page for morning prayers when the phone rang. It startled her, because this was a time in her day when she felt alone and unreachable, safe from the world. She was going to let the machine get it, and then something—a slight lifting of the hairs on the nape of her neck and behind her ears—told her to pick up.

After she answered, there was a pause, during which she could hear voices talking in the background. Then Charlie came on. "Lily?" he said. "I just got some weird news and I wanted to see what you thought. Anna's missing."

"How did you know where I was?"

"You weren't home. Where else would you be?"

"What do you mean missing—missing from where?" Lily asked him. "I thought she was back home."

"So did I. I put her on the bus Sunday, yesterday, after lunch. She was supposed to get in around six but she never showed up."

"How do you know?" she asked.

"Because her neighbor met the bus," said Charlie, "and Anna wasn't on it. He left a message on the guest house machine last night, but we don't listen to that until Monday morning."

"I don't get it," she said. "Would she have stopped off somewhere else?"

"Not without calling him—or me—or someone."

"And there's no message from her there, at the monastery?"

"No. We got everyone to pick up their messages, just in case. There's nothing."

Lily heard the voices in the background again.

"We wondered if you'd be willing to call Tom and ask him what would be the best thing to do."

Tom Casey worked for the Boston Police Department as a photographer in the ID Division. He was a couple of years younger than Lily (in a month he'd turn thirty-four), not quite as tall, and stocky, with brown hair and a kind of generous nonchalance that made the annoying details of life easier to take. Over a year ago, he'd helped Lily uncover the truth about the parish where she worked as interim priest. They had been lovers ever since—but she had her own reasons for not wanting to talk with him at the moment.

"Don't you think she'll turn up somewhere?" Lily asked. She knew she was grasping at straws, but she couldn't stop herself. "She's a grown woman. She probably just—"

"Just what?" asked Charlie. "If you don't want to call Tom, don't. But I'm going to call the police anyway."

"Have you talked with her neighbor again? Are you sure she wasn't on a later bus?"

"I just got off the phone with him. He's worried, and slightly pissed, I think. She's got six or seven dogs that he's looking after. Besides, I left her at the station. The bus was due in ten minutes. Where would she have gone? I can't think of an explanation for this, can you?"

"No," said Lily. "I guess not. I'll call Tom and call you back." Charlie sounded relieved as he said good-bye. "Charlie—" she added, hoping to catch him before he hung up.

"What?" he asked.

"Nothing. I'm sure she's fine," said Lily. But she'd said exactly the opposite of what she felt.

A little more than an hour later, Lily found herself in a small, gray room on the first floor of Police Headquarters on Tremont. Four people—Lily, Charlie, Tom, and a detective from Missing Persons named Murad Gregarian—were crammed into the space. Tom and Gregarian leaned against a table facing Lily and Charlie, who sat in two chairs pushed back against the opposite wall.

"What is this place?" Lily had asked when they first came in.

"A holding cell," said Tom. "I want us to have some privacy, and this was the best I could do."

"Remind me not to get arrested," she'd said.

At the moment, she was trying to concentrate and contribute, but she was having trouble breathing in the close space, and that made the other two jobs a lot harder. Also, she hadn't seen Tom in almost a week—they were taking some "time off," as she'd called it when they last talked. Not his idea and not to his liking. So the whole interview was fraught, for her, with a sense of his presence and his distance.

"Here's what we need to do," Gregarian was saying. "I'm going to take you back to my desk and get you to fill out some forms and answer a lot of questions—names of her friends, business associates, bank account numbers, credit cards. And then I'll get in touch with A-1 and the state police."

Lily thought of steak sauce. "A-1?" she said.

"The district for South Station, where she went missing—or might have gone missing. Technically, you should be reporting this over there, but you're here now, so we'll keep it simple."

"Why the state police?" asked Charlie.

"Because if she got on the bus, it could have happened anywhere between here and Wharton, right?"

"Conceivably," said Charlie. "I don't think—never mind."

"What?" asked Tom.

"I don't know," said Charlie. "I just—I didn't want to leave her sitting there before the bus showed up, but she insisted. She wanted to read. She told me she didn't want to make desultory chat with me in a bus station."

Lily smiled. That certainly sounded like Anna.

"Maybe I just feel guilty for leaving her," Charlie continued. "But how will we know if she even got on the bus? Can we ask the bus driver if he saw her?"

Gregarian shifted his stance against the desk and glanced at Tom. "Here's the story," he said. "We take all this information you give us and put it out over a kind of network. Then, if somebody calls with an ID—you know, there's a woman here who's confused and doesn't know where she is—we check the missing persons list and see if it matches up. But anything beyond that . . ."

"That's it?" asked Lily. "We do everything else? I don't get it."

"Most people turn up," said Tom. "In most cases, especially older people—"

"You know Anna," Lily said to him. "Do you think she wandered off confused? Come on. If she's not where she said she'd be, then something's happened to her. Besides," she began, then looked at Charlie. She wanted to mention the cathedral, their talk at dinner, but as if he knew what was on her mind, Charlie gave her a barely perceptible shake of his head. She stayed quiet.

"There are a few things I'd do," said Gregarian, "if I were in your shoes. Find the bus driver, ask if he remembers her, or anything about that particular trip. Then find out whether or not her luggage turned up at the end of the line, unclaimed. At least you'll know she put her bag on, which means she probably got on herself. Then ask the company if they'll check the ticket numbers, to see which tickets were sold and which were turned in at the end of the run. If there's one missing, and her luggage isn't there, there's a good chance she never got on to begin with."

"Can't you do that?" asked Charlie. "What if they won't tell us anything?"

"Fill out the forms first," said Gregarian. "I'll go on and contact state and the Wharton police, put out a missing persons report. You check with the bus company—which one was it, by the way?"

"Albany Lines," said Charlie.

"That's good," said Gregarian. "They're pretty efficient. Anyway, check with them and get back to me. Then we'll know more about what to do next. What about family—anybody in the area?"

There was a moment of silence in which Lily stared out through a narrow glass panel in the door.

"Nobody anywhere," said Charlie.

Gregarian raised his eyebrows and appeared interested.

"Tell Greg a little about her," said Tom. "Tell him about her background."

Gregarian looked at Lily. He was handsome, she noticed—medium build, thick, dark hair, dark eyes, and a mustache that reminded her vaguely of a young Burt Reynolds. He was probably a few years older than she was, maybe in his early forties. She liked his manner, matter-of-fact, slightly distanced, and his shoes, well-worn work boots. Lily looked at Charlie and said, "You tell him."

So Charlie gave a brief outline of the facts—Anna's childhood in Poland, the arrest of her family, her stay in an orphanage, her time in the family camp in Auschwitz, her years in a French convent, and her college years in the States. "She eventually became a citizen here," said Charlie. "She's very patriotic, and still a staunch Catholic, although idiosyncratic. I mean, she doesn't really agree wholeheartedly with church doctrine."

Gregarian smiled and nodded, as if to say, "I know what idiosyncratic means." "How long was she in Auschwitz?" he asked.

"Not long," said Charlie. "They came and got her and her brothers and sisters out of the orphanage, but it was near the end of the war. You'd think the Germans would have had other things on their minds."

"Yeah, well, in fact, that seems to be the main thing they had on their minds, especially by the end," said Gregarian. "If the Germans had put the resources at their disposal—including Jewish slave labor—toward winning the war, they—But that's another topic." He moved away from the desk again and put his hand on the doorknob. "You want to get started?"

"I guess," said Charlie. "Are you coming?" he asked Lily.

"I'll be right there," she said. "Just give me a minute."

"Right. Okay then," said Charlie, nodding first at Lily, then at Tom, as the light dawned. "So, you just come along whenever. See you guys."

"This is weird, right?" said Tom. He wore a deep green T-shirt and khakis. His brown hair was a little longer than usual. Lily couldn't help but notice that the shirt made his hazel eyes look deep green as well.

"No kidding," she said. "When Charlie first asked if I'd call you, I wasn't sure what to do. But then—it seemed stupid not to."

"It would have been stupid," he said. "What do you think happened?"

For an instant, she thought he meant what had happened between them—why had she needed time apart. But then she realized he was talking about Anna. "I don't know," said Lily. "But Charlie seems really worried. I guess—"

"What?"

"I'm worried, too, but I have no idea why. Common sense keeps telling me she's fine, she's a grown woman, she's been through a lot. You know—she can take care of herself."

"But?"

"But I knew when the phone rang this morning, when Charlie called, that something was wrong. I mean, something was *actually* wrong. I just don't know what it is."

"But you think it's about Anna?"

"I do," said Lily.

Tom was the only person who'd ever gotten the whole story about Lily's messages—the dreams, the physical sensations, the uninvited insights. Once or twice she'd mentioned an occurrence to Charlie, but always with a dismissive laugh. The messages weren't powerful, usually, and they weren't always right. She had a hard time distinguishing between garden variety worry and a useful premonition. But sometimes she knew.

"Why did you want me to tell Gregarian about Anna?" Lily asked.

"Greg's a kind of expert on genocide. He's Armenian and he spent a lot of time studying his family history, tracing it back to Turkey—right, Turkey?"

Lily nodded. "Probably."

"Then he got interested in the whole subject."

"Who can blame him?" said Lily. "It's a great way to

pass a Saturday morning, poring over gas chamber blueprints."

"You should know," said Tom. "You two actually have a lot in common. Anyway, I figured if he knew Anna's story, he might do some work on this himself, instead of passing it on. With old people—we get a lot of calls about older people wandering off alone. Most of the time, somebody finds them in a supermarket five towns over with their shoes on their ears."

"That's not going to happen this time, though," said Lily. "I wish it were."

"So, when do we see each other?" asked Tom, after a brief silence.

"I don't know," said Lily. "How about . . ."

"How about what?"

"How about having dinner soon? This doesn't really feel like a very—"

"Tonight's good," said Tom. "So's tomorrow. I suddenly find myself with a lot a free time on my hands."

Lily smiled. "Let's do it tomorrow. Come over to the office when you're done here. Is that okay?"

"If that's the best we can do," he said, sounding disgruntled. "I still don't see the problem. Are we happy now? Yes. Do we love each other? Yes—"

"That's not it. You know that. I just look ahead, at what's down the road for us, and I don't see anything—anything workable."

Tom stared at her for a couple of seconds, then stood up straight. "You're right. This isn't a good time to talk."

"I'm sorry," said Lily. "I don't want—"

"Just don't make any decisions without telling me," he said. He reached out to touch her cheek, then pulled his hand back. "For now, let's think about Anna."

CHAPTER 7

Out on the sidewalk again, over an hour later, Lily and Charlie stood in the pale sunlight. A cold, sharp breeze had started up. Lily zipped up her black parka and put on her gloves. She felt dazed, directionless.

"So what now?" asked Charlie.

"I don't know," she said. "Let me think."

"I guess we ought to go back to work," said Charlie. "But that doesn't seem right. I want to do something active, you know, start looking for her right away."

"You mean walk around shouting her name?" asked Lily.

Charlie sighed. "You know what I mean."

"I do," said Lily. "Walk me to the office. We'll come up with a plan."

They crossed Ruggles Street and headed for Mass Ave.

"Why didn't you want to mention the cathedral?" she asked him.

"Anna asked us not to tell anyone for a while. She wanted to keep the police away from her friends."

"That doesn't apply if she's in some kind of danger, though," said Lily. "If she doesn't turn up soon, I'm going to say something to Gregarian."

"Look," said Charlie. "If Anna did what she said she

was going to do, if she actually talked with someone from this Catholic bunch to try to get information, then we should probably mention the whole episode to the police. But if not, I don't see the point."

"How will we know?"

"I can ask Larry if she got any messages—he was answering the guest house phone last week. Maybe he can remember who called her. Normally, that would be a breach of—something—but this is different."

"That's good. We'll find out who she spoke with—particularly Sunday morning, before she left. And we can do some research on our own about the group. Then, if she doesn't turn up, we'll give Gregarian what we've found. Maybe the police will get interested enough to do something." Lily watched a city bus stop to pick up a woman, someone Anna's age, but with wispy gray hair that seemed to float off her head like a small cloud. "What have we forgotten? Are you sure she didn't say anything to you about meeting someone?"

"Lily, I just spent over an hour answering these same questions."

"I know. But I thought if I used a badgering tone, I might wear you down."

"You're definitely wearing me down, but you're not helping me think more clearly."

They walked along Columbus in silence; Lily's thoughts ricocheted between fears about Anna and fears about Tom. What if Anna had become confused, had gotten off the bus somewhere, been picked up by—by whom or what? That seemed so unlike Anna.

But what did she really know about Anna? They had become closer over the last couple of years, but they seldom talked about the past. Lily thought of her as a kind of ideal—a woman of principle, on her own, teaching, writing, taking care of her dogs and her garden.

What did she know about anything, if it came to that? Her

whole life had begun to feel flimsy, a jerry-rigged construction that couldn't bear the weight of her confusions. She was being a fool, wasting her time with a younger, Catholic man who had a lot less at stake than she did. As it stood, Tom wanted them to move in together, but Lily couldn't work as an interim priest if she lived with him, unmarried. Meanwhile, he gave up nothing.

On the other hand, Lily didn't much like interim work. She had turned down the last offer, from a parish in Dedham whose rector had decided to leave the priesthood. But Bishop Spencer had let her know that she was risking her standing in the diocese. Unfortunately, the last time she'd worked in a parish—at St. Mary of the Garden—she'd earned a reputation for bucking the system and doing things her own way. So her standing was shaky to begin with.

Lily had long felt like an outsider in the church; her faith barely fit the Episcopal mold. Charlie called her a closet Catholic sometimes, and sometimes a closet Quaker. But she'd always, up until recently, had a few certainties, grounded in the faith of her childhood, enriched by her adult faith. She'd loved the rituals of the church, the liturgy; she'd believed in the power of confession and of prayer; she'd felt moved by the hymns and music. She could take tremendous comfort from lighting a candle in front of the statue of Mary and Jesus in the monastery chapel. But after her father's death and her difficult months at St. Mary's, these certainties had begun to fail her. She'd begun to feel somehow duped. In fact, she'd begun to question her vocation.

During her last talk on the phone with Anna, just before this visit, Lily had confided her doubts. "After I heard about the guy in Dedham, it started me thinking. People do leave, after all."

"But I think of you as the perfect priest," Anna had said. "Why?"

"Because you're full of doubt. You see the church as a human institution, not some precious object. And you're never afraid to argue the finer points of theology."

"It's not so much the finer points that are bothering me now. I just can't get anything out of going to church, you know what I mean? It's as if I've lost the knack."

"Yes," Anna had said. "I've had periods like that. But don't give up yet. Sometimes it takes these periods to push us deeper into our faith, to find new things to believe in. I can't tell you what to do, of course, but it would be a great loss to the church."

"On the other hand," Lily had said, "it's survived almost two thousand years without me."

"Barely," Anna had said. "Look at the track record."

"Good point," Lily had said, and they'd laughed together. Anna knew what parts of a catastrophe were funny—a knowledge not generally shared in religious circles.

The wind whipped a loose strand of hair into her eyes. She remembered the wispy-haired older woman boarding the bus. "What made you think Anna didn't get on the bus?" she asked Charlie.

"I already said, I don't know. How long is this walk, anyway? I thought we'd be there by now."

"A few more blocks," said Lily. "What if someone showed up at the station, right after you left, and offered her a ride?"

"Who would do that? And how would they know she was there?" asked Charlie. "There were only a few people who knew her travel plans. Which reminds me, I need to call her neighbor again. You and I might have to drive out to Wharton."

"Why?" asked Lily. "What good would that do?"

"Somebody's going to have to do something with the dogs. They were like her family. It's about the only thing I ever saw her be sentimental over."

"Won't the neighbor keep them?"

"I'm not sure," said Charlie. "But judging from our talk this morning, I think he's ready to hand them over. Plus, if she hasn't shown up, you and I ought to go through her house, see if we can find anything important, or useful. There's maybe information—even stuff about this group—lying around somewhere."

"I don't think it will come to that, do you?" Lily asked. She meant to sound reassuring, but her voice came out high-pitched and anxious.

"I hope not."

Charlie insisted they pick up something to eat, so they got to the office with a box of Clementines and a loaf of whole-grain, raisin walnut bread. The offices were on the fifth floor—four large rooms, one for office space, two for workshops and classes, and a small kitchen with a table and chairs. An intern was at the ancient copy machine in the entry hall—a skinny white girl with long blonde hair and a butterfly tattoo on her bicep. She wore headphones and stood perfectly still, staring down as the green light scanned the page.

"Who's that?" mouthed Charlie as they walked past.

"I can't remember," Lily whispered as they entered the main room. "Workshops for this session ended on Sunday, so we have someone new. We won't start again until late April. By then, I'll know her pretty well. By August, when we finish next session, I'll know her really well. Then she'll leave."

Barbara Paris, co-founder, co-director, and one of Lily's closest friends, sat working at her computer. When they came in, she took off her reading glasses, stood, and stretched. She was large-framed, broad-shouldered—a couple of inches shorter than Lily—with dark brown skin, brown eyes, and short-cropped black hair liberally mixed with gray. While Lily seldom varied her outfit of jeans with T-shirts and boots, Barbara appeared to have an infinite number of ensembles—all appropriate, elegant, and seemingly impossible for her to own on her income from the center. Lily joked about Barbara's having a second life as an after-hours CEO of a corrupt brokerage firm.

Today, she wore gray flannel slacks with a white silk shirt. A pale blue cashmere cardigan hung over the back of her chair. Her reading glasses dangled from a gold chain around her neck, a chain that matched her gold earrings. "What's up?" she asked.

Lily told Barbara the whole story—where they had been, and why. She felt grateful Barbara didn't go back through the list of obvious questions—Could Anna have changed her plans? Could she have gotten a ride? Barbara simply sat back down and gazed at her computer screen.

"This is so strange," she said. "I don't even feel worried because I can't believe anything's wrong."

"I know," said Lily. "I keep assuming she'll call and say, 'How could you have forgotten I was off to a conference in Madison?'"

"But she's not," said Charlie. "She was on her way home, I left her—"

"We know this," said Lily. "You've told us this a few times now."

"I think I feel responsible," said Charlie. "As if I lost her."

Barbara looked at Charlie over the top of her glasses. "It's not your fault. Nobody thinks it's your fault. We just have to pray for her safety—and find her."

Lily had put the tangerines and the bread down on her desk and was returning from the kitchen with a knife, a cutting board, and a plate. "We decided we needed some food to help us search."

"That's not food," said Barbara. "Let's make a plan, then I'll go get something we can actually eat."

"Thank you," said Charlie. "Lily had me convinced this was a lunch."

"We need to find out if she talked with anyone," said Lily. "Told someone where she was going, even got a last-minute ride."

"We can start with our own phone list," said Barbara. "It's the same old liberal church group that Anna knows."

"You mean call everyone?" asked Lily.

"Everyone who knows her. The three of us can do it in a couple of hours."

"I'll talk to Larry," said Charlie. "He'll know who left messages at the monastery."

"Gregarian said to see what we could find out from the bus company," said Lily. "I'll do that."

"Good," said Barbara. She took her gray cashmere coat off a hook on the back of the door. "I'll be back with subs."

"We're also going to drive over to Wharton at some point," said Charlie. "You want to come along?"

"No thanks," said Barbara, as she wound a pale blue cashmere scarf around her neck. "I don't go anywhere there's a possibility I could be the only black woman in town. It's how I've gotten to be this old."

"How old is she?" Charlie asked after Barbara left.

"I never can remember exactly," said Lily. "We had her sixtieth birthday party, when, about two years ago? I know her kids were in school here in Boston back in the sixties, during busing. That's when she became an activist." Lily sat at her desk and peeled a tangerine while she waited for the antique computer to boot. "They'd just moved from Arkansas, and she couldn't believe she hadn't gotten away from all of it—picketing, spitting—here we go." The computer sounded a chord, announcing its readiness. She sat up and put the tangerine on the plate beside her.

In a few minutes the printer made a whirring sound and

began printing out numbers and addresses. Lily looked up and saw Charlie staring down at the machine as if he'd never seen anything like it before. "Charlie?" she asked.

"What if she got sick—she wasn't looking too great this visit. Did you notice?"

Lily paused, one foot up on the chair, tangerine section in hand. "I noticed she was pale, but only at times. Do you think that's what happened?"

"I don't know," said Charlie. "It's possible. If I'd stayed—"

"Charlie," said Lily. "Listen to me. No one blames you for this. And I'm positive, no matter where she is, Anna isn't blaming you for this. It's not her style. If she got sick, someone probably helped her. She may be in a hospital at the moment, and for some reason she can't tell people to call us. When Gregarian puts that stuff out over the network, someone will make the connection between her name and the little old Polish lady in the south wing, and we'll find her. This might all be over tomorrow."

Charlie sat down in Barbara's chair, put his elbows on the desk and his head in his hands. "God, I hope you're right," he said. "I just can't shake the feeling that something's very, very wrong."

"I know," said Lily. She might as well come clean with Charlie. "The truth is, I feel the same way. But the best thing we can do right now is start looking for her and, like Barbara said, pray."

"It doesn't seem like enough," said Charlie.

"It never does," said Lily. "But you work with what you got."

CHAPTER 8

Lily hung up the phone as Barbara entered the office, carrying a large brown bag, grease spots showing through the paper.

"What do you think Albany Lines has to hide?" asked Lily. "I feel like I've been after the fail-safe code from the Joint Chiefs of Staff."

"Did they tell you anything?" asked Barbara.

"Sort of. I think—although I can't be sure—that the two o'clock bus to Wharton on Sunday was full, and there was no unclaimed luggage, from that run, in Wharton."

"And you can't be sure because—?" asked Charlie.

"Because the gentleman would only repeat in a flat, nasal voice, 'This is what the computer is giving me.' He wouldn't call to verify any of it. He wouldn't give me numbers so I could call. And he wouldn't give me the bus driver's name."

"If it's true, though," said Charlie. "That means Anna did get on the bus."

Barbara had unpacked the bag. The smell of french fries and eggplant parmesan filled the room. "Not necessarily," she said.

"But I stood with her while she bought her ticket. I carried her suitcase to the gate."

"Maybe she gave someone her ticket," said Barbara. She unwrapped a cardboard container of fries and passed them to Charlie.

"But why?" he asked.

"Who knows?" said Lily.

"Yes. Who knows," said Barbara. "That's what we're about to try to find out."

By four o'clock that afternoon, Lily, Charlie, and Barbara had called everyone on the address list who might have seen or spoken with Anna. The three of them had worked out a story, a modified version of the truth, so as not to spread premature panic: I've been trying to reach Anna and can't remember if she headed home from Boston or not. Did you talk to her? Did she say anything about her plans?

A few people had spoken with her. Anna had called Frank Leslie on Sunday morning to be sure he was all right, but they hadn't talked about much other than that. In fact, Frank was fine and reissued his own diagnosis—too little food, too much heat. He said he would make some calls as well, though, to check with other friends.

Anna had also met with Bishop Spencer on Saturday morning, before the service, to discuss taking a leave of absence from the Ecumenical Council. According to him, she was excited and exhausted by the work she'd been doing recently—dredging up memories. She wanted to focus on that work for a while, without interruption.

"I assume there's nothing wrong here," Spencer had said to Lily.

"I hope not," she said. "I'll let you know when I find her." She'd left it at that, and he had let her. One of Spencer's finest attitudes was a working assumption that his friends were honest, thrifty, and reliable. He trusted people. Of course, he wasn't always right, but he continued to expect adult behavior anyway—a kind of willed obtuseness on his part, maybe, but an admirable one.

Now Lily sat with her elbows on her desk, peeling her fourth tangerine of the day. She didn't like talking on the phone at the best of times; she felt defeated and worried. "So we don't know anything," she said, addressing not so much Charlie and Barbara as the room itself, dim, high-ceilinged, the air filled with dust motes caught in slanted afternoon light from the tall windows.

"We know she didn't tell anyone she was going somewhere exotic when she left Boston, at least no one we've talked to so far," said Barbara. She stood with her back to Lily and Charlie, making copies of the list of people they'd called, with notes on who'd said what and who hadn't answered or called back yet.

"Good point," said Charlie. "And if the guy at the bus company is right, she might have gone to Wharton after all."

The copier stuttered and began a series of short, high beeps. Barbara groaned, kneeled down, and opened the side of the machine.

"You want me to do that?" asked Lily.

"No. I want to feel like I've fixed at least one thing today," said Barbara. After she wrestled a crushed piece of paper out of a roller, she closed the door, stood, and added, "I'm starting to believe it's real."

For a moment, no one spoke.

"So if she got off in Wharton," Charlie finally said, "we ought to be talking to the police over there. And to the neighbor."

"Who is this guy, the neighbor?" asked Barbara. "How did he sound?"

"Taciturn," said Charlie. "But I figured it was a kind of mountain-man thing. He definitely did not want to take care of the dogs anymore."

"How about Larry?" asked Lily.

"I didn't get him," said Charlie. "He's supposed to call me here this afternoon. If I don't hear from him, I'll find him tonight. I probably ought to go soon anyway. I've been out since this morning." But he stayed where he was, leaning on his elbows at the extra desk, staring down at an old copy of *Essence*.

When the phone rang, Lily sat up so fast she knocked over a stack of fund-raising letters; they flooded down onto the floor, a small cascade of paper.

She answered and waved to Charlie. "It's Larry," she said.

Charlie picked up the phone on his desk and talked quietly for a few minutes. As she cleaned up the letters, Lily couldn't hear everything he said, but she saw that he made a few notes, which she took to be a good sign.

"So?" asked Lily, as soon as he hung up.

Barbara had finished at the copier. She handed a list to Lily and one to Charlie, then sat down at her desk. "So?" she echoed.

Charlie scanned the sheet of paper Barbara just handed him. "Who talked to Jeffrey Tatum?" he asked.

"I did," said Lily. "Why?"

"This says he didn't think he'd spoken with Anna before she left, right?"

"Yeah," said Lily. "He said he wasn't sure, because he'd talked to her earlier in the week. But not since the service on Saturday."

Charlie continued to stare down at the paper.

"What?" asked Barbara.

"Larry said Jeffrey'd called a few times, and he was almost sure they talked Sunday morning, because Anna had been at chapel when the call came through. She told Larry she was going upstairs to call Jeffrey back. Larry seems to think she'd been waiting for the call."

Lily looked at Barbara, who widened her eyes and arched her eyebrows.

"So who wants to call Brother Jeffrey?" asked Barbara.

They decided Charlie should call, because he liked Jeffrey the most. But Jeffrey was not at his house, a large, old clapboard building on Garden Street where most of the teaching brothers of St. Joseph's Seminary lived; he taught a Monday night seminar.

"Keep trying when you get home," said Lily.

"I'm not going to hound him," said Charlie. "I've left a message. He'll call me back. He probably just forgot he'd talked with Anna the second time."

"Maybe one of us better call him," Barbara said to Lily.

"What do you think?" Lily asked Charlie.

"Do it however you like," said Charlie. "But I know him best, and he's most likely to be comfortable with me. Let's start with the assumption that Jeffrey's not a hardened criminal, shall we?"

"I think that's fair," said Barbara. "I just wish he didn't have such a stick up his butt."

"You are definitely not calling him," said Charlie.

"Can you take tomorrow off, too?" Lily asked him.

"I don't know for sure. I've got two people I'm seeing for spiritual advising—but that's early. I might be able to be gone for the rest of the day. Why?"

"I'll come in first thing and try to talk with anyone we missed today. You see if you can get Jeffrey. Then we ought to go see Gregarian. He needs to know the whole story—everything we've found so far, and the scene at the cathedral. Yes?"

Barbara nodded. "She's right," she said. "Y'all shouldn't keep this to yourself, no matter what you think about Jeffrey."

"Did Lily tell you all of it—Beth Shalom, the cathedral, Anna's plan?"

Barbara nodded. "We talked yesterday."

"What do you think?" Charlie asked her.

"If it's a coincidence, it's a weird coincidence."

"Very weird," said Lily.

"I'll call in the morning as soon as I'm free," said Charlie. "We'll go back over and tell Gregarian what we've got." He stood and placed the magazine on a pile on top of a filing cabinet. "Something about leaving makes this all seem final. I thought we'd know more by now, I thought we'd have found her, or found something—"

"I know," said Barbara. "I feel the same way. Are you taking the T?" she asked him.

"Yeah," he said. "You want to come?"

"Give me five minutes. I'll finish the budget. I'm just moving zeros around anyway. Then we can go together."

"What about you?" Charlie asked Lily.

"I think I'll stick around for a while. I haven't gotten anything done, besides this, and I could use some work time."

"Where's what's-her-name?" asked Barbara.

"The intern?" asked Lily. "I thought you knew her."

"I don't keep track of them after the first session. I get attached and then it tears me up when they leave," said Barbara. "I think this one's Annie, or Minnie, or Frannie—"

"Never mind," said Lily. "She appears to be gone. We should make more of an effort. This gives nonprofits a bad name."

"I don't think so," said Barbara. "The more we resemble a corporation, the more people like us." Barbara shut down her computer, took a compact out ofher Coach bag, put on fresh lipstick, then replaced the compact and stood up. "Okay," she said to Charlie. "Let's go."

Lily ended the work day the same way she'd begun it—alone in the office, feet up on her desk, the prayer book in her hand. The late winter sky was turning from azure to deep blue. She could hear the wind; it surged around the corner of the building and rattled a window behind her, the one with the broken lock. And she could hear the rush hour traffic below on Mass Ave. Everyone was going home. Everyone but Anna.

Lily couldn't bring herself to say the prayer for a person in trouble—that would mean Anna was in trouble—so she chose the prayer for travelers: ". . . Preserve those who travel, especially Anna; surround her with your loving care; protect her from every danger; and bring her in safety to her journey's end . . ."

As usual these days, the words didn't bring her much comfort. She finished and sat quietly for a long time, listening to the wind, the cars, the elevator bell, people saying good-night in the hallway. If she finished her prayers, she'd have to know what to do next. Finally, she got to her knees and put her elbows on the desk chair, but she was out of practice. It had been a long time since she'd asked God for anything, honestly, from her heart. She didn't know how to do it.

Finally, she opened her eyes, stood, and looked up at the ceiling. "We need a miracle," she said out loud. "We need Anna to be fine."

CHAPTER 9

At ten A.M. the next day, Lily waited for Charlie in the lobby of police headquarters—a pair of tall, new buildings joined by a breezeway. The lobby was gray and shiny, full of marble, glass, and metal; it reminded Lily of a refurbished train terminal. Four long benches formed a square in the middle of the vast floor space. Lily sat on the bench facing the door across from the T-stop, the door through which she expected Charlie to emerge at any minute. Through the glass wall, she could see piles of dark clouds moving fast, obliterating a pale blue sky.

Normally she would have waited in Tom's office, but she'd called before she came and found he'd gone to the morgue—his least favorite duty, photographing autopsies. She had asked for Gregarian and arranged a meeting, feeling both guilty and relieved. She'd had a restless, dreamy night, filled with images of Tom—at one point he was trying to push a huge trunk of clothes, kitchen utensils, cameras, through the (what had suddenly become) tiny door of her (what had suddenly become) garret-like apartment. She felt as if she'd been wrestling with him on and off for the past eight hours, and was grateful for the break.

She'd also dreamed of Anna—or almost Anna, an older woman with pale skin and two brilliant spots of red on her cheeks—getting on the bus on Columbus Ave. The woman had left her suitcase—army green with brown trim and wheels attached to the bottom—on the sidewalk. Lily had tried to drag the suitcase to the bus, but she'd been too late. As the bus pulled away, Lily had seen the woman's face in a window, framed by her hands pressed against the pane, her mouth a perfect O.

Lily had lain awake a long time afterward. This morning her mind felt jangled, intensely alert. So when she heard someone call her name, she jumped to her feet and turned.

"Whoa," said Gregarian. "Guilty conscience?"

"I always have a guilty conscience," she said.

"Why don't you absolve yourself?" he asked her. His voice was bantering, but he had dark half circles under his eyes.

"It's not based in reality," she said. "Absolution doesn't help."

He nodded, as if he recognized the symptom. "Charlie called," he said. "He's running late. He said we should go on and meet, which surprised me, because I didn't know you were here."

"I was waiting for him," she said. "But that's fine. It's just—"

"What?"

"There's some stuff I need to add to what we told you yesterday. I was hoping Charlie would help."

"I suspect you can handle it," he said. "Let's go." And he bowed, slightly, as if ushering her into a formal drawing room.

Lily caught herself smiling and blushing, not a common reaction for her.

They walked past the front desk, and Gregarian waved to the sergeant on duty, a heavyset black man with pock-marked skin. "She's with me," he said.

"I've still got to get her ID," said the sergeant.

Gregarian sighed. "Give him your driver's license," he said.

"I didn't bring it," said Lily.

"You don't drive?" Gregarian asked her.

"Not usually," she said. "I live in the city. I walk or take the bus to work."

Gregarian exchanged a glance with the desk sergeant. "What do you want to do?"

The man shook his head in exasperation. Lily couldn't tell if he was joking or not. "Keep an eye on her."

They sat at Gregarian's corner desk in a large room filled with other desks and people, ringing phones and voices. A few feet away, a small Asian man—Lily assumed he was a detective—was talking on the phone; the person on the other end was either deaf or drugged, because the Asian man yelled everything at least twice.

"Is she there with you now?" he screamed. "I said, is she there now?"

Lily's chair faced the back wall, but she was intensely aware of the hubbub behind her. She stared for a moment at the pictures on Gregarian's desk—two framed school photos, a boy and a girl, dark hair, large dark eyes, sky-blue background. She didn't know where to start; she felt awkward, as if she were trying to have an intimate conversation in a public place.

"So what's up?" Gregarian asked.

"We got some information yesterday, but I want to start with what we left out when we first talked to you."

"Good place to start."

"The reason Anna was here, in Boston, as you know—we told you that part, right?"

He nodded.

"So," said Lily. "She was here for this event at the cathedral—the one we'd planned together, about the Holocaust." For some reason, Lily felt tongue-tied and self-conscious.

Gregarian nodded again, this time with an encouraging smile, something like a small grimace.

"So, we were at the Holocaust Memorial, over by Faneuil Hall, but then Anna and Charlie and I left early to walk to the cathedral. We got there before anyone else, and when we got there, we found some kind of . . . a sort of . . ." She raised her hands towards the ceiling to indicate the doll hanging from the cross beam. She couldn't find the words to describe it.

"Airplane?" asked Gregarian.

"No," said Lily.

"Take your time."

"We found this horrible thing, this doll, sort of dummy, dressed like a concentration camp child, in striped clothes, and a hat. He was hanging by his neck from a rope—"

Gregarian's face changed as she spoke, his expression moving from mildly amused tolerance to something impassive, something she couldn't read.

"And the Nazi flag was draped over the altar . . ."

"Does this have something to do with Banieka?" he asked.

Lily had never heard anyone refer to Anna by her last name only. It sounded wrong, and it chilled her.

"Anna told us afterward that she might know who was responsible. No, not exactly that—she said she might know people who might know who was responsible."

"Did she contact them?" Gregarian asked.

"We're not sure. Charlie checked with the brother who had been answering the guest house phone over the weekend. We found a couple of people she'd talked with, but no one knew anything, or admitted to knowing anything—except, maybe, Jeffrey Tatum. Charlie's supposed to talk with him today."

"And Jeffrey Tatum would be—?"

"A Jesuit, and a friend of Anna's. He teaches over at Saint Joe's and lives in one of the teaching brothers' houses on Garden Street."

"And he might be helpful because—?"

"I don't know why exactly, but he lied when we first talked with him, so I'm guessing he might have something else to say. Also, Jeffrey's—"

"What?"

"Here's the deal—"

"The deal, at last," he said, his voice regaining a touch of its usual irony.

"Anna met some people in college when she first came to the States, a conservative Catholic group—I don't know much more than that. Evidently, she thought this group—or some aging version of this group—might be connected to the incident in the cathedral, and an earlier one at Beth Shalom. She said she was going to make some calls, talk to some people, and find out what she could. I think she even hoped to stop the vandalism somehow, without getting the police involved."

"Stop it how?"

"I have no idea," said Lily.

"When was that—the thing at Beth Shalom?"

"A few months ago. But Charlie would know for sure, because he was there for that one, too."

"And he was there this time, right?" asked Gregarian. "I don't suppose Charlie could be, in any way—"

"No," said Lily. "No way. Trust me."

"And the Tatum guy is involved how?"

Lily shrugged. "At the very least, he's known Anna since she arrived in the States. And, frankly, it's not too hard to imagine him as a member of a 'conservative Catholic group'—if you get my drift."

The phone on the desk buzzed once, loudly. Lily startled, reached to grab it, pulled her hand back. Gregarian answered, said a few words, and hung up.

"Now we can ask him in person," said Gregarian.

"Jeffrey?"

"No, Charlie."

"You're going to ask him if he's part of this group?" asked Lily, her voice getting higher and louder on the last few words.

"No," said Gregarian. "You said to trust you and I do. I'm going to ask him for details about Beth Shalom."

Charlie didn't have much to add. He'd actually arrived late on the scene at Beth Shalom. He knew there'd been a flag, a doll, and a Bible. The doll had been nailed on a cross. He'd thumbed through the Bible—red cover, lots of red print, and at least one book printed in gold—which was why he recognized the one in the cathedral. He explained that the police had been called, but that, as far as he knew, they hadn't found who was responsible, at least not yet.

"Are these the only two incidents you know of—like this, I mean?" asked Gregarian.

"Yes," said Charlie.

"Me, too," said Gregarian. "This is the first I've heard of it—this group, this method. And I know most of them—or I like to think I do. So you didn't report the second incident, the one at the cathedral, because Banieka didn't want to get someone in trouble. How close to the group is she?"

"Not at all—not close at all," said Lily. "She just knew some of them in college. I think it's a shared history loyalty sort of thing. And it wasn't my impression she thought members of the group were actually responsible for any of it—just that they might know who was. So what's next?"

"Depends," said Gregarian. "What else did you find out yesterday?"

Lily and Charlie gave him the list of people they'd called, along with the responses, and ideas for follow-up. Charlie said he'd let Gregarian know what he learned from Jeffrey Tatum—if anything. Gregarian stared down at a notepad on his desk; occasionally he'd make a few marks.

To Lily they looked like Morse code notations. After Charlie finished talking, Gregarian sat silently, still studying the pad.

Lily restrained herself from interrupting the silence.

"I'm thinking," he finally said. "It sounds like Banieka may have gone home after all. I'll let the Wharton police know. You never talked with the bus driver, right?"

"No," said Lily. "Just a man in the office of Albany Lines. He looked up everything on the computer. But he wouldn't give me the bus driver's name."

"Okay, I'll see if I can find the driver. And I'm going to get you a list off our database—I'll pull all the hate groups that sound Catholic, or even a little bit Catholic, look for any similar incidents in the past few years. But since you already know people, and have this guy Tatum lined up to talk with, I'm going to leave that part to you."

"Which part?" asked Lily. "You mean trying to find out Anna's connection with the group?"

"Yeah," said Gregarian. "And finding out anything you can about who they are, where they are, if she ever talked with them. I'd be interested to know more about them, even if it turns out they have nothing to do with Banieka."

"Could you not call her that?" asked Lily. "Please?"

"Sure," said Gregarian. "Sorry. Do you know anyone in Wharton?"

"Not exactly," said Charlie. "But we've got to drive over there to meet her neighbor and figure out what to do about her dogs."

"Is this the same neighbor who was supposed to meet her at the bus?"

"Yes," said Charlie. "I talked to him on the phone, and he sounded—I don't know—surly."

"Do you remember his name?" asked Gregarian.

"Hatcher," said Charlie.

"What about the first name?"

"I can't remember. But I can call you with it when I get home."

"Do that," said Gregarian. "When are you going?"

Charlie looked over at Lily. She shrugged.

"This weekend?" she asked him.

"Probably," said Charlie. "Maybe Saturday."

"Good. Get me his name, and I'll run a check. And I'll try to talk with the driver."

"I thought you guys didn't do this kind of work in Missing Persons," said Lily. "I thought the missing person was supposed to show up down in the lobby and ask to be found."

"Naturally," said Gregarian, "those are the cases we prefer. But let's say I've taken a personal interest in this one. Also, her possible involvement with a hate group means there might be—" He glanced over Lily's shoulder at the Asian man, now talking loudly into the phone in another language—Lily thought it sounded like Portuguese. "It makes it worth looking into."

CHAPTER 10

By 11:30 Lily was back in her office. She tried to outline the new workshop schedule for the fall, but the dates and descriptions felt slippery and insubstantial, as if she were dealing with water instead of words and numbers. Barbara was out for lunch, Tuesday wasn't an intern day, so Lily had the place to herself. She stopped work and said the noon devotion. She used to feel comforted by the passage from Isaiah—"for in returning and rest we shall be saved; in quietness and trust shall be our strength." But lately it was as if she'd thought and read and argued so much about religion that she'd lost the ability, or the willingness, to practice it.

The first collect—"Blessed Savior, at this hour you hung upon the cross, stretching out your loving arms"—reminded her that Easter was just around the corner. And over the years, Easter had come to be her least favorite holy day. She could understand Jesus as a rabbi and a teacher. She could even *believe in* that Jesus—the Jesus who struggled and made mistakes and knew forgiveness first hand; the Jesus born without a human father; the Jesus who was tempted; the Jesus who cruelly dismissed the Syrophoenician woman, then had to take it back; the Jesus who asked that the cup be passed from him; the Jesus who protected the adulteress, who welcomed the tax collector, who forgave the Roman soldiers—but not Paul's Christ surfing down on a sunbeam, his identity obscured by the language of sin and sacrifice. And she didn't like all those Easter hymns about triumph, either.

She got caught up in her resentments, lost the thread of her prayers, and didn't hear Barbara come in. When she looked up, Barbara stood across from her.

"You don't look like you're praying," she said.

"I'm not," said Lily. She closed the prayer book and stuck it back in her desk. "I hate Easter."

Barbara chuckled. She took off her pale blue scarf and cashmere coat and hung them on the hook. "You can't hate Easter," she said. "You're a priest. You have to hate things like swear words and crack houses."

"You know the truth?" asked Lily. "I've never actually understood it."

"What?" asked Barbara. "Crack?"

"No, Easter," said Lily. "To begin with, I've never actually understood what it means, that Jesus died for our sins. What does that mean? I know about the goats and the sacrifices and all that, but I don't know how to translate that into anything useful for my life. And it's the holiday that brings out the worst in the church—all that king stuff, all that triumphalism. If there's anything I don't like it's a room full of well-fed white people being triumphal."

Barbara laughed out loud this time, then she sat down in her desk chair and started sifting through the stacks of mail. "I'll tell you what," she said. "If you don't like being in a room full of triumphal white people, you should come to church with me. You can be in a room full of triumphal black people—black Catholics at that. You want triumphal, we do triumphal."

"Could I?" asked Lily. "Would that be okay? I couldn't take communion, but that doesn't matter. It would just be—"

"A nice change?" asked Barbara.

"A very nice change. I love your church. And it's been too long since I visited. Can I come Palm Sunday, too? Then I've got my holidays covered, in case other things come up."

"Come as often as you want. Come as you are, as Father Ralph says. God won't have you any other way."

"Does it bother you that he's so corny?" asked Lily.

"No. But it bothers me that he's so white. Still, you work with what you got, and we got Father Ralph. As priests go, he's a pretty good one. He stays out of the choir's way and keeps the sermons short."

"Where are all the black Catholic priests?" asked Lily.

"I assume they're both busy," said Barbara. "So tell me how it went with the Armenian detective."

Lily reported on their conversation and the resulting plan. When she finished, Barbara looked up from the letter she was reading.

"Where do you think she is?" Barbara asked.

"I don't know," said Lily. "And on some level, I don't want to know anymore. I mean, I just want to keep hoping everything's all right."

The day passed slowly. Lily got some approximate version of the fall workshop schedule mapped out, but she was suspicious of the results. She felt almost certain that when she looked at the arrangement tomorrow it would make no sense. Around three o'clock Tom called to say he would come by her office at 5:30. But for some reason, Lily didn't want him to come to her office, so she suggested they meet halfway between. They decided on one of their regular spots, a small trattoria on Newbury, across Mass Ave, around the corner from the Women's Center.

About half an hour later, Gregarian called to say he had a printout of that list of hate groups for her. Should he bring it by? Or did she want to meet for a drink after work? He could go over it with her then.

Her first impulse was to say, "Sure, let's meet," and then lie to Tom. She told herself she was eager to have the information, but she knew better. She wanted to have a drink—or dinner—with Gregarian. Admitting this to herself threw her into more confusion than ever. She forgot for a moment what they were talking about. Then she recovered and said she already had plans but that she could come over the next day and pick up the list, maybe around lunch time—and they left it at that, said good-bye, and hung up.

Until Lily had met Tom, she'd been single for a long time, so long that Charlie regularly grilled her about her social life and her sexual identity. "It's okay to be a lesbian priest, you know," he'd said to her once. "You'd be in great company."

"If I were a lesbian, I'd be happy to be a lesbian priest, but I'm not going to pretend to be one just to make you feel better. You know how old-fashioned you're being? You think any woman who isn't married is gay?"

"Then what's this about? You're great looking, smart—you know the list."

"Everyone I like has taken holy vows," she'd said. "What's a girl to do?"

Then she had met Tom, and they'd fallen in love, and that had kept Charlie quiet for a while. Until he started asking her why she and Tom didn't live together, or get married. And then Tom had started asking the same questions, and Lily had found herself feeling short of breath when she was around him, having mild versions of the panic attacks she used to have in graduate school, especially in her tiny, airless study carrel. Sometimes when she and Tom were talking about the future, she'd have to open a window in midwinter, or she'd insist they take a walk, just so she could breathe.

And now this—Gregarian? Gregarian wasn't her type,

if she had one. She suspected he was divorced (no ring), paying alimony and child support (the pictures on his desk), a heavy drinker (ruddy complexion, deep circles under his eyes). But all the same, she had wanted to meet him for a drink, even though she didn't drink anymore—at least, that was the plan. As she turned out lights and shut down the copy machine, she tried to make sense of it, found she couldn't, and gave up for the moment.

It was almost 5:30 when she locked the door to the office and rode the elevator to the first floor. Outside, the dark clouds that had rolled in that morning had never left. The air was cold and raw, with a fine drizzle that slicked the city streets and caused cars to slide precariously into intersections jammed with rush hour traffic. This particular form of New England spring made Lily homesick for the rough heat of Texas.

When she reached the restaurant, she glanced in through the plate glass window and saw Tom sitting at the bar, drinking what looked like water in a shot glass. Grappa, she thought. And just for that instant she could feel it slide down her throat and hit her stomach, knocking out a few lights in her brain, dimming the system. It sounded like a great idea, except she might not stop there. If she started on grappa now, she might end up on tequila or cognac or Jim Beam at 3 A.M., God knows where, and eventually find her way home, to spend the next day in bed, having called in sick with the flu. She'd had the flu a lot in seminary.

She closed her eyes and took some deep breaths. The cold mist felt good just then, clean, a reminder of real life. When she looked at him again, Tom had taken out a pen and was drawing something on a napkin, something he showed the bartender and the waitress, who both, at the same moment, threw back their heads and laughed. He wore an old anorak, navy with drab green lining, and his hair was curlier than usual from the damp air. Her heart contracted, like a fist; she wanted never to lose him.

"I called today before I came over," Lily was telling him. "Someone said you'd gone to the morgue." They'd gotten a table by the window, technically for bar customers only, but, for Tom, the owner bent the rules.

"What do you mean, came over?" he asked. He cocked his head to feign mild interest, but she could see it was more than that.

"I came back to talk with Gregarian today—Charlie and I came back together. I'd planned to visit you but you weren't there."

"What brought you back?" he asked.

"We did some research on our own yesterday, and I wanted to give Gregarian the results. Also, we left out something when we first talked."

"What?" asked Tom. "Or can't you say?"

"No," said Lily. "I mean, yes, of course I can say. We just didn't mention it yesterday because Anna had asked us not to talk about it with anyone." And she told the story of the cathedral, and of Anna's reaction, again for Tom.

"So you think she actually knew who did it?" he asked.

"No," said Lily. "Not knew, exactly. This is only a theory, but the more I remember about it, the more I think— When we first walked in and saw the doll and the rest, she didn't seem all that surprised. She was shaken by it, but not surprised, almost as if she'd been worried something like this might happen. Then she started talking about the theological content, which was kind of a weird response—not the first thing that came to mind—at least, to my mind."

"You think she expected it?" he asked.

"Not exactly," said Lily. "More like, she understood it, or had some idea what it was all about. Also—"

"What?" he asked.

"That thing about not reporting it. She said she didn't want to call attention to the group, because that's what they want. She said something about bad children, when children go through a stage when they want attention—I don't know. That's not my area of expertise. But it sounded familiar, somehow, almost protective."

"Sounds like a good place to start," said Tom.

"Does it?" asked Lily. "I'm not sure."

"Speaking of which, Greg asked me to give you this." He reached into the inside pocket of his jacket, hanging on the back of the chair, and handed her a thick, white envelope with the Boston Police Department insignia in the upper left-hand corner. "I forgot. Sorry."

"That's okay," said Lily. Her heart took a little plunge. She wouldn't be walking over there at lunch tomorrow. "It's just a list of hate groups—ideas to get us going." She started to scan the names and descriptions, but nothing sounded familiar. "Look how many there are. They've even got their own printing presses."

The waitress who'd been at the bar earlier brought a glass of red wine for Tom and a bottle of sparkling water for Lily. She was small boned, olive skinned, with thick dark hair pulled back into a long ponytail. She made Lily feel as if they were actually in Italy, at least until she spoke. "Ready to order?" she asked. Her Boston accent made the last word sound like *ahduh.*

Lily looked sheepish. "I forgot to look at the menu," she said. "Give me another minute."

"Sure," she said.

"So," said Tom. "Decide what you want to eat, then—"

"I know," said Lily. "We need to talk." Her guilt made her voice sound clipped.

"Actually, I've been thinking," said Tom. "With everything going on, maybe we should just enjoy the meal. You could use a break, right?"

"Right," said Lily. She felt tears in her eyes—a mixture of gratitude, relief, worry, sadness, and hunger. "I could definitely use a break."

"So let's think of this as a date. We haven't had one of those for a while. How does that sound?"

"Like divine intervention," said Lily. She reached over and took his hand. "Thanks."

He blushed slightly, a faint pink tinge, and patted her hand. "No problem."

CHAPTER 11

By Saturday, March had undergone its annual identity crisis. Charlie and Lily left Boston under blue skies, the cherry and apple and sycamore trees along the Charles in early bud, the scullers out in full force. But Lily found the whole scene irritating, as if the people—as well as the sun and the trees and the skinny boats and the birds and the romping dogs—should know why she and Charlie were on this trip and should tone it down.

Every day that passed without news of Anna made Lily more certain that something was very wrong. Her fears felt shapeless and unfathomable. Lily didn't picture Anna dead or bound in a dark room or even wandering blankly around downtown Albany. She couldn't picture Anna at all, not since the dream of the bus. Lily slept little, and badly, and when she woke, she knew she'd been dreaming—but not dreams she could remember or visualize. Anna had disappeared from Lily's psyche. Though Lily felt as if she thought about Anna constantly, she couldn't *see* her anymore.

Spring receded before them as they drove northwest on Route 2. Once they reached the Berkshires, the fields looked winter sere, and only a few trees showed tiny flecks of pale green on their limbs. It was like watching a Disney slow-motion recording of seasons running backwards.

"I smell something," said Lily.

"You always say that when you're in this car," said Charlie.

"No, no. I mean something—different."

"Yeah, I smell it now, too. I think that's Syro. That *is* different." The monastery dog, a black, one-eyed, long-haired mutt, part Lab, part setter, lay asleep next to the luggage in the back of the station wagon.

"If we wake him up will he stop making that awful stink?" asked Lily.

"No," said Charlie. "If we wake him up, he'll try to bring the stink up here into the front seat with you."

"I don't understand why we brought him," said Lily.

"Because we're going to the country and when you go to the country you take the dog. Also he's my responsibility for the time being. I'm doing dog-walking and -feeding duty for the moment. Besides, he loves Anna. He sometimes sleeps in her room when she stays at the monastery guest house." They both fell silent at the mention of Anna's name. Lily noticed that Charlie put all the verbs in the present tense.

Charlie glanced at Lily. "Does this indifference of yours to animals and small children ever concern you?"

"I'm not indifferent. I just don't find *all* animals and small children inherently charming. I take them as they come, on a case-by-case basis." In the silence that followed, Lily looked out the window at the landscape, the rugged fields, the gray barns and houses, the swollen creek that wove its way along the roadside. "Anyway, I love Syro."

Though Lily didn't want it to, the silence stretched out over minutes. She tried to picture Anna's face, but it eluded her again. She and Charlie had talked to almost everyone on their list by now—except Jeffrey Tatum, who had been impossible to find. When Charlie hadn't heard back, he'd called Jeffrey on Thursday, but Jeffrey had gone on retreat and wouldn't return until the following Sunday, the same day Lily and Charlie returned from this trip to Wharton.

Gregarian had talked to the bus driver who hadn't remembered Anna but said that didn't mean anything—the bus had been full most of the way, at least as far as Wharton. He had remembered something weird about the Wharton stop, a family—he thought they were Chinese, maybe Japanese, something like that—who'd been on the bus, he thought it was that same day. One of them—the mother he thought—had to get off in Wharton to buy the rest of her ticket to Albany. The bus driver couldn't understand them well enough to learn the whole story. If it was the run he thought it was, the bus had definitely been full, so he couldn't remember everyone on there. But he did remember that family, the Chinese mother with the ticket to Wharton who had wanted to go all the way to Albany, who'd bought the rest of her ticket at the Wharton station.

When Gregarian told her all this, he and Lily had been eating at a sandwich shop around the corner from her office. It was the only time they'd gotten together outside the police station. He had called her to report on what he'd found out, and Lily had asked him to lunch. "I'm going pretty soon anyway," she'd said—a lie. She'd planned to make a sandwich and get work done. She had no idea what she was doing, but whatever it was, it wasn't good. She remembered how Gregarian had imitated the bus driver's voice, how perfectly he'd captured the Albany accent, how much they had laughed.

She caught her reflection in the sideview mirror, a slight smile on her face.

"Did you look over the list from Greg?" she asked Charlie.

"Greg?"

"Detective Gregarian," said Lily. "Did you check out the list of hate groups?"

"Greg?" Charlie repeated.

"Forget it," said Lily.

"I looked at it," said Charlie. "But nothing especially caught my eye. What about you?"

"Same here. It seemed like the usual suspects—Aryan-nation skinhead white supremacist ZOG types—except for a group west of Boston. Did you see them? They have a printing press that puts out some pretty sophisticated stuff."

"Like what—homophobic villanelles?"

"No—more like biblical tracts and historical studies—how the Bible Code proves the Zionist takeover of the world, how you can tell the Holocaust never happened. What do you think the median IQ is in that group?"

"I'd say it's somewhere around the national average," said Charlie.

She looked over at him. "Come on, you know these people are dumb dumb dumb."

"Don't underestimate your opponent," said Charlie. "Just because people don't agree with you, doesn't mean they're stupid. We're almost there," he added. "Let's go to Anna's first, then we can get food and stuff at the general store down the road from her, okay?"

"Yeah, fine," she said. "Do you think the Chinese family had anything to do with Anna?"

"What Chinese family? You mean the people on the bus? No—or I guess I mean I don't see why they would. I think it's just a coincidence. The driver told Gregarian—I mean Greg—there were a few students coming back, too, that a few people got off there. I think he just can't remember her face."

"If she got on," said Lily.

"If she got on," echoed Charlie.

Because all tickets had been turned in, the bus had been full, and the suitcase had never showed up, Gregarian and the police were working on the assumption Anna had gotten on the bus and gotten off in Wharton. Lily didn't feel so sure. Neither did Charlie. But those conversations, that careful sorting through of the facts, seemed to belong to the days when Lily still had hopes of finding Anna, even hopes of the whole thing's being a monumental mistake. Now, in some way, the rehashing of details seemed like a lie, another method for delaying the truth.

Wharton lay just off Route 2, in the far northwestern corner of Massachusetts, almost to the Vermont border. About fifteen minutes after they turned off the main highway, Lily and Charlie passed a row of clapboard houses. A small creek—a tributary of the Hudson—ran behind the houses on the left. Lily could glimpse makeshift bridges, pulleys, and rafts rigged to connect the backyards to a maze of wire pens and wooden paddocks in the field beyond.

"I love this place," said Lily.

"Wait until you see Anna's house," said Charlie. "*That* you will really love. It's just your style."

They drove through the center of town, past the college buildings clustered at the foot of a small hill, at the top of which stood a white church with a spire, and then out into a series of broad meadows. Syro had woken up when they left the highway. The back seat of the station wagon was down, so he now stood in his usual position, directly behind the front seat with his head resting on Charlie's shoulder.

At an intersection where a dirt road crossed the main road, Lily spotted a general store with two gas pumps outside and a gray shingled house next door. Charlie turned left onto the dirt road and they climbed slowly, passing the occasional gray farmhouse, red barn, smattering of black and white cows. He turned left again onto a road whose sides were overgrown with pine seedlings and waist-high grasses.

After almost a mile, Charlie turned left yet again into

what looked like a natural break in the roadside flora. In front of them stood a shack—a small, flat-roofed wooden structure.

"This is just my style?" asked Lily.

"Wait," said Charlie. "You'll see."

From around the corner of the house came the dogs. The leader of the pack, who looked like a miniature wolf, ran at the car, barking. Lily turned and saw that Syro had hunkered down behind the back of the seat and was staring up at Charlie. If he'd been a child, he would have had tears in his eyes.

"Syro's terrified," said Lily.

"Who isn't?" asked Charlie.

They sat in the car together, windows up, doors closed, until a young man appeared, also from around the corner of the house. He was small and wiry, probably in his late teens, with a full head of straight black hair, longish in the back.

He walked up to the wolf-like dog and grabbed its collar. The dog yelped, then got quiet. The young man turned the dog around, half pulling, half walking it back to the house, then whistled once, sharply, and the other three dogs followed them.

Lily and Charlie still sat in the car.

"Shouldn't we get out?" asked Lily.

"I'm not sure," said Charlie. "Who was that?"

"The neighbor?" asked Lily.

"No," said Charlie. "The neighbor sounded like an older guy. I think."

"Let's go see," said Lily. She opened her door, climbed out, and stretched. Then she leaned back in and grabbed her parka off the seat. "It's cold," she said. "But I think it's safe. You can emerge."

Charlie got out and called Syro, but the dog stayed where he was, scanning the horizon. So they closed the doors and left him for the moment. As she walked toward the house, Lily glanced back and could see Syro's ears over the top of the front seat.

Then she stopped. What had looked like a shack from the driveway turned out to be a small, graceful one-story cottage. The house stood most of the way up a long, gradual slope. The front yard was a fenced-in field of grasses—soon to be wildflowers, Lily thought—and a large rectangle of freshly turned earth. Lily could only begin to imagine this scene in summer, with the asters and cornflowers and tall tomato plants at their peak.

Across the front of the house stretched a deep, screened-in porch with a variety of furniture—a faded armchair, a glider, a small wooden table, and a pair of white metal bunkbeds against the far end. A black and tan mutt lay on the armchair, two yellow dogs on the floor, and the largest dog, the wolf-like shepherd leader, lounged on the bottom bunk. Now that they'd been called off, the animals seemed content to watch.

The man had disappeared. Lily walked to the door of the porch and yelled "hello." After a moment of silence, she heard footsteps, but they were from outside. She wheeled around to see him materialize behind her, a heavy wrench in his hand.

"I'm about to shut off the water," he said. "I was just checking the outside line. If she's not going to be here, the pipes will freeze—at least, they might." He had large, dark eyes, thick eyelashes, and an olive complexion. Lily could see he was part Asian; his face would have been beautiful if there'd been any warmth in it at all.

"But we were going to stay here tonight," said Lily. For a moment no one spoke or moved. Charlie cleared his throat. Then Lily walked toward the stranger and held out her hand. "I'm Lily Connor, a friend of Anna's, from Boston. I thought Charlie had called to say we were—"

"I did," said Charlie.

"I didn't talk to you," said the man. He moved the

wrench from his left hand to his right, but didn't appear to see Lily's outstretched arm.

"Are you Mr. Hatcher?" asked Charlie.

"I'm one of them—Andy," he said, then shifted the wrench back to his right hand. Lily had slowly lowered her own hand and wiped it on her jeans.

"I called earlier this week to say we'd come up this weekend and figure out what to do about the dogs. I talked with someone—"

The man's eyes narrowed, just for an instant, and Lily was almost sure he suddenly remembered the call. "Is it okay if we stay here?" she asked. "We're trying to get things in order for Anna, see to the dogs, make sure the house is all right."

"That's what she pays me for," said Hatcher. "But it's okay with me if you want to take it over. Looks like I'm not going to get paid anytime soon anyway."

Apparently, he thought of Anna's disappearance as an interruption in his pay schedule, and not much more. Lily tried to imagine Anna making friends with Mr. Hatcher, but she couldn't.

Hatcher walked past Lily and onto the porch; she smelled cigarettes and something else—vodka?—she wasn't sure. Inside, he knelt next to a large red metal tool kit. He put the wrench into the bottom and closed the lid, snapping both clasps shut. After which he stood, picked up the tool kit, and walked back out into the yard.

"You'll have to feed the dogs," he said. "The food's in a barrel in the kitchen." He started down the driveway, tool kit in his left hand, his right hand swinging out from his body, slightly, to balance the weight. "Let me know when you leave," he called back over his shoulder. "So I can shut the water off." From behind, he looked like a young boy carrying a tackle box.

Charlie opened his mouth to call out after him, then closed it.

"I wouldn't bother," said Lily. "We can find out more on our own." Then she opened the door and stepped into the porch. The smallest dog, a little yellow lab mutt, got up, trotted over, and sniffed her shoes, her pants, and, finally, her hand. Lily could feel his soft, warm nose in her palm. Then the dog walked back and lay down, with a deep sigh.

CHAPTER 12

The older section of the house included one large room with a small kitchen, a woodstove, a table and chairs, and a platform bed that Lily guessed, judging from the dog hair, served as the pack's winter nest. Off the back, behind a curtained doorway, Lily discovered the bedroom, with a double brass bed that almost filled the tiny cubicle, leaving just enough space for an oak dresser. This part of the house was snug, a hermit's hut. But just past the kitchen, through a wide doorway, Lily found another, newer space, a high-ceilinged room with two tall windows facing out across the sloping meadows. The room held a minimum of furniture—an overstuffed sofa, a high-backed rocking chair, and a long trestle table, obviously Anna's workspace, that stretched across the far wall.

Lily wandered through the house, retracing her steps more than once. The three smaller dogs joined her from time to time, sometimes alone, sometimes in pairs, sometimes all three together. As she roamed, she talked to them quietly, cataloging the house's contents, commenting on surprises—the glass box full of perfect sand dollars, the collection of delicate, etched wine glasses. She thought of how much she would have enjoyed this same tour if Anna had been with her.

Lily didn't like being there alone, without Anna; it was like being in a house with a ghost. She found the thermostat and turned up the baseboard heat, then crossed the porch into the yard again and called to Charlie, who was trying to lure Syro out of the station wagon with a dog biscuit they'd discovered in a tin on the refrigerator.

"How's it going?" she yelled.

Charlie shrugged and pointed to Syro, who sat in exactly the same place he'd sat when they'd pulled into the drive.

"Where's the wood?" she called. "Do you know?"

"In the shed, around the side of the house," he yelled back, this time pointing in the direction from which Hatcher had appeared with the wrench.

Lily returned to the front and then continued around the corner. She saw a small lean-to next to the house. Inside, almost a cord of wood had been neatly ricked against the back wall. On a shelf along a side wall stood some tools, a couple of cans of paint, a jumble of string, nails, grease rags, a pack of cigarettes—Andy Hatcher's stuff. The place felt like it belonged to him—cold and hostile.

Lily filled her arms with wood and carried it inside to the box by the stove. She went back for her second load, but as she was pulling a log from the pile, she saw something shiny, silvery, wedged between the bottom row of logs and the wall of the house. She leaned over to get a better look. It was a small bottle of clear liquid, and she thought she saw something else beneath it.

She hunched down against the wall and grabbed the bottle—it came out easily enough and proved to be a pint of vodka. Though it was cheap liquor and though Lily had never drunk vodka, even when she drank, for a second she wanted to take a swig from the bottle. The impulse passed quickly, but it surprised her, and she noticed her hand shook slightly as she lay the pint on the ground beside her.

On her second try, she felt something cold and hard,

something metal. This time, she pulled out a black handgun with a long barrel and a fake wood handle. She knew plenty about shotguns—on the ranch, she'd gotten her own rifle when she was twelve—but not much about handguns. She could see that the serial number had been partially defaced—a less than thorough job—and, on inspection, she discovered the gun was loaded. She checked to be sure the safety was on, then picked up both the bottle and the gun and went to show Charlie.

The gun and the pint lay at one end of the table near the woodstove. Lily and Charlie sat at the other end, finishing off the homemade tomato soup, cheese, apples, and whole wheat challah that Charlie had brought from the monastery. Syro remained in the car, but the other dogs had hopped up onto the platform bed, where they lay curled around one another.

"What do you think we should do with it?" asked Charlie, staring at the gun.

"I think we probably ought to put it back," said Lily. "I guess I could try to read what's left of the registration number, but I suspect it belongs to the young Mr. Hatcher and doesn't have much to do with us."

"How do you know?" asked Charlie. "Couldn't it be important?"

"You mean couldn't it have something to do with Anna?" asked Lily. "I suppose. We probably ought to let the police know he has it, just in case. What should we do about Syro?"

"I give up," said Charlie. "He can live in the car."

"Yeah, but he can't poop in the car."

"We'll cross that bridge when we come to it. Have you looked around inside?"

"Everywhere but the closets, dresser, and desk. I thought we should do that together. It feels so—"

"Private?" asked Charlie.

"Private—yes," she said. "I was thinking eerie." What she was really thinking was *final,* but she didn't say that to Charlie.

"When we finish eating, we'll look together. Then we need to get down to the store to get stuff for tonight and tomorrow." He stood and started to wrap up the rest of the bread and cheese. Because of their similar build and coloring—tall and slender, dark hair, dark eyes—Lily and Charlie had occasionally been mistaken for brother and sister. At the moment he wore a red pullover, a white shirt, black jeans, and Lily speculated that no one would ever know he was a monk—except for his fresh-faced quality, that mix of innocence and enthusiasm that had always lent him a slightly otherworldly air. Charlie was a natural, meant for priesthood and monastic life. He had known it when they first met, in seminary, and had never wavered in his plan. His faith was complex but constant; he never lost it, at least as far as she could tell. But then, what did she know?

"And what about the police—and the newspaper?" he asked her.

"Gregarian talked with them both yesterday," she said. "The local police know we're here, and the Wharton paper's going to run a story about Anna, telling about her disappearance, asking anyone who knows anything to get in touch with them. The *Globe*'s been harder to convince, but Gregarian's going to keep trying."

"Is there a reward?" asked Charlie.

"I don't think so," said Lily. "Who would offer a reward? I mean, who knows her well enough and has the money to do that?"

"Maybe we should do it. We could raise the money from her friends."

"Maybe," said Lily. "If nothing comes of this one, we could get them to run a second story about the reward. And do the same thing in Boston."

"I have a feeling we're the only people left who think she might still be in Boston," said Charlie. "Everyone else is assuming she got on the bus and got off with her luggage, that she's around here somewhere."

Lily didn't correct the tense this time either.

"I know," she said. "But that doesn't mean we're wrong."

"No," said Charlie. "Just stubborn. It's not like we've got anything to go on. It's a hunch."

"It's the power of deduction," said Lily. "If she'd gotten off the bus in Wharton, someone would have seen her. She's lived here for twenty years. She taught at the college all that time. It's not reasonable to think she could have been out here for a week without bumping into someone she knows. And you talked with the neighbor, right? He said he was there, waiting for her. What are the chances he could lie about that and get away with it? Someone must have seen him."

"I'm beginning to wonder though," said Charlie, glancing at the gun.

"About what?"

"About the neighbors."

"That guy?" asked Lily, nodding toward the end of the table. "He's your basic ne'er-do-well. Probably lives with his father, done some jail time. They're both drunks, and they make their living plowing driveways and taking care of summer houses—and Anna. Why would they put an end to one of their few sources of income?"

"Then why are you getting the serial number off the gun?" asked Charlie.

"Because you never know," said Lily. She pushed away from the table and stood. "I'll get whatever numbers I can figure out and then put the stuff back in the woodpile. Then let's go through the closets and desk before we go to the store."

"How come?" asked Charlie.

"I'm not sure. I guess I'm eager to see if we can find anything useful, anything that tells us where she might be."

"Like what?" he asked. "What are we looking for?"

"I don't know—a diary, address book, appointment book, list of things to do with phone numbers on it. Any kind of information about this week, about her plans."

"Doesn't it seem like the police should be doing this?"

"Yeah," said Lily. "It does. But they're not. So let's start."

They began in the bedroom closet, a small niche with a curtain across the front. Anna's clothes exactly filled the space with little room to spare. Lily pushed through the hanging clothes to peer in behind, but didn't find much of interest—a neat stack of shoe boxes (the top one containing a pair of black dress pumps) and some thick folded sweaters on a small shelf near the floor. The dresser held no surprises either—plenty of long underwear, flannel nightgowns, thick socks.

"There aren't any pictures," said Lily. "Have you noticed?"

"What do you mean?"

"No bedside photos, no snapshots. I just realized. It's kind of weird."

"But it makes sense," said Charlie. "Given her past."

"I guess," said Lily. "Though it's not as if she doesn't have one. Let's try the desk."

Along with an older computer—large and square, with a separate modem and a printer on the floor underneath the table—they found a cordless phone and an answering machine, which showed that it held seven messages. Lily hit the replay button. First they heard the voice of a man—stiff, formal—asking politely if plans had become confused.

"That's the neighbor," said Charlie. "That's the one I talked to."

Next, they heard Charlie's voice, once, twice, three times, and after that the neighbor again. The sixth message started in silence, then they heard a sigh, and maybe a word, distorted and unintelligible. Then the person began to cry, slowly at first, then harder. Between the sobs Lily thought she could make out the words "I can't" or "I am." The message ended abruptly, as if the tape had cut off.

Charlie stopped the machine. "What in the hell was that?" he asked.

They looked at one another. "I have no idea," said Lily. "Play it again."

They still couldn't make out the words, but Lily felt worried and frightened. "We should take this to Gregarian," she said.

"Why?" asked Charlie. "What would he do with it?"

"I'm not sure. Maybe it will convince him to stay involved."

They listened to the final message—from the secretary in the English Department at Wharton College—then Lily took the tape out of the machine and stuck it in her pocket.

Since the desk was a trestle table, there were no drawers. In the large wooden boxes on top, behind the computer, they found recent letters—two of them from colleges inviting her to speak, but none inviting her to speak during March—four or five legal pads filled with notes—and, in the largest box, file folders, labeled with dates and places. On inspection, these appeared to hold essays and talks delivered over the past couple of years. As Lily looked through the files, her eye caught sight of a door in the wall next to the desk—it was small, about three feet high, and had a simple wooden latch.

She put the cover back on the file box, leaned over, and

opened the door. In the light from the tall windows, she saw a crawl space lined on three sides with shelves. Every shelf held a long row of audio tapes in their clear plastic cases, and every shelf was labeled. Lily recognized Anna's square, solid handwriting on the labels: Poddebice/childhood; Poddebice/1939–1943; Lodz/Nov.'43–Nov.'44; Nov.'44–Jan.'45; Lodz/1945; Giverny/1947–48; Boston/1948–.

Lily pulled out a plastic case from the far end of the second shelf, marked "Poddebice/1939–1943." In the same handwriting, on a small white label on the cassette itself, she read, "the arrest, Nov.'43," and on the next line, "first tape."

The tape recorder was on the floor of the crawl space, under the bottom shelf on the right. Charlie set it up on the desk, plugged it in, and put in the tape Lily still held. The sound quality was bad, tinny and blurred, so Charlie turned down the treble and turned up the volume. Anna's voice filled the room.

". . . later, Sonia and I decided it must have been the old Dembowski woman who told them about us. She had always hated my mother, because she was beautiful, and because she married my father, whom the Dembowski woman had hoped to marry. Once when Jan and I went to her house to deliver eggs, she hit me with a switch. I don't remember why. Maybe no reason.

"They came at night. I can remember the sounds. They pounded on the door, and it seems to me I'd never heard that noise before, because we never locked our door. People just walked in and out."

Charlie suddenly stopped the tape. Lily looked up, surprised, and saw tears in his eyes. Then she saw that all four dogs stood in the doorway, their heads cocked, ears raised, staring toward the tape recorder.

CHAPTER 13

It had begun to rain—a thin drizzle that coated the trees, the high grasses, the turned earth. The view from Anna's windows looked vague, as if in need of fine tuning. Lily set down her mug of tea and turned on one of the desk lamps. She sat in the office-style desk chair and rewound the tape to the beginning. Charlie had gone to the store; he hadn't wanted to listen. But she had. When the tape stopped rewinding, she pushed play.

Again, Anna's voice filled the room. "I had the impression, as a child," she said, "that everyone in the world was related to everyone else." This time, only the three smaller dogs came trotting to the door and stared in the direction of the voice. "My father had nine brothers and sisters, and seven of them were married with children. Both sets of my grandparents were still alive. So almost everyone in my town was related somehow—at least, that's how it seemed to me then."

Anna stumbled at the beginning of the next sentence. Then, after a short silence, she said, "My father believed—and my mother—that being a Christian meant you helped other people. My whole family believed this—that being a Christian meant you behaved in certain ways, that you helped people in trouble. And then, of course, most of the people we knew were relatives, so you would help them anyway." She had laughed when saying that last sentence. Lily saw her, wry smile, dyed hair, round, lined face.

"After Germany invaded Poland, most of my family hid Jews. My father wouldn't let his parents, or my mother's parents, because they were old by then, and he knew they could be caught and punished. I think I can remember my mother saying we had fifty Jews living among us—in barns, cellars, worksheds. I understood that they were in danger and we were helping them. I only felt confused—it was confusing to me because—" There was another pause, and a click. She had stopped recording. Lily looked up and saw that the dogs had settled down this time on the rug in the middle of the room.

Then a second click, and her voice returned. "We didn't have Jewish friends; they didn't come to our house. But my father traded with them—milk, potatoes, eggs from our farm for shoes and leather—that's what I remember—we got our leather from the Jews. At Easter our church put on a play. Every year Judas would come on stage dressed like a Jew of our village, someone I recognized, a different Jew each year, I think. Once I remember he looked like the man with whom we traded for leather. When we would go to trade, his daughter and I would take the scraps of leather from the floor and make rings and bracelets and necklaces for ourselves.

"In the play, the other Jews in the crowd yelled and screamed, in a sort of frenzy, for Jesus to be crucified. I recognized some of them, too. I thought the Jews of our village had crucified Jesus. As I got older, and I suppose I understood the play better, I became afraid of them. I stopped going with my father to trade for leather. When we traveled to Lodz, I would stay just next to my mother, because there were so many Jews around. I thought, if they'd kill Jesus, then surely they'd kill me. I didn't want to be hanging on a cross and have vinegar shoved into my mouth.

"One year—after the Germans had come to our town, come to stay—my father left this play before it was over. But he never spoke about it to us, so, of course, as a child, I thought he had left because he felt so mad at the Jews." There was a pause, during which the tape ran. Lily could hear, on the tape, in the background, the tap-tap sound of one of the dogs paws on the wood floor. Anna said something, off to the side, in Polish—it had the tone of an endearment. Then she began to speak in English again, into the tape recorder.

"So I didn't understand, the whole time—why were we saving these people? We had never eaten with them, or had them to our home, and they had killed Jesus, and suddenly they're living in our barn. And in my favorite auntie's cellar. And in our cousins' attics. My mother said our family had fifty Jews living among us—more Jews than family members. Once when I asked where the Jews came from, my father told me Lodz, 'the ghetto in Lodz,' he said. And I thought, so these are the Jews that might kill me. No one explained it to us, or to me, at least.

"My father built a false ceiling in our barn, above the hayloft, and they lived way up there. Usually my father or my oldest brother took food out and emptied the waste buckets. One evening I wanted to see what it was like, what happened, so I climbed into the hayloft and waited. I got down under the hay and waited until my father came. It was getting cold, and I began to shiver, but I kept quiet. My father dragged a ladder out from under the hay, climbed it, knocked on the ceiling, and, from within, someone pulled up a plank. My father handed in food and took a bucket from them. Everyone was completely silent. It was like watching from a long distance away, or from behind thick glass.

"My father bent down, and when he did, I saw the face

of the leather man up in the ceiling space and, beside him, a girl, his daughter. But she looked completely different, her skin very white. And I remember her eyes. I gasped. I hadn't thought about children—I hadn't thought about my playmate from all those years ago. So I made a noise.

"All three of them turned toward me—as I say this, I see their faces. I had never seen adults afraid like that. I had thought only children could be so afraid. My father, who had a ruddy complexion, went pale. I got up on my knees from where I had been lying on the ground. I must have been covered in hay.

"The girl waved at me. But it was the wave of someone very far away, in a different world. I didn't wave back.

"All the color came into my father's face. He got very red. But the other man, the Jewish man, looked so relieved, as if he might cry.

"That night, my father and mother talked to all of us, my brothers and sisters and me, and explained what was happening, and why. But I don't remember their saying anything about Jews—I don't remember their using the word 'Jews.' They may have. I only remember their telling us about the Germans. In my mind, I think I just added Germans to the list of people who would kill me. And so in that way I never really got my thinking straight about what was happening, or about the Jews."

Again, the tape clicked off, then on, and the next section was the place at which Lily had first heard Anna's voice, the story about the Dembowski woman, and about the soldiers coming to Anna's home in the night. The next morning the Germans had taken her entire family—grandparents, parents, brothers, sisters, aunts, uncles, cousins—to the paved courtyard in the middle of their town. The wind was fierce, the temperature below freezing.

"We had no coats, none of us. I tried to wrap my skirt around my youngest brother, Stephan, to cover his shoulders. But I couldn't do it and remain covered myself. Still, I kept trying.

"The Germans brought the grown-ups, two or three at a time, to stand in front of the wall of our church. A row of German soldiers stood facing that wall. All the children stood to the side, close enough so that the gunshots hurt our ears. Then I tried to cover my brother's ears, and his eyes, and his shoulders—everything, but I couldn't. More than once, soldiers had to move the bodies aside in order to make room for more."

Silence on the tape, the sound of a chair on casters, probably the chair Lily was sitting in at that moment, as she listened. Then the recorder switched off, then on, and Anna's voice began again.

"My mother and father were the last. I think they had been identified as the ringleaders. They were both small people, fine-boned. They didn't look like ringleaders.

"My father had a sign hung around his neck. It said—it was in German, of course—but it meant 'He helped the Jews.'

"My mother was in her underwear. I remember how old-fashioned it looked to me; she still wore some sort of bloomers. Her skin was purple from the cold."

The tape ran for almost a minute.

"Afterward, everyone left but two soldiers. They made us stand there a long time, maybe until dark. I'm not sure. At some point, we were all taken to the orphanage."

The tape ran again; there was the sound of the chair rolling across the wooden floor. Then Lily could hear some rustling, the sound of papers being shuffled. Then the tape clicked off.

CHAPTER 14

Sunday morning Lily took the dogs for a walk and left Charlie to listen to one of the tapes. The weather had cleared overnight. The sky was bright blue, cloudless, and there was a strong breeze from the north. Lily walked down the driveway and turned left, letting the dogs lead the way. The night before, Syro had been enticed into the house with a beef-scented chew toy; he had stood still, petrified, until the other dogs were through sniffing him, and he had stuck next to Charlie from then on. At one point during the night, Charlie had woken up and found Syro trying to crawl into the sleeping bag.

But now Syro traveled with the pack. The road led them up into the woods. Lily discovered minuscule signs of spring: green shoots in sunlit patches along the road, tiny red buds on a few of the maple branches, and a fluty sonata of birdsongs.

Soon the dogs veered off onto a steep path. Lily saw a sign that read "Lookout" nailed to a tree at the intersection; she would have missed it had she been alone. At first glance, she read it as two words, then, irritated, corrected herself. The route led straight to the top, and Lily wondered at Anna's having made this climb. She remembered standing at the foot of the stairs to the cathedral a week ago, worrying about Anna, about her ability to make it as far as the portico. She remembered the gray cast of Anna's cheeks. I'll never see her again, thought Lily; her stomach lurched—she stopped and put her hand on a nearby tree. She waited, but nothing happened, no tears, no more feelings, so she continued up the path.

Soon she saw bright light through the trees ahead. Twenty yards on, the ground leveled and fell away, so that the whole valley lay exposed, earth readied for new crops, fields marked by hedgerows and barbed wire and riprap walls, houses and barns set in clusters of maple, oak, chestnut. On the farm at the foot of the hill, Lily could see chickens in a pen behind the gray house and, next to the barn, a paddock with two chestnut horses. The sun filled the bowl made by the surrounding mountains. Lily sat with her back against a wide white pine and breathed. She started her morning prayers, "Open my lips, O Lord, and my mouth shall proclaim your praise. Create in me a clean heart, O God—" But a sudden eruption of barks and growls kept her from getting any farther.

She got to her feet and walked toward the path to see what had happened. Syro appeared at her side, then hung behind. The other three smaller dogs milled aimlessly, keeping a distance from the leader, the big shepherd, who lay at the base of a huge fir tree in a clearing off to the right. When Lily walked toward him, he bared his teeth and rumbled, a low, thoughtful sound, a canine suggestion that she not come any closer.

She didn't. This must be a spot the dog owned, where he'd come with Anna countless times and stood guard while she rested from the climb. Lily felt surprised he'd barked at the other dogs if that was the case, since they were part of the family, but maybe Syro had unknowingly come too close. He certainly wouldn't have done it knowingly.

Suddenly, the three smaller dogs ran down the path,

barking. Someone was coming. The shepherd never moved, just bared his teeth again, but this time with a growl that was deep-throated and serious. Lily couldn't decide whether to call out or step back into the trees.

Then she heard Charlie's voice, shaky and distant, calling to the dogs, calming them down. His head and shoulders appeared, then he was in front of her on the path. She knew that he hadn't seen her and that she would startle him if she called out, so she stayed quiet. To Lily's surprise, he walked over and sat next to the shepherd, who stopped growling and licked his face a couple of times. Lily could see Charlie was crying, had been crying for a while, judging by his red nose and the soft hiccuping sounds he made as he sat with his arm around the dog. Syro did a kind of canine tiptoe up to Charlie's other side, and Charlie remained there, staring off toward the ridge, flanked by the dogs.

"Maybe when we're home, it will be easier," said Lily. She and Charlie sat together against the white pine on the ridge, facing the valley. "I think we need to hear them, especially the later ones, the ones about college. I'm not sure how far they go, but there could be some useful—"

"I don't think I can," said Charlie. "That's what I'm saying. I'm really sorry, but you're going to have to do it. I can't stand to hear her voice like that, disembodied, to say nothing of the content. It's too hard."

The sun had just begun to reach them through the trees, but the wind was constant and cold. Lily studied the gray farmhouse at the base of the hill. As she watched, a young man slammed a screen door (could she hear it or just imagine she heard it?) and walked across the yard toward the barn. She heard a deep voice, a grown man's voice, yelling after him. Then another, louder slam after the young man reached the barn, and everything got quiet.

"That's okay," she said, still secretly assuming Charlie would change his mind once they got back to Boston.

"What should we do today, though? We ought to at least visit the police and talk with the Hatchers. And what about the dogs? If the Hatchers really don't want to—"

"Lily," he said. "Can we just sit here for a few minutes? Then I'll make plans, I promise. But I need a few minutes first."

"Okay," she repeated. In the silence, she understood that Charlie wouldn't change his mind about the tapes. Gregarian would help for a short time, but he'd have to move on to other cases. (And she didn't know how she felt about working with him, anyway. Casual dalliance was so far from her style, the idea made her laugh. She needed some distance.) She felt lonely and resentful; she was going to have to find Anna on her own.

The road to the Hatchers' house was just past Anna's driveway, off to the left. Charlie had seen the name on one of the four mailboxes nailed to an old telephone pole. They decided to walk down to the Hatchers first, to get that out of the way, to be sure the dogs and the house would be watched over. At least, that's what Lily had on her mind. She could tell Charlie had something altogether different on his, that he felt suspicious of the family. In turn, Lily felt irritated by those suspicions, as if they drained energy from what really mattered—the tapes, the past.

Charlie and Lily stopped by Anna's and put her four dogs inside the porch. Syro they kept with them. The wind had lessened, and Lily could feel the sun on her back, soaking into her black parka, reaching all the way to her skin. As soon as they turned onto the side road, Lily saw a woman working in a large garden, next to a white house with green shutters and windowboxes, still empty this early in the season. Maybe that's the Hatchers' house, thought Lily, and we're both wrong about them. But no. According to the woman, who seemed both confused and disgusted by the idea of someone visiting the Hatchers, their house was the last on the left, past the rest of the houses, back up off the road.

As it turned out, the Hatchers' place wasn't so much a ramshackle rural bachelor pad as an austere New England hermitage. From the front, it looked like a white box, with two gray-trimmed square windows and a single gray door. The vinyl siding was clean, if not cheerful, and the porch empty. She noticed a stack of wood in the yard and, beyond that, a fenced-in rectangle of turned earth.

The door opened as they walked up the drive and the elder Mr. Hatcher, or so Lily guessed, stood framed by the plate-glass storm door. He was short, shorter than his son, and square-shaped himself, with thick white hair and tan skin. He wore a flannel shirt, blue jeans, and work boots. Not until Lily stepped onto the porch did she realize he was Asian, probably Japanese.

He opened the door and came out onto the porch.

"Mr. Hatcher?" asked Charlie.

The man nodded.

"We spoke a couple of days ago. I'm Charlie Cooper, a friend of Anna Banieka's. This is Lily Connor."

"Do you know where Mrs. Banieka is?" asked Mr. Hatcher. Like his son, he didn't shake hands.

"No," said Charlie. "That's partly why we're here, to try to figure out where she is. And to make sure her house is okay, the dogs, the garden, the pipes."

"Andy takes care of the house. Mrs. Banieka pays him to do that."

"Yes," said Charlie. "He told us that. But when you and I spoke a few days ago, I had the impression you were doing the caretaking. In fact, I had the impression—"

"A few days ago, Andy was gone. Now he's back."

"We met him," said Charlie. His manner, which had

started out hopeful and polite, was shifting to grim and impatient. "Where's he been?"

"You'd have to ask him that," said Mr. Hatcher. "But now he's back, and he can take care of the house and the dogs."

Lily glanced through the window beside her. She couldn't see much because of the thickness of the storm glass, but the front room looked almost empty—no couch, no bookshelves, no recliner—only a woodstove and a wooden table with two folding chairs.

"I know you've already talked with the police," said Charlie. "But you don't have any idea where she might be, do you? She didn't mention that she was going anywhere, to you or your son?"

"No. I went to meet her at the bus station, and she wasn't on the bus. There was no suitcase, either. I waited, thinking she might have gotten off somewhere and then not gotten back in time. But there was no suitcase."

Lily took a small step toward the man. "Did you notice a large Asian family on the bus—maybe Chinese?"

Mr. Hatcher looked at her. His eyes were like his son's, large and dark, but not as cold. "A woman and a child got off the bus to buy a ticket, I think," he said. "But they weren't Chinese." Lily thought Mr. Hatcher might have suppressed a smile. "They were Korean."

"Did you speak to them?" asked Lily.

"I heard them speaking to the ticket woman. I went in to make sure this was the right bus, that I had come to meet the right bus. The woman's English was not very good, so her child translated for her. They spoke Korean."

There were a few seconds of silence. Lily thought Charlie was disappointed. The man didn't seem very villainous; it was impossible to imagine him knocking Anna on the head and dragging her to a hideout in the woods.

"Is Andy here?" asked Charlie, trying to look over Mr. Hatcher's shoulder into the house.

"No."

"If he comes back, will you ask him to stop by the house today? We have to drive back to Boston this evening, and we want to make sure the house and the dogs—"

"Andy will take care of them," he said, then repeated. "Mrs. Banieka pays him to do that."

"But if Mrs. Banieka isn't here," said Charlie, his voice rising in pitch and volume, "he won't be getting paid. So we should arrange for him to send us some kind of bill. And if he decides to go away again—"

"You don't need to make any arrangements," said Mr. Hatcher. "Mrs. Banieka can pay him on her return. He'll take care of the house. He's not going anywhere."

CHAPTER 15

Lily put the box of tapes in the back of the station wagon. It was not quite four o'clock, but the sun had gone behind the hill and the air had grown colder in the last twenty minutes, making it feel like evening. As she walked toward the house, she thought she heard a car on the road, so she paused and looked back over her shoulder. An old red Ford pickup pulled into Anna's driveway and parked behind the station wagon. Lily turned and waited. A barrel-chested, middle-aged man in a down vest and a black scarf and watch cap climbed out and waved. She was almost certain she didn't know him.

"I'm glad I caught you," he called as he approached. Then he stuck out his hand. "I'm Paul McPherson. I've been hoping someone would show up."

Lily introduced herself. "I'm here with another friend, Charlie Cooper. We thought we ought to come check on the house, make sure everything was okay."

The man's face fell. "Then she's not with you?" he asked. "You haven't seen her?"

"Anna?" said Lily. "No. We don't know where she is."

He shook his head, like someone who's talking to himself, and looked toward the top of the hill. "Well, hell," he said.

"I guess you haven't heard from her either?" asked Lily.

He shook his head again.

"Do you want to come in? We're just finishing packing some stuff." She began to walk toward the house with the man beside her. "Are you a neighbor?"

"More or less," he said. "I live near the college. I went into the store down the hill today and they told me someone was here, someone who'd come in to buy groceries. I guess I got my hopes up." He had a faint accent, maybe Southwestern, definitely not western Massachusetts.

"So you know Anna . . . ?" Lily let her voice trail off.

"Sorry," said the man. "I'm the Catholic chaplain at the college. Anna and I started there the same year. We've worked together a lot, with student organizations—you know, two good old liberals." He smiled ruefully at Lily, then looked away. "I was supposed to have dinner with her the night she got back, so I came up, but the house was dark, the dogs were nuts. I let them out, fed them, and then went over to Hatcher's. Have you talked to him?"

They walked into the kitchen just as Charlie finished sweeping. He leaned the broom against the wall, and Lily introduced the two men.

Then Lily asked, "By 'him,' do you mean the father or the son?"

McPherson looked blank for a moment, then smiled again. "I thought you were asking me a theological question. When you work with undergraduates, you're ready for almost anything. Hatcher, the grandfather, actually—the grandson's not around."

"Unfortunately, he is," said Charlie. "We met him yesterday. He was up here shutting off the water, or so he said."

"No kidding. So he's back."

"From where?" Lily asked.

"County jail, over in Pittsfield. He's been there for about

three months. I guess they let him out. I visited him a couple of times—it didn't seem to do either of us any good."

"Do you know what he was in for?" asked Charlie.

"A collection of things—a couple of OUIs—"

"OUIs?" said Lily.

"Operating under the influence. He was busted twice, then this time they caught him on foot, drunk and disorderly with some dope on him—less than an ounce. He got tanked and tried to walk out of the White Hen Pantry with a quart of ice cream. They only sent him away for six months. He must be out on parole."

"And what's his grandfather's story?" asked Charlie.

McPherson leaned against the kitchen counter. Lily felt she ought to invite him to sit down, offer him something, but she also wanted to get going. They still needed to stop by the police department in Wharton and then drive back to Boston. The man seemed nice enough, but he didn't appear to know anything helpful, and she felt impatient with him for feeding Charlie's suspicions about the Hatchers.

"I'm not sure," said McPherson. "They've been here a while. I think Coby Hatcher came when the boy was little, three or four, just the two of them. Anna knows them better than anyone—she's had Andy doing work around here for a long time, since he was at the elementary school."

No one said anything. Finally, Charlie shifted his weight, offered McPherson something to drink.

"No, thanks. I've got to get over to the college anyway." But he took off his cap and unwrapped his scarf, letting it hang loose. Lily saw his collar for the first time. For some reason, she hadn't thought of him as a priest until that moment; he suddenly seemed more substantial.

"You can't think of anything—you know, where she might have gone, or anyone who would have—just anything?" Lily asked him.

He rubbed his eyes with his left hand, then shook his head, slowly.

"Not right this minute. I've probably been avoiding that line of thought, but it makes sense at least to try—" He stuck his hat in the pocket of his vest. "It's been good to meet you. Now that I think of it, she talked about you, both of you." He headed for the door.

Lily moved forward to walk him to his truck, but as she did, he turned. "Have you talked to the police?" he asked.

"We went to the Boston police first, because Boston's the last place anyone saw her, when Charlie dropped her off at the bus station."

"I wanted to stay," said Charlie. Then he glanced at Lily and added, more quietly, "She didn't want me to."

McPherson nodded. "And you've talked with Miller, here?"

"Is he the chief of police?" asked Lily. "Because I think the Boston detective who's working with us talked with the Wharton chief of police."

"Yeah," said McPherson. "Not that it would do much good. They're just dumb as posts over there, at least half of them—but Miller's the worst. There's one young deputy who seems pretty smart—Thompson, Tomlin, something like that."

"Where are you from?" Lily asked him.

"Oklahoma," he said. "Enid. How about you?"

"Texas—Benton, outside of Houston."

He nodded. "I thought so. And you're a priest, too, right?"

Now Lily nodded. "Ostensibly," she said. "I haven't done any parish work for a while, in over a year, and that didn't turn out too well. But I guess I'm still a priest. I was last time I checked."

"Someday we'll have women, too, you know," he said. "I'm sure of it. It's just going to take time."

"Maybe you're right," said Lily. She tried to smile, but her face muscles weren't up to it, so she gave him a little grimace.

Once more he turned to go, then turned back. "Why don't I just take your numbers? That way, if something does occur to me, I can call you. There's no point calling Miller."

Charlie found a pencil and pad and wrote down both numbers for him.

"I hope I see you again," said McPherson.

"Me, too," said Charlie.

Lily walked McPherson partway to the truck, stopping in front of the station wagon.

"So what do you think?" he asked her.

"I don't know what to think," said Lily. "But it's not good, whatever it is. I know that."

"I'm afraid you're right," he said. "Do you know much about her past, I mean, what she got up to when she came over here?"

"Not much," said Lily. "She told us a little. Do you think it's connected to all this?"

"I don't—let me think about it," he said. Then he patted her awkwardly on the shoulder, a gesture that reminded her so much of home, of the men she grew up around in Benton, that she wanted to hug him. "We'll be in touch."

Lily watched him leave, then walked toward the house. It was getting dark in the east, and the view from the front yard was shaded in blues. A couple of white houses reflected the dying light and gleamed like polished silver.

Once the car was packed, and Syro had said good-bye, a ritual that included getting out of the car twice to go stand in front of the porch and stare through the screen at the other dogs, Lily and Charlie drove slowly down the hill in the twilight. When they arrived, the town of Wharton felt deserted. Lily asked directions at a Cumberland Farms store, the only place that appeared to be open. The high-school student at the counter gave her directions that, though vague and mumbled, turned out to be accurate. There were few lights on in the police station when they pulled up outside.

"Why don't I just run in?" asked Lily. "All we really want to do is check with them, right? No one's going to be there, anyway—no one important. What should I say?"

"Ask them if they've learned anything, and you probably ought to mention the Hatchers, and the gun. Also ask them if the paper has run a story yet, and give them both our numbers in case—"

"In case what?" she asked.

"I don't know. I guess they can just call Gregarian. I mean Greg."

Lily slammed the door and walked up the steps to the brick building. There were lions on either side of the concrete stairs, and a bright blue light above the entrance, over a painted wooden sign that read, *Wharton Police Department,* and in smaller letters underneath, *Jonah Miller, Ph.D., Chief of Police.* Inside, a large oak desk stood on a low platform to the left of the entrance. Straight ahead was a waist-high wooden partition with a hinged gate, and beyond that three or four smaller desks. No one was at the front desk, but Lily noticed a couple of officers talking in the hallway and someone at the desk farthest away, against the back wall.

That officer stood and turned—it was a young woman, in her mid-twenties, with thick, curly black hair, cut close to her head, and olive skin. She was tall and broad-shouldered, almost Lily's height. Lily thought she saw a hint of recognition in the woman's eyes, a silent acknowledgement of all the years of taunts and slouching and dateless weekends. But the officer came only as far as the middle of the room, and she didn't smile.

"Are you Officer Thompson?" asked Lily, on a hunch.

"Thompkins," said the woman. "Can I help you?"

"Paul McPherson suggested I talk to you." It was close

enough to the truth. The officer's face relaxed a notch. Lily explained who she was, who Charlie was, and what they were doing in Wharton. By the time she finished, Thompkins had become entirely businesslike, no longer closed and protective. While Lily had been speaking, the young woman had picked up a pad and pencil and walked to the small desk nearest the partition.

"You can come through there," she said, pointing to the gate. "Have a seat. Do you want coffee?"

"No, thanks," said Lily.

"Good," said Thompkins. "I never have any made, but I always feel like I'm supposed to ask."

"What would you have done if I'd said yes?" asked Lily.

"Make instant," said Thompkins. "So let me get your name and stuff. I'll give this all to Captain Miller when he comes in tomorrow." After she'd written down the information, she asked, "Do you want the captain to call you?"

"Not especially," said Lily.

Thompkins looked up quickly, as if to check the expression on Lily's face. "Have you spoken with Captain Miller?"

"No," said Lily. "But Paul McPherson suggested it might be a waste of time."

Thompkins's face never changed. "Depends on what you're after, I guess." Then she widened her eyes slightly, and Lily nodded. "Anyway," she continued, "what should I tell him?"

"We just wanted to be sure someone had our names and numbers. And to be sure, too, that somebody's watching out."

"For her house, you mean?" asked Thompkins.

"Partly. And for any information, any ideas about where she might be."

"Do you have any idea where she might be?"

"No," said Lily. "None. My friend, Charlie, is suspicious of her neighbors, the Hatchers, but I don't really see anything there that—why would they want to hurt Anna?"

"Could have been an accident," said Thompkins.

"I suppose," said Lily. "But then why not tell someone?"

One of the officers Lily had seen in the hallway earlier walked through at the front of the room. He stood for a minute at the large desk by the door, then left.

Thompkins waited until he was gone before she continued. "Because you've already got a record, and no one would believe you."

"Do you know him, the grandson?"

Thompkins shook her head slowly. "No, not really. My youngest sister went to high school with him for a couple of years, but they weren't in the same grade. He used to make honor roll, I remember that. But he drinks and does drugs, so brains don't have much to do with it anymore."

"He's just out of jail, right?" asked Lily.

"Miller busted him for possession, among other things. I heard that Miller got rough and Andy threw a punch. Of course, Andy's been a pain in the ass for a long time—shoplifting, disturbing the peace. But some people wouldn't have done anything, just given him another warning. Not Miller."

"So he's out on parole now?" asked Lily.

"Probation," said Thompkins.

"Then if he had a weapon—a gun—he'd be breaking probation?"

"Does he have a weapon?" asked Thompkins.

"I don't know. This is a hypothetical," said Lily.

Thompkins nodded again.

"What would they do to him?" asked Lily.

"Nobody around here—well, hardly anybody—wants to put a kid like that away for any amount of time. He's not a criminal, unless it's a crime to be a loser, and in that case, we'd have a full jail. But if he violated probation, they'd have to. So, hypothetically, if such a person had a weapon, it would be best for the weapon to disappear."

"Do you think he'd hurt anyone, Anna, on purpose?" asked Lily.

"I can't make that kind of judgment," said Thompkins. "But if I had to guess—only a guess—I'd say no. He doesn't have any history of violence."

"What about hitting Miller?"

"That's different."

"Okay," said Lily.

"We'll be watching him anyway," said Thompkins. "Or I will. I'll let you know if anything happens, one way or the other. And I'll call you if we find out anything else about Professor Banieka."

"Did you know her, too?" asked Lily.

"I took a course from her at the college. I liked it, and her."

"I don't suppose you have any ideas about where she might be?" asked Lily.

Thompkins shook her head. "No, sorry. She always seemed pretty—I don't know—reliable. I don't see her running off to Vegas."

"Me neither," said Lily. "Did they put a story in the paper already—about her being missing?"

"Yep," said Thompkins. "On Friday. It told about the bus ride and asked anyone with information to let us know. Do you want me to see if I can find it? We keep all the ones that are related to cases."

"No," said Lily. "That's okay. Do you think it would help if we could raise some reward money?"

"It depends on what's happened," said Thompkins. "It depends on who's involved."

"Right," said Lily. "I guess that's it, then." She started to stand and leave, but she wasn't quite ready. She wanted something from this woman, some reassurance that they'd keep looking until they found Anna, no matter what it took, that they wouldn't stop until they found her.

Lily looked up and saw Thompkins staring across the desk at her. "Sorry," said the young woman. "I wish I could be more help."

"Yeah, me, too," said Lily. "I mean I wish someone could." Thompkins walked her to the door of the police station where they said good-bye.

CHAPTER 16

One week later, on Palm Sunday, Lily stood on the steps of her apartment building in the cool, spring sunshine, waiting for Barbara to pick her up and take her to church. The week had been hard; there had been no news of Anna. Charlie had finally spoken with Jeffrey Tatum but hadn't learned anything helpful. Jeffrey described the conservative Catholic group as a dwindling collection of elderly monastics who couldn't possibly have had anything to do with Anna's disappearance. The report had left Lily feeling suspicious and dissatisfied.

On their return from Wharton, Lily had met with Gregarian—she'd called just before lunch, again, and arranged to get together at the same sandwich shop near her office. She'd told him everything they'd learned on their trip—or almost everything, omitting the part about the gun, because she still wasn't sure what to do about that. But she'd given him the messages from Anna's answering machine and told him about Anna's collection of tapes, promising to keep him posted as she listened to them. She was finding that part—the listening—very slow going; it was harder than she'd thought it would be, though she hadn't yet admitted this to Charlie.

The most surprising thing had been her response to seeing Gregarian—which was no response at all. She couldn't quite figure out what had happened to her the week before. Was this the same man who had made her blush and stammer and laugh out loud? She liked him; he seemed like a smart guy, a decent person, but lonely and a little lost. None of this behavior was normal for her—not the crush, the teenage physical symptoms, or the crush's sudden disappearance.

Lily had lived alone most of her adult life, except for her second year in seminary when she'd had a sad, drunken affair with a charismatic ethics professor. That relationship had ended with his moving to Vermont with another man. Lily looked for him after she graduated and finally located him in a town outside of Montpelier, where the two men moved in a blur of Jim Beam and some kind of ecological spiritualism. But she was still a little in love with him, and she remained a little in love with him for years afterward. He was delicate—a few inches shorter then she was, skinny, small-boned—and handsome and a great believer in causes. In any case, she had dated since, some, but never seriously.

Tom had not been her idea of a love object—solid, down-to-earth, helpful, Roman Catholic, a good listener, someone who thought she hung the moon—not her type. But it had turned out she was wrong, or not wrong so much as narrow-minded. Tom wasn't her type, but she loved him and had never met a man whom she so admired as a species, someone male and decent and linear-thinking.

Then why couldn't she take the next step and live with him? She'd had no problem moving into the mostly unheated and unfurnished house of the ethics professor. Somehow this was different. For one thing, she wasn't drinking, so she knew what she was doing—more or less. And she was older, more than ten years older. And maybe she didn't like the idea that this was it, the end of the line, as good as it was going to get. Or maybe her dissatisfaction with herself was affecting her judgment about everything and everyone. Or maybe—what?

She had gotten to the *what* when Barbara's Honda Civic appeared on Commonwealth. Barbara would know, or be able to lead her to knowing, but Lily wasn't ready to talk about all this yet. She'd looked forward to today for a while. Ironically, she felt at home in the black church in a way she never did in white Episcopal services. There were no thin-voiced plainsongs in this service, no watered-down liberal-speak. She felt like a freeloader, borrowing spirit from the black congregation, but she liked to believe there was enough to go around.

As always, Barbara was dressed for church. In her honor, Lily had done her best, a clean pair of black wool pants and a tweed blazer. But next to Barbara's pale blue silk suit and bone colored sling-backs, Lily felt like an impostor.

"Do I look okay?" she asked when she got in the car.

"You look very nice," said Barbara. "You look like you're going to a funeral, but you look fine. What is it with white people and color?"

"When I grew up, only the Mexican kids got to wear bright colors. You couldn't wear bright colors, or people would think you were Mexican—or white trash."

"Nice," said Barbara.

"Isn't it?" said Lily. "Anyway, I guess it stuck with me. I can't imagine buying anything red."

"I've had a hard life," said Barbara. "But at least I didn't have to grow up white."

"You think I'll be the only white person there?"

"No. We still have a handful of good, earnest Catholic liberals. They keep hoping Martin Luther King will appear at the altar and bless them. Well, who doesn't? They're regulars. Never miss a Sunday."

"I wish I could take communion," said Lily.

"You can take communion," said Barbara. "Who's

gonna know? Just, when they ask for visitors to identify themselves, don't stand up and say you're an Episcopal priest. That's kind of a giveaway."

The church was packed already, but Lily followed Barbara to her usual place, halfway down on the right. They squeezed into a space for one. Palm Sunday was the preparation for the big event, the rising action, and even though everyone knew the crisis and denouement by heart, in this church it seemed like a surprise every time, as if no one knew what would happen next.

A short, older man with light-brown skin, wearing a beautifully tailored navy blue suit and a white usher's carnation in his lapel, began to walk down the center aisle, passing out palm branches. Ushers on the side aisles did the same, so by the time the organ sounded the first few chords of the anthem, everyone held a long, green branch. Despite herself, Lily felt caught up in the surge of voices and the spectacle of the choir, stepping in, waving the branches. If she'd gone to the monastery service, she'd already have had to keep from rolling her eyes—something about the Anglicanism itself, the inherent restraint, simply didn't mix with the enthusiasm required for the procession of the palms.

But here, Lily felt free to sing out with the rest in "All Glory Laud and Honor." Barbara had been right; this triumphalism didn't ring false—or, worse, ring too true. Parishioners grabbed up jackets and palm branches and got in line. Then the entire congregation processed through the church door, down the sidewalk, and around to the side entrance, in through the office hall, and finally back into the chancel, singing and waving palm branches, giving the sinners on Ruggles Street something to think about.

For this moment, in this context, Lily's faith didn't seem to be an issue. She just believed, and that felt like a big relief. A group of parishioners read the Passion, and everyone cried "Crucify him" together. In the midst of the play-acting, Lily felt something stir, a childhood, but not necessarily childish, sense of being there, in Jesus' last hours, when he accepted his death. By the time they all stood together in the now solemn church, singing "Were You There," she felt ready for whatever came next.

They had coffee hour in the large meeting hall next to the church offices. It was a subdued gathering, because of the nature of that last half of the Palm Sunday service, but not too subdued. Lily saw four or five kinds of coffee cake, fresh fruit, and urns of coffee and hot water in two different places. She stuck with Barbara for most of the time, but whenever she stood by herself for a moment, someone came up to greet her and make sure she had food and coffee.

At one point when Barbara had been taken away to change the date of some committee meeting, Lily stood near the end of the buffet table, against the wall. After a few minutes, she noticed a woman watching her from the other end of the table, a small, older woman, light-skinned, with short gray hair and a deep blue beret that matched her suit. Lily smiled, but the smile wasn't returned, so she blushed slightly and looked in the other direction.

Within seconds, the woman stood in front of her.

"I'm so sorry," she said, "to be caught staring. I want to welcome you to our church."

It took Lily a moment to understand that the voice she'd just heard had come out of the woman—the sound was deep, a bass or baritone from the center of the chest. She found herself wondering if the woman was black or white, or maybe a very small Latino man in drag.

The woman held out her hand. "I'm Betty Carl. Have we met before?"

Lily shook hands with her, but when she tried to draw her own hand back, the woman held on and patted it. "Good to meet you," said Lily. "I'm here with Barbara."

"Barbara's a good girl. Some people don't like the work she does, but I do. Is that how you know Barbara, through her work?"

"Yes," said Lily. "We work together. I hope that doesn't mean I'm leading her astray."

Betty Carl didn't smile. "I don't think so. Do you? You're not from here either, are you? You're from Barbara's geographical area, I think."

"Texas," said Lily.

"I spent some time in Texas. Many years ago, during the war."

Lily assumed she meant World War II, but she didn't ask. The other woman didn't seem to expect her to, and Lily thought it might seem rude. But she also felt slightly apprehensive, as if the woman might say "Civil War" or "War of Independence."

"Yes, I think Barbara's doing good work," Betty Carl added. But she sounded distant, distracted.

The woman still hadn't let go of her hand, and Lily wasn't sure what to do. In truth, she didn't really mind having her hand held. At the moment, her hand felt warm and comfortable, but she wasn't sure of the etiquette for this sort of thing. Then something else happened: Lily got an image of Anna's face, briefly, almost too fast to register any details. Before Lily could make any sense of the image, Barbara appeared.

"Miss Betty," said Barbara. "Good morning."

Betty Carl dropped Lily's hand. "I'm meeting your colleague," she said.

"That's good," said Barbara. "How are you today?"

"Just about the same," she responded. "Just about the same. Bring your friend to see us again, why don't you? I like her." And with that she returned to her post at the end of the buffet table.

"What'd she do, ask you if we were sleeping together?" asked Barbara.

"No," said Lily, feeling a need to defend her new acquaintance. "She seemed nice, she just—"

Barbara laughed quietly, a kind of snort. "I'm not sure nice exactly captures it. She knows every piece of business of every person here. They say she has the sixth sense. I've never been so sure—I think the source of her sixth sense is more telephone than telepathy. Still, though, I wouldn't mess with her." Barbara gazed in Betty Carl's direction. "And I wouldn't tell her anything."

"Okay," said Lily. "I'll keep that in mind. Can I ask you something?"

"Sure."

"Is she Black?"

Barbara smiled. "Miss Betty says we're all the same color under our skin—you know the line. But, yes, she's Black. Now let's go get some real food. I'm starving."

Lily followed Barbara toward the door, but when she glanced back over her shoulder, she saw Betty Carl staring at her through the crowd.

CHAPTER 17

When she reached the third-floor hallway, Lily could hear the phone ringing in her apartment. She and Barbara had eaten lunch at one of Lily's hang-outs, a deli on Commonwealth, two blocks from her building. Then Lily had walked home in the windier but still sunny Sunday afternoon, trying to enjoy the weather and the day. But she couldn't shake the image of Anna she'd had at the coffee hour.

The machine had picked up by the time she got the front door opened. She heard Charlie's voice, calling her name, assuming she was home and not answering—a safe assumption in Lily's case.

She grabbed the phone with one hand and unbuttoned her blazer with the other. "Hi," she said. "I'm here."

"No kidding," said Charlie.

"As a matter of fact, I just walked in the door. I went to church with Barbara and we had lunch afterward."

"You're a closet Catholic," said Charlie.

"No," said Lily. "I'm a closet person of color—well, maybe both."

"Lily," said Charlie. "God loves you just the way you are."

"Yes," she said. "God and Mr. Rogers."

"Can you come over here tonight?" he asked.

"Why?"

"Frank Leslie called me. He wants to see us. He seems to have convinced Jeffrey to tell us the whole story. I can't get away until this evening, so I told him we'd meet them both for dinner in the Square."

"Yes," said Lily. "I'll come. Where should we go?"

"The usual. The Indian restaurant at six."

"Did he say anything else, like what Jeffrey had to say, or why he was so hard to locate?" she asked.

"No. I didn't like to press him. He seemed embarrassed about Jeffrey's behavior. I guess he and Jeffrey know all about that group, the group Anna mentioned at dinner, the one from her college years. In fact, I think you were right—it sounded to me as if Jeffrey had been a member. Anyway, Frank doesn't think it's directly related to her disappearing, but he says we ought to know everything, just in case."

"But do they still exist? I mean, are they the people responsible for the stuff in the cathedral?"

"I don't know," said Charlie. "He said it was a long story, and he didn't want to go into it on the phone."

"It sounds to me as if Frank has talked Jeffrey into telling the truth."

"Maybe. Or maybe Jeffrey's thought of something else that might be helpful."

"Yeah," said Lily. "Like the truth. See you at six."

"God, you're exasperating."

After she hung up and changed clothes, she checked her messages. Tom had called twice. She made a cup of tea and sat in the viewing chair, an old, swivel armchair that had been in her father's house for decades, now draped in a blue ticking slipcover and placed in front of one of the windows in the living room. She loved her apartment, the high ceilings and tall windows, the kitchen that got morning sun, the bedroom that got evening sun, the pale yellow she and Charlie had painted the walls.

She leaned over and put her elbows on the window sill, her viewing position. The maple tree in front of her building was in full bud now, and Commonwealth Avenue was crowded with people ready for spring—Lily watched a couple walking together, the woman pushing a stroller, flattened out to form a cot for a bundled, sleeping baby, the man pushing an elderly woman in a wheelchair. As Lily watched, the man bent down, and the woman in the wheelchair said something that caused him to laugh. Then he appeared to repeat it to the woman walking beside him. She laughed, too, and leaned down to speak to the woman in the wheelchair, and the circle was complete.

Lily felt the stirrings of jealousy—a family group, connected to one another—the life Lily didn't have, maybe never would have. She also knew there were things she couldn't see—the details of illness and age and care, of money and strain and work, the general process of disillusionment that life turned out to be.

Over the past few weeks, she had watched herself hurting Tom, someone she loved, and misleading Gregarian, a man she didn't even know, and she had no clear idea why she'd done either thing. What did she want? she wondered. Did she want to live with Tom, get married, have a family? She'd ignored the larger question for years. Maybe she couldn't ignore it anymore.

She used to turn to prayer for decisions like this, but prayer felt far away from her these days. She had to force herself to get to one service a week at the monastery. She still read the offices of the day in the Book of Common Prayer, but the practice had become more rote than religion. Since her father's death, almost two years ago, she had a vague notion the church had failed her, that God had failed her. Some part of her knew she needed to move on, to take her faith to a different place, but she couldn't find that place, or even imagine it.

As an experiment, she got on her knees and put her elbows on the seat of the viewing chair. It tipped toward her precariously, but she found a balance, closed her eyes, and tried to quiet her mind for prayer. But before she could focus, the image of Anna returned, the image she'd seen while Betty Carl was holding her hand—Anna's face, eyes closed, lips white, dark hair matted with pine needles.

Jeffrey, Frank, and Charlie were already at their table when Lily arrived.

"So, the elusive Father Tatum," she said as she sat down.

The three men looked up at her.

"What?" asked Charlie.

"Nothing," said Lily. "Don't let me interrupt you."

"We're just catching up a little," said Frank. "I haven't talked with you and Charlie since—when? We couldn't remember." Frank wore his black suit, which seemed more in need of cleaning than ever. Lily saw a white smear on the lapel and dandruff on the shoulders. She also saw deep circles under his eyes. He usually reminded her of a clean-shaven Santa Claus, with his round face and white hair, but at the moment he looked drawn, and old.

"Are you okay?" she asked him.

"Frank's been sick," said Jeffrey. "He really shouldn't be here." Jeffrey, on the other hand, looked immaculate.

"Sick with what?" Lily asked Frank.

"A flu—the same flu everyone's had this spring," he said.

"Because—" Lily began.

"No," said Frank. "Don't even ask. It has nothing to do with the humiliation in the cathedral. And no, I don't need a CAT scan, and no, I don't have a brain tumor." Though

Frank appeared bumbling and ineffectual, Lily had noticed, especially in ecumenical meetings, his clear mind and strong will.

"Well," said Lily. "That settles that."

"Let's order," said Charlie. "I'm starving."

"You're hungry," said Jeffrey. "People in Bangladesh are starving."

Lily kept herself from rolling her eyes. Jeffrey's particular brand of social consciousness made her want to argue on the side of trickle-down economics and increased defense spending.

"My mother used to say that," said Charlie.

"Your mother was a wise woman."

"Right," said Charlie. "What shall we have?"

The waiter showed up and they ordered, Frank asking Lily and Charlie to order for him, since he'd never had much Indian food. She suspected from his tone of voice that he'd never had *any* Indian food. She imagined frozen dinners and Bible study and a few favorite TV programs—the life of a celibate priest.

"I may as well start," Frank said, after the waiter left. "Since this was my idea. As I told Charlie on the phone, I don't think any of this information we're about to give you is connected to Anna's disappearance. But it seemed wrong—to Jeffrey and to me—to keep it a secret any longer. We were protecting Anna, really. But I'm certain she'll understand."

"The point is," said Jeffrey. "Anna's past involves other people, people with whom I'm also friends, so I don't see any reason for this information to get out if it isn't necessary. That is, I'll leave it up to you about whom to tell, but I ask, at the same time, for discretion."

"I don't know what that means," said Lily.

"All right," said Jeffrey, slowly. "Let me say this—for many years, Anna—and a number of us—have kept our earlier involvement with the Becket Movement to ourselves."

"That's the name of the Catholic group?" asked Lily.

"Yes," said Jeffrey. "And it's not something one would talk about with other Catholics, for instance. In any case, I hope you respect her privacy. I suppose it means only talk about this if it seems absolutely necessary. Perhaps you'll understand better after you hear the story."

Lily felt a surge of impatience, and something else—fear? She didn't like the use of the word *involvement.* Anna hadn't been involved, she'd simply known people there. But before she could say anything, the waiter returned with the first course, a plate of fried vegetables and potatoes, with a green pepper sauce, a red pepper sauce, and a yogurt sauce. Charlie went into a disquisition on the eating and savoring of Indian food, and Lily looked out the windows—or the wall, since the whole wall was glass. The restaurant was on the second floor, overlooking a small park and a busy street in Harvard Square. The sky had already turned dark blue in the east, with a few streaks of light left in the west. Enough warmth lingered in the evening air to keep people outside—students, tourists, aging graduates.

Frank tried a chunk of the fried potatoes, dipped in the green sauce, but Lily could see he didn't like it. He didn't say that, though. He said, "Well," a few times, then took a drink of water. "Anna is a very adventurous eater," he said. "When I knew her best, when we first met, she'd try anything."

"Was that in college?" asked Lily.

"Yes," he said. "We were at Holy Cross together for one year."

"We were all there together," said Jeffrey. "Then Anna and I—this is where my story begins, I suppose—transferred to the Thomas Becket Center. We intended to get our degrees from the center, but that quickly became impossible."

"I don't understand," said Lily. "Anna told us she knew people in the group. But I never had the impression that she was part of this whole thing."

Jeffrey took a sip of water, patted his mouth with his napkin, then returned his napkin to his lap. "As I said, most of us have chosen to keep our involvement to ourselves. There was a great deal of misunderstanding at the time."

Lily waited for more, but there was no more. Jeffrey stared at his water glass. She felt a mild panic; nothing she'd imagined or understood about Anna fit with this story. "So what was the Thomas Becket Center?" she asked.

"The center was a place for the more orthodox members of the church to hear lectures on issues of interest to Catholics, have tea, feel comfortable," Jeffrey explained. "This was right after the war, you understand—1945, 1946—and the country, and the church, were changing tremendously. I know the two of you will have little sympathy for this, but there was a certain innocence about it, and fervor. We were so certain we were right."

"But what happened? And what did Anna have to do with any of it?" asked Lily.

"What happened is a very long story, indeed," said Jeffrey. "Long and complicated and difficult. And Anna and I were in the middle of it all."

CHAPTER 18

According to Jeffrey Tatum, the Becket Center saw itself as a gathering of the faithful elite come together to keep the church on course. After a few years, the center attracted the attention of a powerful, charismatic Jesuit teaching at Holy Cross, Father Sebastian O'Riordan. He had been in trouble, on and off, for years; he opposed the teaching of Darwin's theory of evolution, the ecumenical movement, and a whole raft of other liberal interpretations of Scripture and church tradition. But at the Center he found an enthusiastic audience, and O'Riordan and the Followers flourished, with blessings from the diocese and support from a handful of wealthy Boston Catholic families.

"There was really nothing in those first few years to warn us—there was no way of knowing what it would come to," he said.

Lily could see he felt uncomfortable, even ashamed.

"That's when Anna arrived—1948," said Jeffrey. "I still took some courses at Holy Cross, and I met her at the college. I brought her to one of O'Riordan's lectures. She was mesmerized. Well, we all were. He was a superior performer."

"You should have seen her," said Frank. "You have no

idea how beautiful she was, and brilliant. She was four years out of the camp. She had no family. She'd been taken in by a French convent, along with some other child survivors. She spoke perfect English, but with this odd little accent." He paused and looked down at his plate.

Lily could see he had been in love with Anna. Maybe he still was.

"While the rest of us had been stealing kisses and going to confession," Frank continued, "Anna had been reading. She'd read everything, most of it in the original language."

"Did you get involved with this group, too?" Lily asked him.

"Moderately," said Frank. "I admired some of what they did, what they believed. But at heart, I'm not a radical—at either end of the spectrum. Anna tended, then, at least, to live large. She liked extremes."

"Her scars were internal," said Jeffrey. "She was vulnerable to the kind of rigid, rule-bound Catholicism that O'Riordan began to preach. It provided an ego-structure for her—perhaps for all of us. And her feelings about those outside the Catholic faith had become complicated during the war. She was . . . confused." He searched for that last word and then stopped speaking.

In the silence, Jeffrey suddenly became three-dimensional for her. Something about the way he said that last word made Lily see him as a human being, someone who'd wanted things he couldn't have. And, now, someone whose past was catching up to him and, possibly, to a dear friend.

The waiter removed the first course and brought plates of basmati rice, chicken *saag, raita,* mango chutney. Charlie made a plate for Frank and explained what everything was. He's so much nicer than I am, thought Lily. I wonder why he puts up with me at all.

Frank tried a little of everything, but what he liked best was the *nan,* a soft, buttery flatbread. He ate carelessly, Lily noticed, dropping crumbs in his lap and down his jacket.

Meanwhile, Jeffrey continued his story of the Becket Center. His voice became businesslike; he didn't mention Anna again. He thought it best to summarize at this point. The Center and the diocese quarreled—primarily over issues of doctrine. The Center split with the church—at about this point the group also lost its scholastic accreditation—and founded its own order on a farm in Lester, west of the city.

"Anna and I, and a few others, left the order not long after the move to the farm," said Jeffrey.

"Anna had joined the order?" asked Lily. "This just doesn't—I'm not sure I understand exactly what this order was. I mean, was it official? Were there vows of poverty and chastity and obedience? Did she wear a habit?"

By the time she finished, Lily's voice had grown louder. Jeffrey hesitated. He glanced at the table next to them, where a large group of Indian students were celebrating some event—Lily couldn't tell what, exactly, except that there was a lot of toasting going on and it seemed to be directed at a long-haired, young woman at the head of the table.

"The thing is," said Frank, "that this is really Anna's story. Jeff and I wanted to let you know about the group—for a specific reason. But I think we ought to let her tell you anything else more—personal. You see what I mean?"

"Okay," said Lily. She couldn't make sense of this information. It was as if Anna were disappearing for a second time. And Charlie had remained silent for the whole telling, except to explain the food to Frank and ask for more water from the busboy. "So what's the specific reason?"

"That weekend," said Jeffrey, "before she left Cambridge, she called to say she thought she would go out to the farm in Lester on her way home."

"From Boston?" asked Charlie. "I don't understand."

"It was on the bus route. She said she might just get off the bus and stay there for a night."

"But why didn't you tell us earlier?" asked Lily. "She might be there now. She might have gone there—"

Jeffrey raised his hand, shaking his head. "I called them immediately. She's not there. She never went. They haven't seen her in months."

They walked out together into the March evening, chilly, but chilly like spring, not winter—a small reserve of warmth still lingering close to the earth. The three of them strolled together as far as the Harvard Coop in the center of Harvard Square, then Charlie made a point of saying good-bye to Frank and Jeffrey before he accompanied Lily across the street to the T stop.

Lily watched Frank and Jeffrey as they walked away together. Before they turned the corner onto Church Street, Frank stopped to put money in a cup in front of a middle-aged man sitting on the sidewalk, playing a desultory, shapeless melody on a harmonica. Frank took out his wallet and loose change fell in all directions. Three or four people stopped to help, while Jeffrey stood a few feet away, gazing into a store that sold bath essences.

"Laurel and Hardy," said Lily.

"We need to get tea somewhere," said Charlie.

"We just had tea," she said.

"We need to have it again," said Charlie. "I've got to talk to you."

They crossed the street, passed the T station, and ended up at Au Bon Pain. A few hard-core chess players sat hunched over games in the courtyard, but Lily and

Charlie chose to sit in the noisy, neon-lit room inside the building.

"So what is this?" she asked, once they were settled. "I've got work tomorrow." She felt angry at Charlie for getting her into the meeting with Frank and Jeffrey, as if Charlie were somehow responsible for what she had just learned about Anna.

"So do we all," he said. "You never heard of The Followers?"

Lily shook her head.

"I don't know the details," said Charlie. "But Jeffrey's version is extremely watered-down. It was before my time, of course, but people talked. I learned about them from my parents—who were staunchly opposed. I just want to be sure you know that."

"Charlie, I've known your parents for years. They're my favorite Catholic family—since my dad died. I'm still lost."

"O'Riordan was a hate-monger, an anti-Semite, a Coughlinite, really, although he developed his own style. According to O'Riordan, nobody was saved except him and his group. That meant everyone—Protestants, Masons, Quakers, atheists, but especially Jews, and liberal Catholics, people who didn't agree with him. He preached eternal damnation for all of us."

"But what was the group, exactly?" asked Lily. "I still don't understand what they did, who they were."

"It's like Jeffrey said—they started as a sort of tea and sympathy center for conservative Catholics around the Boston area. The idea was that Catholicism had been perverted by places like Holy Cross, Harvard, Boston College, and that there was no place for serious young Catholics to learn doctrine, unpolluted by American liberalism. A couple of diocesan leaders took their side for a while."

"So what happened?" asked Lily.

"They had a lot of power after the war. They published a newspaper, started a school, and eventually constituted themselves as a religious order, with O'Riordan as their leader. They used to hold these outdoor rallies around the city. My parents said it was terrible for Boston Catholics. People—non-Catholics—got the impression the whole church was like the Followers, that they represented mainstream Catholicism. O'Riordan and his bodyguards and all his flock would gather on the Boston Common on Sunday afternoon, wearing black—he'd preach and they'd recruit. People would heckle him. He called them perverts, Jew-lovers, infidels. There were fistfights, I think, real brawls—"

"Nice," said Lily. "But it doesn't make sense—Anna's being a member, does it? I think there's a mistake somewhere, or Jeffrey's lying, which is a lot more believable than Anna's joining a hate group. Jeffrey I can see—but Anna? Anyway, this afternoon I went through the tapes, sort of scanning them for information about this period in Anna's life. There's nothing there. Or, at least, I haven't found it yet. If this had been really important to her, it would be on those tapes."

"Jeffrey said they all kept it a secret."

"Secret from whom? I'm sure Anna never imagined anyone else would be hearing this stuff. I hate listening to them—it feels like such an invasion of privacy. And who's 'they all,' anyway? Do you think it's people we know?"

"I have no idea. Do you think—?"

"I think we have to tell Gregarian everything. This is weird—"

"What?" asked Charlie.

"For the first time since she—left, I guess—I feel hopeful."

"What do you mean?" Charlie asked.

"What if Anna stayed in touch with this group in order to keep tabs on them? And someone found out—"

"And what?" asked Charlie. "Jeffrey said the place is a geriatric ward."

"I don't have the absolute faith in Jeffrey's word that you seem to have," she said. "What if that's not entirely true? What if they're holding her hostage somewhere? Then she may still be alive."

CHAPTER 19

"Listen to this," said Lily. She sat in her office with her feet up on the desk, reading out loud to Barbara. *"When a child broke the rules, he would be punished. Sometimes he would be forced to kneel on a broom handle on the concrete floor of the dormitory. There was also The Box—a small wooden crate where the children who misbehaved were often forced to sleep overnight . . ."*

Barbara shook her head. In honor of the promise of spring, she wore a pale pink silk shirtwaist dress and a white silk cardigan. She was at her desk, posting the new schedule for workshops and classes on the Women Center's Web site. "The Box," she said, then glanced over at the book. "Where did you get that thing?"

"I got it Monday at the library. It's the only book about O'Riordan and the whole episode, but the writer—he's a sociologist—did a lot of research. They took monastic vows, even the married couples. And the children were raised separately, in a separate dormitory by a group of nuns and unmarried members. Supposedly, these kids were all being trained for monastic life."

"White people do some crazy shit," said Barbara. "Well, everybody does crazy shit, but there's something about the white thing, the Nazi thing, you know?"

"I think so," said Lily. "You mean the self-hatred in it?"

"I guess—you want to know the truth? You and I teach about this and talk about this and are supposed to have a handle on it. And I'm sure you'll agree that *nobody's* more articulate than I am on the subject. But underneath all that, I sometimes feel I can't quite get a hold of the real thing, the cruelty."

"And this is a special brand, this stuff," said Lily. She held up the book. "Because it's Catholic."

"What's that supposed to mean?"

"First of all, it's all caught up with sin, with somehow beating the sinfulness out of ourselves, out of small children. Think of it. Just imagine doing that, actually making a five-year-old child kneel on a broom handle. What's that about?"

"And second?"

"I'm not sure how to say this, but it's not as if anti-Semitism in the Catholic Church originated with this group."

"That is definitely true," said Barbara.

"Anyway," said Lily. "They started off as a Catholic culture center, where Catholics can congregate and revel in being Catholic—music, art, literature."

"White Catholic," said Barbara.

"Right," said Lily. "Conservative white Catholic—although it's interesting to note that they held quite liberal social policies in some areas—anti-atomic-bomb, feed the poor, house the homeless."

"House the white, Catholic homeless," said Barbara.

"Yeah, probably," said Lily. "Anyway, then this priest appears, O'Riordan. Among other things not mentioned anywhere else except in this book, the guy's a drunk. The church has moved him from place to place to help him dry out. Of course, it hasn't helped, but the church doesn't acknowledge that detail. He's also brilliant, a kind of literary figure, and a tremendous speaker, evidently. Charismatic. With a huge ego."

"Sounds Baptist," said Barbara. "Except for the alcoholic part."

"He becomes the sun, you know, the central gravitational pull for all these wandering souls. Everything begins to form around him. He gives lectures every Tuesday night, and soon they're packed. People are converting all over the place. And now Boston's a little scared. Boston feels it has enough Catholics already. What it doesn't need are more Catholics, especially rich, powerful Catholics. So a group of Protestant ministers—as well as some Harvard administrators—appeal to the diocese to get O'Riordan and the center under control."

Barbara has turned back to her computer.

"Do you want to hear this?" asked Lily.

"I don't mind hearing it," said Barbara. "But are you going to finish the labels for mailing the schedule or not? Because it needs to go out today."

"I'll stay late."

"If you stay late to do them, you can't get them in the mail today."

"Barbara, I think this has something to do with Anna. Plus, there are at least two different splinter groups, according to this guy. And the book is almost ten years old. So there may have been other groups established since then. Any of these people may know where Anna is."

Barbara turned again and faced Lily. "I understand that's what you think. But let me say this. And I'm not trying to be mean. Today's Tuesday—it's been more than two weeks since she went missing. If she's still alive, why hasn't anyone heard anything?"

Lily stared at the page in front of her. She didn't know what to say, and she couldn't have spoken even if she did.

"You want to have hope," said Barbara. "I do, too. I didn't know Anna that well. I've only met her with you a couple of times. But I've always admired her. And she means a lot to you, so she means a lot to me. But you need to get clear about what you're doing here, because you also have a life, and a job, and other responsibilities. Besides, you don't even know if these were the people who vandalized the cathedral, much less whether Anna got in touch with them, much less whether they have anything to do with this—"

"I was just wondering about that last night," said Lily. "What made her so sure they would know about the vandalism? Because, if you think about it, she seemed pretty sure. She told Jeffrey she was going to stop at the Followers' place on her way home. Something in the cathedral, something she saw, or—I don't know."

"Are you going to do the mailing?" asked Barbara.

Lily put down the book and rubbed her eyes with both hands. "Yes," she said. "I'm going to do it. And then, I have an idea." She opened her eyes and looked at Barbara. "How about we get the mailing done and then take a ride out to Lester?"

"What's Lester?" asked Barbara.

"The Followers. The Becket Center. Their farm."

"Have you lost your mind? What have you just been telling me about these people? How do you think they're going to feel about a visit from a woman priest and her black sidekick?"

"Good point," said Lily. "Can I borrow your car?"

"I don't drive it to work, you know that. But if you get the mailing done, you can borrow it tomorrow. I'll drive it in."

"You don't mind being on your own tomorrow?"

"First of all, given your input the last few days, it won't be that different. And second of all, even if I did—" Barbara was interrupted by the ringing of the telephone on her desk.

"You better get that," said Lily, glad to be spared the rest of Barbara's insights. Lily put down the book and turned to her own computer to finish the labels. After a few moments, Lily got the impression that Barbara and the caller were talking about her, Lily, and that Barbara wasn't any too happy with what was being said.

Her final words were, "I'll talk to her, but I'm not making any promises. We're awfully busy here, and she has a business trip planned for this week."

"Who was that?" asked Lily, after Barbara had said good-bye and hung up.

"You remember Betty Carl?"

"The woman I met at the coffee hour?" asked Lily. "She's pretty memorable."

"She wants to talk to you," said Barbara.

"About what?" asked Lily.

"She wouldn't say. But she said it was important, and the sooner the better."

"What should I do?" asked Lily.

"I'd stay away from her if I were you. She's probably after information."

"What information?"

"No telling. But if you're serious about getting those labels done, you'd better not call her back now. You'll be on the phone for the rest of the day."

CHAPTER 20

At home that evening, Lily found Lester on the map. It lay about sixty miles west of Boston. But specific directions were a problem. She didn't want the people at the Becket Center to know she was coming. And she was afraid if she called Jeffrey for information, he would warn them. So she decided to go ahead on her own and assume that the town was fairly small and the farm would be easy to find. She felt hopeful, revved-up, for the first time in days.

She woke early the next morning, picked up the car keys from Barbara, and headed west on Route 2. Just before ten she arrived on the outskirts of Lester and stopped at a Mobil station off the highway. Two men were working on a dark green Mustang convertible in one of the garage bays. Actually, one man appeared to be working. The other man—skinny, with a sallow face and a clipped, red beard—stood leaning against the driver's side of the car, telling a story about some escapade involving lighter fluid and earwax—at least that's what Lily thought she heard.

"Sorry to bother you," she said. Neither of them had moved when she pulled up in Barbara's car. And neither of them had turned around when she walked over to the garage.

"That's quite all right," the mechanic said, his head still under the hood. The other man got quiet. "How can we help you?"

"I'm looking for the Becket Center. Do you know where it is?"

The mechanic stood up straight and turned toward her. He was young, in his twenties, and his face was round and flushed, probably from bending over the engine. Something about him—his build, his general air of decency—reminded her of Tom. "Becket Center?" he asked. "What is it?"

"It's a kind of farm," she began. "Run by a Catholic order."

"She means the Followers," the other man said.

"Isn't that what you mean?" asked the skinny one. "The Followers of the—whatever it is. Highway to Heaven. Something. I can't remember."

Lily felt as if she'd stepped into Wonderland; in fact the skinny guy—with his whiskers and red-rimmed eyes—looked a little like a rabbit.

"Oh yeah," said the round-faced man. "Is that what you mean?"

"Yes," she said. "That's it."

"You mean the one in Lester?" asked the mechanic.

"Is there another one?"

"Not here in Lester. There's another group up in Ahearn."

"Another Catholic group, on a farm?" asked Lily.

"I don't know about the farm part. But I know that some of the people from the Followers moved out and started something else up in Ahearn."

"He'd know," said the skinny guy. "He's Catholic."

So he had that in common with Tom, too. Maybe they're related, she thought, but that was too weird a line of questioning to follow. "Well let's start with the one in Lester," said Lily. "Can you tell me how to get there?"

"Sure," said the mechanic, and he gave her careful instructions, which, when followed, led her down a side road to a white gate across a dirt driveway, beside which a sign read Followers of the Way of the Cross. Sort of like the Highway to Heaven, thought Lily.

The gate was latched, not locked, but another smaller sign on the gate post read *Please Stop Here and Wait for Assistance.* She couldn't tell what that meant—wait for assistance. For how long? And who would assist her? To the left of the driveway stood a large white farmhouse; the siding looked dirty, with streaks of green mildew, but there were curtains on the windows and two green Adirondack chairs on the front porch. A few hundred yards behind the house and to the right stood a red barn. Beyond, the land sloped down to a large cleared field and a couple of one-story prefab buildings. Though the barn doors had been left open and three trucks were parked in the drive, there was no one in sight.

She felt foolish just standing there, so she got back into the car. After a few minutes, she pulled the car onto the road and parked on the grass next to the fence. She got out, this time with her backpack, and returned to the driveway. There was still no sign of anyone coming to assist. She unlatched the gate and walked through.

She half-expected a sudden upheaval of action, a pack of German shepherds followed by a man in military uniform, but nothing happened. She knocked on the door of the farmhouse. Through the window, she could see into the front room; it was a sort of old-fashioned parlor, sparsely furnished, with a formal carved love seat, a rocking chair, an end table with a doily. The house looked like the home of an elderly farmer and his wife—maybe a little too much like the home of an elderly farmer and his wife, now that she thought about it, more like a stage set.

The lifelessness of the place felt eerie. No one came to the door, no one left the barn, no one started a tractor or called a dog. In fact, she hadn't seen any dogs, or cats, or chickens, or goats. Lily stepped down off the porch and walked around the corner of the house toward the field. There were actually four modern, pre-fab buildings, she saw now—two long houses facing each other, and two shorter ones, forming a rectangle. They reminded her of covered wagons circling the fire at night.

Lily gazed down from the top of the hill and wondered what to do. Maybe, she thought, she *should* go back and wait. Then the sliding door of the closest building, the shorter one facing the farmhouse, opened, and two people stepped out, a man and a woman. The man wore a black cassock, the woman a full-length black habit with a wimple and veil. They walked up the hill, their eyes on the ground in front of them; maybe they were talking to each other, but Lily couldn't tell. She felt relieved she'd dressed conservatively—a nice pair of brown cords, a cotton turtleneck, a tan pullover, and her clean windbreaker. She'd even brought a relatively new, unsoiled daypack, instead of her old leather backpack. Barbara had said she looked like a model in a Lands' End catalog—except for the cowboy boots.

Finally, the woman raised her head. The hair visible under her wimple looked thick and dark, and though she smiled at Lily, her eyes never lost their look of cold scrutiny. Lily waited until they were in speaking range, then offered an explanation. "I'm sorry to intrude. I couldn't find anyone at the house."

"Did you not see the sign on the gate?" asked the woman, still smiling.

"I did," said Lily. "But there was no one to assist me, so I wasn't sure—"

"Ah," said the woman. The expression on her face had never changed. "I'm afraid you caught us at the changing of the guard."

"I beg your pardon?"

"Everyone was in the chapel for tierce. What can we do for you?"

"I'm a friend of Jeffrey Tatum," said Lily. "I was looking for a quiet place for a day-long retreat. I don't really need meals or anything—just some nature and a chapel."

The man—his round, balding head reminded Lily of some kind of vegetable—answered her. "I'm afraid we don't have the facilities for that sort of retreat. I'm surprised Father Jeffrey would suggest—" He was about the same size as his companion, both a few inches shorter than Lily, but his voice sounded like that of a much taller man, deep and resonant.

"He didn't, actually," said Lily. "He had told me about the farm, and it sounded perfect for what I had in mind, so I came up with the plan on my own. I tried to call him last night, but I couldn't get him. He was teaching."

"I thought his evening class was on Monday," said the man.

"All I know is that when I called his house, they said he was teaching." He was right, Lily remembered. Charlie had tried to get in touch with Jeffrey on a Monday and been told he had seminar. So she added, "But I guess even monks can make mistakes."

"You're welcome to take a walk," said the woman. She turned and pointed down the hill to a break in the line of trees at the edge of the field. "There's a cleared trail, a loop, that starts right there. Take your time. But we'll have to ask you to leave afterwards. We do have visiting days. Stop by the house on your way out, and I'll give you our schedule."

A short way along the trail into the woods, a vernal pond reflected the pale blue sky and surrounding trees—but Lily wasn't interested. She turned back and lingered on the edge of the forest, watching the farm. If the man and woman had been coming from tierce, that front building must be the chapel. She wanted to get in and look around.

She couldn't see any activity around the building now. She watched and waited, then shouldered her pack and set out from the trees. She walked directly to the sliding doors, opened the one on the left, and went in.

At first, she couldn't see clearly. Then she noticed the opulence. It looked like the side chapel of an elegant cathedral—the pews of dark polished wood with burgundy velvet seat cushions, the walls covered in the same burgundy fabric, tall candlesticks that shone like gold. The crucifix on the wall behind the altar seemed enormous, an ivory cross with a carved wooden Christ figure, blond and pale skinned. The blood that flowed from his side and streamed down his arms seemed to sparkle as if fresh.

Because of the light—she could see that, but she couldn't tell where it came from. There were no windows in the walls, no lamps or chandeliers, only the candles on the altar. But jewel-toned patches of light glowed throughout the chapel. Then she looked up and saw two stained-glass skylights. She walked quietly to the center aisle and studied them: the one on her right depicted the betrayal in the Garden of Gethsemane—a prominent black-robed Judas stood to the side, pointing a long, bony finger at the blond Christ of the crucifix, while Roman soldiers, in full battle regalia, looked on; the one on her left showed Jesus, in golden robes with a crown-like aura of gold, allowing Thomas to touch his wounds. Thomas's finger seemed to be all the way inside Jesus' flesh.

Lily had become so transfixed by the drama of the skylights that at first she didn't hear the noises. By the time she noticed that someone was about to enter the chapel, she didn't have a chance to hide. She knelt in the pew closest to her and bowed her head. A door opened behind her. She willed herself not to move. She thought it would be a good idea to pray, but she couldn't think of what to pray for. She prayed the person would go away and leave her alone—which seemed the obvious petition, but not quite right. She couldn't come up with anything better. After a few moments, she heard the closing of the heavy door and the echo of footsteps, growing fainter.

She knew she didn't have much time left. When she opened her eyes, she saw the books on the rack in front of her, attached to the back of the pew. Then she picked up the oddly familiar Bible—heavy, bound in red, with gold lettering on the cover—and turned to John 19, where she found all the words spoken by Jews printed in bright red ink.

Lily stuck the Bible in her pack and left. As she opened the sliding glass door, she heard footsteps in the hallway again. But she was gone before anyone came back.

By the time she knocked on the door of the farmhouse, she had a strange sense of calm. The woman she'd met earlier appeared and led her into the front room. Beyond the tidy parlor Lily saw a hallway with a row of doors, at least four or five, all identical. Something about them made her uneasy. The woman handed her a schedule of visiting days and a brochure offering a short history of the farm and the order.

"Did you enjoy the trail?"

"Yes," said Lily. "Very much. But I'm afraid I got a little confused."

"On the trail?"

"No, no," said Lily. "I didn't have any trouble on the trail. But when you said for me to stop by the house, I thought you meant the house you'd just come out of. So I ended up in your beautiful chapel."

"That's all right," said the woman, too quickly, Lily thought. "It's usually empty at this time of the morning." She pointed to a small table that held an open book with lined pages. "Would you sign our guest book before you leave?"

"Sure," said Lily, although, she didn't want to. She wrote her name, address, and phone number and then immediately regretted it. When she finished, she stood and headed for the door. "I'll plan to come back on a visiting day, then," she said. "Thanks a lot."

As she walked toward the gate, she realized she'd gotten away with lies and theft, and she felt quietly elated. She also felt certain that Anna's disappearance was connected to the events in the cathedral and the events in the cathedral were connected to the Followers; this Bible proved that. Underlying those certainties she discovered a larger certainty—that she could do this on her own. If no one would help her, she'd find Anna by herself.

CHAPTER 21

As long as she had the car, Lily thought, she might as well use it. The mechanic at the Mobil station did not seem surprised to see her. He stood inside the glass office, talking on the phone. She came in and waited by the door until he'd finished. After he hung up, he asked, "Did you find them?"

"Yes," said Lily. "Thanks. Now I was wondering if you could give me directions to the group up in Ahearn."

He looked out the window behind her. He reminded her more of Tom each time she saw him. Finally, he said, "I can't. But I know someone who can. Hold on."

He dialed a number and let the phone ring a long time—at least, that's what Lily assumed was happening. Finally, he shouted into the receiver, "Hi, Mom. It's me."

He looked at Lily with a slight, apologetic shrug.

"Yes, yes," he said. "I know. I heard. Terrible. Listen, do you remember that group from the Followers who moved up to Ahearn? You have any idea where their place is? Is it a farm, like the one here?"

After a few seconds, he said, "No, no. I'm not going. But there's someone here looking for them." He listened, smiled, put his hand over the receiver, and asked Lily, "Are you intending them harm?"

"No," said Lily. "I just want to ask them about a friend of mine who was a member. I don't know where she is. I'm hoping they can help me find her."

"She's looking for a friend," he yelled back into the phone. "Yeah. She seems really nice." He smiled at Lily again, then took a pencil from behind his ear and began to write.

When he hung up, he went through the directions with her.

"How does your mother know so much about them?" asked Lily.

"She's a Catholic, and kind of a—oh, I don't know—she's always done things her own way," he said.

"Was she a member?"

He laughed, a short chuckle, a lot like Tom's laugh when you caught him by surprise. "Not hardly. But she liked their politics. My mother's an activist. She's been fighting nuclear power, and the military industrial complex, and working for poor people around here for years. The Followers had a lot of the same ideas, at least when they first got here. My mother used to go to services there a lot, and she had a spiritual adviser out there."

Lily had read about the Followers' activism, their antinuclear stance, their horror over the bombing of Hiroshima. But she had set it aside and forgotten it, as if she couldn't contain so many contradictory messages.

"She doesn't go anymore?"

"Well, she can't drive. She can't hardly see. As you probably noticed, she doesn't hear too well either. But they brought her communion for a long time. They were good to her. Now their numbers are down, so they can't do as much as they used to. I take her to Mass on Sunday."

Lily thought he might have blushed, slightly, after admitting the last part.

"Were you ever involved with them—with the Followers?" she asked him.

"No," he said in a flat voice. "Too weird for me."

"Weird how?" she asked.

"I don't know," he answered. She could tell he didn't want to talk about the Becket group anymore. "It's just an impression."

A red SUV pulled up on the full-service side of the pumps. The young man excused himself and left. She took the directions to the Ahearn farm and put them in the pocket of her cords.

As she walked past the gas pumps, she waved and called out "thank you." He waved back and then seemed to be about to say something. At that moment the pump clicked off, so instead he replaced the hose, took a credit card from the dark-haired woman in the driver's seat, who talked in a loud, singsong voice to three children strapped into car seats in the back. He went into the office, glancing over his shoulder at Lily one last time.

Lily found herself wishing he'd said whatever had been on his mind. She had a feeling it would have been helpful.

Once again, the directions the mechanic had given her were detailed, easy to follow, and accurate. They led her to another farmhouse, larger, also white with green shutters, also with a red barn. This one had a fence, but no gate. Lily pulled into the driveway and parked to the right of the front walk.

As soon as she turned off the ignition, a man appeared beside the house. She couldn't tell where he'd come from. She had decided to try the same line about being Jeffrey's friend and hope it worked; she had a backup story in case she needed it. When she got out of the Honda, the man walked across the lawn and stood on the path to the porch. Like Lily, he wore a pair of cords and a pullover, both black, with a black down vest. He was broad shouldered but slender, a little shorter than Lily and, she thought, a little older, with black hair, buzz cut, large dark eyes, and a broad mouth. In fact, as they got closer, Lily saw he had the features of a beautiful woman and would have been remarkably handsome if not for the extreme pallor of his skin. They met halfway down the path.

Lily put out her hand. "I'm Lily Connor," she said. "A friend of Jeffrey Tatum."

His hand felt cold to the touch. "I'm Steve. I'm sorry, I didn't get the name of your friend—" His voice was deep and a little self-conscious. He seemed shy, maybe not all that used to talking to strange women.

Lily caught herself staring at his face—at the white skin and dark eyes. "Look," she said, "I'm not sure I'm in the right place. I'm putting together a list of retreat houses, places with a chapel and a quiet spot for walks and meditation. I visited the Followers this morning, over in Lester, and got a schedule of visiting days from them. The guy at the filling station off Route 2 mentioned your place, and I thought I'd at least give it a try. Is that something you do here?"

He looked confused. "I'm not sure what they told you at the filling station, but there's not much *here* here. Our group is very small. Many years ago, some of our older members were affiliated with the Followers, but it's been a long time since we've thought of ourselves as a religious order."

"So you're—what—more of a group home for Catholics?" she asked.

"That's a good description," he said.

"And I assume you don't do retreats."

"No, we never did. There's nothing to retreat to." He didn't seem irritated or impatient. "Look, I'd ask you in, but my mother's here for the week, and she's not feeling great. Otherwise, you could—"

"No, no," said Lily. "I've really gotten this mixed up. Sorry."

"We do have an informal newsletter—just a letter,

really. You want to leave your name and address? I'm happy to put you on the mailing list."

"Sure," said Lily. "That's fine. But not if it's any trouble. I'm not—"

"No trouble," he said. He took a small, leather notebook out of his back pocket and produced a matching ball-point pen from the inside flap.

"That's cool," said Lily.

"Yeah," he said. "I love this thing. I never go anywhere without it. Just write your info here, and I'll add you to the list."

Lily wrote her name and then thought better of giving her home address, so she wrote down the address of the Women's Center. When she handed it back to him, he read it and asked. "The Women's Center—is that the group putting together the list of retreat spots?"

"No," said Lily. "It's for a small publisher in Cambridge—Huron Press." Lily had no idea where the name came from, but it sounded convincing, even to her. "You've probably never heard of them. They do religious stuff, retreat centers, inspirational books. Someone was telling me you've got a place like that out here, a small press that does religious stuff. Do you know anything about that?"

"No," he said and shook his head. "Sorry."

"I'm full of misinformation," said Lily. "Okay, well, I'm not going to waste any more of your time. Thanks. Take care." She turned toward the driveway.

"You're welcome," he said. "I wish I could have been more help. But I'm glad you made the mistake. It was a nice break in my day."

Lily could feel the color rise to her cheeks—something in his voice. She waved good-bye and got into the car. He walked to the driveway and stood until she'd backed out onto the road.

In her hurry, she turned right, away from the highway,

but she didn't want him to stand there watching her reverse direction, so she drove off as if she knew where she was going. The road led up a short rise then down into a valley. She passed another farmhouse on the left, not as grand as the one she'd just visited, but cozier, with pale green shingles, a wraparound porch, and a huge garden already staked and planted—or so it looked from the road.

She rolled her window down and drove slowly. Her father had loved the Texas hill country, the broad expanses of land and sky. But this was Lily's terrain, the rural hills of New England, the mountains of western Massachusetts and Vermont, where Anna lived.

Lily had admired Anna's style, how she lived out there in the mountains, alone, in a cabin. Lily could imagine living like that—in fact, part of her craved that solitude. Then she remembered Tom, and her mind sort of buckled under the weight of the conflicting desires. Anna had arranged it all so cleanly. But she wouldn't think about that now.

She had driven farther than she intended, so she pulled onto the shoulder and turned the car around. She hoped the man wasn't still standing out front. She didn't want him to think she was spying—even though that had been her plan. But mostly, she didn't want him to see her, though she couldn't have said why.

When she crested the hill before his farmhouse, she thought she'd gotten lost and ended up, impossibly, back at the Followers' farm. In a small valley behind the house stood four prefab buildings, not visible from the driveway, identical to the ones at the Becket Center. Once she saw that she was in the right place, she told herself it made a kind of sense—this group had been part of the Followers, so they'd reconstructed the community buildings. Nothing wrong with that, but she felt a chill as she drove by. She rolled up the window and didn't slow down. There was no one in sight.

CHAPTER 22

When Lily got off Route 2 in Cambridge, she rolled down her window. The trees around Fresh Pond seemed to have leafed out since that morning. There were at least twenty shades of green—from the pale yellow of the willow to the deep blue of the spruce—and a spring breeze gave the whole scene a festive look, as if the trees were being waved about in celebration. She thought maybe she would call Tom later, see what he was doing for dinner. The visits had shaken her; she missed him.

She found a parking place in the lot behind the center's office building—something that seldom existed after eight A.M. Barbara was on the phone when Lily came in. The intern sat at Lily's desk, updating the membership list. Unfortunately, she had to use Lily's computer to do it, so Lily made herself tea and brought the mug and her pack into the smaller workshop space. She shut the door and took out the Bible.

As far as she could tell, it was a lot like the one they had found in the cathedral—a red, fake-leather cover with gold embossed letters, THE HOLY BIBLE, and below that, in smaller capital letters, WITH NECESSARY REVISIONS AND ADDITIONS. Charlie might still have the Bible he'd found on the altar. Lily couldn't remember—if she'd known in the first place—what they'd done with the flag and the Bible. That last day with Anna had begun to seem farther and farther away.

Lily thumbed through the pages, which felt thicker than those of a normal Bible; the paper looked expensive and made the book heavy. The red print was scattered throughout. In Revelations, she found whole passages printed in gold, impressive but hard to read. She also found brightly colored maps in the back; the modern one showed Israel as a large red stain on the area marked Holy Land.

At the bottom of the title page, she discovered the printer's name and logo—a semicircle of stars over the words Philadelphia Press, with a semicircle of torches below. Lily felt disappointed. The city of Philadelphia lent the book an air of respectability. She had been hoping for something lurid and despicable. Also, she had been hoping the print job was local. She would like to talk to the person producing these things.

She picked up her mug of tea and went to the window. The breeze had gotten stronger; the people below on the sidewalk were clutching shopping bags and keeping their hands on their hats. They all seemed to be walking purposefully, with definite destinations in mind. Her sense of mission flagged.

She must have sighed, because when Barbara opened the door, she asked, "That bad?"

"I don't know. No. Yes. Never mind."

"So that's settled," said Barbara. "Miss Betty called here again."

"Did she say what she wanted?"

"Not exactly," said Barbara.

Lily noticed something in Barbara's voice, a kind of uncertainty. "What?" she asked.

"Did you tell her anything—about anything?" asked Barbara.

"I have no idea what you're talking about."

"Did you mention Anna?"

"No. Of course not. Why would I?"

"She has a way of getting things out of people. You might have said something and not even know you said it."

"But I didn't. I'd remember. Why?"

"Because the message is she wants to talk to you about your friend."

"What friend?" asked Lily.

"Your friend who's missing."

When Lily came back in the room, Barbara had on her reading glasses and was turning the pages of the red Bible. "What did she say?" Barbara asked.

"She said she had to talk with me in person. I'm going over there tonight."

"You want me to come?"

"No. I don't think she's dangerous. She wouldn't tell me anything else. I still can't figure out—"

"I wouldn't worry about it. She has a lot of grapevines. She probably snooped around and found out who you were, and then heard about Anna." She held up the book and studied the spine. "What's this lovely thing?"

"A Bible from the farm. I stole it."

"How come?"

"Because I thought it was exactly the same as the one we found in the cathedral. And if it was, then these were the people who had hung up the dummy and kidnapped Anna. I thought I'd solved the whole thing by myself."

"But now—?"

"Now I'm not so sure. I don't remember the other Bible that well, except that it had a red cover and red print all through John 19—this one does, too. But beyond that—"

"Where'd you steal it from?"

"The chapel."

"I think that takes it from venial to mortal," said Barbara. She wore a navy blue linen skirt and a white silk pullover, navy sandals, and a rope of pearls. She put on her reading glasses—today attached by a white cord—and started to read.

"I know," said Lily. "I don't—"

"What's all this red print?" asked Barbara.

"I'm not sure about the Hebrew Scripture, but the word Jew and most of the stuff said by Jews is in red throughout the New Testament."

"Yeah," said Barbara as she continued to study the book. "What do these people do about the fact that Jesus was Jewish?" She turned to the back of the book. "And what's all this gold shit?"

"I think that's just in Revelation."

"It's too bad Revelation was ever recorded," said Barbara. "It gives these folks more material than any other printed matter in existence. Who does print these things, anyway?"

"Someone in Philadelphia. The logo looks fairly staid."

Barbara didn't answer. She stood staring down at the title page for a few seconds, then she flipped again to the back of the book. "That's the problem with you liberal white folks," she finally said. "You don't know your Bible."

"What do you mean?" asked Lily, walking over to stand beside her.

"Seven stars? Seven lampstands? The sixth church? Philadelphia?"

Lily shook her head. "Revelation?" she guessed.

Barbara began to read, "'And to the angel of the church in Philadelphia write'. . . . Let's see. Here we got gold and red. . . . 'I will make those of the synagogue of Satan who say that they are Jews and are not, but are lying—I will make them come and bow down before your feet, and they will learn that I have loved you. Because you have kept my word of patient endurance, I will keep you from the hour of trial that is coming on the whole world to test the inhabitants of the earth.'"

"So it's *that* Philadelphia?" asked Lily.

Barbara nodded. "That's my guess."

"I wonder who they're thinking of as the Jews who say they're Jews and are not?"

"It depends on who you mean by *they*. I'm not sure what this guy was talking about," said Barbara, pointing to the text. "But I suspect your new friends are thinking of Jews—as in the people who don't get it that Christ is the Messiah—you know, the ones who missed the Jesus bus."

"It certainly fits with the rest of their thinking."

Then Barbara showed Lily the back of the title page. "And it's not in Pennsylvania," she said. "It's in Ahearn."

Lily took the book out of Barbara's hands and studied the copyright page.

"I just got back from Ahearn," she said.

"I thought you went to Lester."

"I went to both."

"Did you see any printing presses?"

Lily thought of the buildings behind the Followers' farm and the matching set behind the second farm she visited. "I might have."

CHAPTER 23

Betty Carl lived just off Columbia Road near Upham's Corner in Roxbury. Her street climbed a hill crowded with tall, thin triple deckers, some freshly painted, some with new siding, a few showing patches of bare wood and a boarded window or two. Betty Carl's house was a mix—the siding looked new enough, but the porch slanted down toward the street, as if undecided about whether or not to be part of this structure. There were two front doors.

Lily's watch said seven o'clock exactly. As she climbed the porch stoop, Miss Betty opened the door on the left. She smiled at Lily and ushered her in.

"I knew you'd be on time," she said. "I like it when people are on time."

They walked directly into the living room, small and bright, with white walls, four table lamps, and a standing lamp in the far corner. Lily felt relieved. She'd had the notion that older women with a sixth sense lived in shuttered rooms crammed with heavy furniture.

"Do you mind helping me a little bit?" asked Miss Betty, although Lily could tell the woman had already assumed the answer. "I've got everything ready, but I don't want to risk carrying this heavy old tray."

In order to reach the kitchen, they walked through the

dining room, more of an alcove or passageway. Lily stopped and stared. The wall to her right was covered with pictures of children—contemporary color snapshots, older black and white photos, sepia-tinted portraits from another era. Most of the children looked African-American, around the same age, eight or nine, many dressed in white, and a lot of them stared straight out from their photographs, directly at the camera, directly at Lily—or so it felt to her for a moment.

"My wall," said Miss Betty.

"Are they family?" asked Lily, not knowing what else to say.

Miss Betty laughed. "Yes," she said. "I suppose you could say so. They're the children of our church, most of them. I always get a first communion picture. And then I started finding other old pictures in antique stores and estate sales. I've had a long time to look." She chuckled again, that deep-throated sound Lily had been so taken with when they first met. "They're my angels."

Lily made herself follow Miss Betty into the small kitchen. Its bright yellow counters and white appliances seemed incongruous after having seen the wall of pictures. There was something disconcerting about that collection of young, solemn faces, as if the viewer had stepped not forward or backward in time but out of time entirely.

On the counter by the sink sat a painted wooden tray, and on the tray were a collection of assorted antique cups and saucers, a beautiful creamer of translucent porcelain, a plate of shortbread cookies, a plate of melon slices, and a teapot.

"I took you to be a tea drinker," said Miss Betty.

"I am," said Lily. "How did you know?"

"You didn't have any coffee at coffee hour last Sunday. And—oh, I don't know—I can usually spot a fellow tea drinker." She poured some milk into the creamer then put the carton back in the refrigerator. "Now, if you'll just carry that tray out to the front room for me, we'll get started."

Something about that last phrase made Lily feel edgy. "When you say, 'get started—'" she began.

But Miss Betty cut her off. She rapped once lightly on the tray and waved her hand in the direction of the front rooms. "Figure of speech," she said. Then she walked over and held the kitchen door opened so Lily could pass through.

Lily didn't look at the wall of photographs. But still she felt the watchful presence of the children. Even when she had set down the tray and settled into the comfortable floral couch against the front windows, even as Miss Betty poured tea and began to talk about her own days in Texas, Lily was aware of those rows of faces in the next room.

Miss Betty's husband had served in World War II and had been sent to west Texas for boot camp. "I was a young girl, so I went along with him. I didn't have anywhere else to go. Oh, I hated it. The nights were so hot you couldn't sleep. And the air was so dry and dusty. I didn't last long. He sent me back up here to be with his family."

Miss Betty didn't seem to require responses; she poured out the cups of tea and offered Lily cookies, never interrupting her flow of speech.

"I was afraid of his mother back then. But she became my closest friend. When Walter died—he died over in the Pacific. They sent home what they could find of his body. I stayed here, in this house with them. And it was from Mrs. Carl—everybody called her Mrs. Carl. We wouldn't have imagined calling her by her first name."

She looked up at Lily and smiled. "She did domestic work, so did her husband, and they had to listen to their first names being called out all day long. So they always addressed one another as Mr. Carl and Mrs. Carl. I kept the house here, for them. They started calling me Miss Betty, since we couldn't have two Mrs. Carls in the house."

She gave her low chuckle. Lily could tell this was a joke she'd told many times, but never tired of. The continuous flow of speech surrounded Lily, as if she were in a warm bath, floating.

"It was from Mrs. Carl that I learned about my abilities—she called them her insights and treated them as a precious gift. She was a regular churchgoer, of course, never missed a Friday, Saturday, or Sunday—if she could help it, if her work didn't keep her late. She knew right away, when we met, that I had them, the insights, but she didn't say a word about it for the first few years.

"Then, on the second anniversary of Walter's death, I had the same dream I'd been dreaming on and off ever since he died. I could see him on a beach—the details don't matter so much. Just that he struggled in the sand, trying to carry something down the beach. I never could see what it was, but I could tell it was heavy."

Lily shifted on the couch, as if trying to get farther away from Miss Betty's voice. She felt a slow sadness building beneath the restlessness.

"It seemed to me I had that dream all night long," Miss Betty continued. "When I came down to make breakfast the next morning, Mrs. Carl was already up and dressed out there in the kitchen. She was sitting at the table, and she said, 'Miss Betty, I dreamed about my Walter all night.' And I said, 'So did I.' She hadn't talked with me before about any of this, but that day she took my hand, and she asked me, 'Can you see what he's carrying?' And that moment the dream was there in my head just as clearly as it had been in the middle of the night. It was like she had sent it to me." She paused for an instant and looked directly at Lily. "You know why I'm telling you this, don't you?"

Lily felt the sadness began to press upward, into her throat. She shook her head.

Miss Betty nodded. "Well, you will," she said and went on with her story. "Back then, I was flabbergasted. I asked her how did she know my dream, and she explained it all to me, how she had these insights, and I had them, and how she'd known it when we met, but hadn't said. She was so pleased that Walter had chosen someone like me. At any rate, she said it was a body he was carrying down the beach, a white man in uniform. And I asked her, of course, why would he be doing that. I remember she looked a little surprised when I asked—I think she must have believed I was farther along in my understanding than I was back then. Then she said, well, he must have died trying to save a white man's life.

"That night I had the dream again, but I saw the body. It was a white man, just as she had said, an officer, I told her that later. I could see those stars on his shoulder. After that day, she just took for granted I knew the things she knew. I didn't always; sometimes I knew different things."

Miss Betty stopped talking.

Lily had the sensation of standing undressed in front of a stranger. That wasn't exactly right, exactly what it felt like, but the feeling made Lily want to hide. Instead, she spoke in order to fill the space between them.

"How is this about Anna?" she asked.

"When I held your hand, I knew you'd lost someone close, and I didn't think it was family, because then you would have been more, oh, affected. Then when I started seeing the images, I felt pretty sure they were about you, about your loss."

"What images?"

"Your friend's face, very white, with pine needles in her hair. Did she have black hair?"

"Yes," said Lily. She didn't say anything about her own image of Anna. She thought Miss Betty probably already knew, although she couldn't be sure. In any case, she didn't want any more information, because she did, in fact, know why Miss Betty was telling her all this.

"I'm sorry," said Miss Betty.

Lily shook her head again.

"I know you don't want to hear it, and I can certainly understand that. It doesn't mean you should stop looking for her, though, because it might be I'm seeing something that hasn't happened yet. I've never been entirely sure how that works. I just try to keep my mind clean and fresh—and always with the Lord—and let Him worry about the details. If she is still alive—I'm not saying she is and I'm not saying she's not—you need to find her soon."

"But you think she's dead, don't you?"

Miss Betty stood and walked into the dining room. "Come over here for a minute."

Lily followed her reluctantly.

"What do you think about my angels?" asked Miss Betty.

"I—" Lily began. She had planned to lie, but changed her mind. "I don't like looking at them."

"No," said Miss Betty. She pointed to a small snapshot on the top row, a little boy with a round, dark face and a solemn smile, wearing a white suit jacket, white shirt, white tie. "He died just last year—November. Right around the corner here. He was delivering pizzas. They robbed him, shot him in the face. Had to have a closed casket." Then she pointed to a light-skinned girl with cornrows. "She was trying to keep her brother out of a fight. Somebody came up behind her, stuck a knife in and twisted it." She pointed to the picture below that of the girl. "That's her brother. Killed him that night, too."

Lily wanted to put her hands over her ears, leave the room, get out. "Are they all dead?"

The famous chuckle. "Not hardly. Most of these children have gone on to become parents and lawyers and doctors and dry cleaners and policemen—we have quite a few policemen, and servicemen." She took Lily's arm and linked it through her own.

"Aren't there things you just don't want to know?" asked Lily.

"There are," said Miss Betty, still gazing at the picture on the top row, the first one she'd mentioned.

"But what do you do with it?" asked Lily.

"I pass it on. What we can't bear here on earth, God bears for us in Heaven."

Lily felt a resistance built up over years of late-night theological arguments and layers of disappointment. "I wish I could understand that," was all she said.

"You don't mean understand. You mean believe. You have to believe it. I think that's why they call it faith. But that's hard for you, isn't it? Sounds too simple and unsophisticated. You're smart, and you rely on that, and your pride gets in the way, doesn't it? Was your friend in a lot of pain? Let's sit down."

"You mean when she died?" Lily asked; she felt befuddled by the lightning change of subject. She walked Miss Betty to the chair and then sat on the couch. She didn't like having been seen so clearly.

"All the time," said Miss Betty. "Did she have children?"

"No. But she had—she was Polish. Her parents were shot by the Germans for helping Jews. Anna and her youngest brother were sent together to Auschwitz, right at the end of the war. She lost all her family—her brother died in the infirmary."

Miss Betty nodded. "Have you ever been to the wailing wall, that wall in Jerusalem?"

"No," Lily said. "I've always wanted to go to Jerusalem."

"Yes," said Miss Betty. "So have I. I've always wanted to go to that wall. Everybody needs a wailing wall. That's my wailing wall in there." She tilted her head in the direction of the dining room. "I go in there when I need to and I celebrate the ones who've made it and mourn the ones who haven't. Because both those things are true—the celebration and the mourning. We've got to be willing to do both, to offer them up, to offer all of it up."

Lily stood on the porch with Miss Betty. The air had cooled, but again there was the faint promise of spring in the darkness. Lily took a deep breath and smelled cigarette smoke. A group of teenagers—girls and boys—were up at the top of the hill, leaning on cars, smoking, talking, listening to music.

She just wanted to get someplace where she could be alone. She'd always understood those animals that dragged themselves off into the marsh to lick their wounds. After a moment of silence, Lily started to walk down the steps, then stopped. She wasn't sure how she felt about Miss Betty as a source of information, but, even so, Lily wanted all the information she could get.

"You don't know where she is, do you?" asked Lily. "Or where her body is?"

"No," said Miss Betty. "I might know later."

Lily nodded.

"I do keep seeing a hill, so maybe whatever happened to her happened on a hill, with a view of buildings and people. Now, about the police—"

"What?" asked Lily. She was trying to think about hills, with views of buildings and people.

"They won't do a thing about this," said Miss Betty, "if all you have to give them are some pictures in my head."

"But it's a homicide now," said Lily.

"Possibly," said Miss Betty.

"I have a—friend. He's a photographer in the ID division. If I tell him—"

"What you and your friend need to do is come up with

some evidence, even if you have to make it up. I've been down this road with the police before. Don't mention my name over there. That won't get you anywhere. I promise you that."

"Like what?" asked Lily. "What would we say?"

"You'll come up with something. Before you go to sleep, you just put this problem before the Lord. Never practice your abilities without the Lord's guidance. But that won't be a problem for you, since you're a priest."

Lily suspected Miss Betty of sarcasm, but she couldn't be sure. The woman knew her too well already.

"You just put this problem before the Lord tonight," Miss Betty repeated. "When you wake up, you'll have some good ideas."

"You think it's okay to do that if you're planning to lie?" asked Lily, only half joking.

Miss Betty gave her now familiar chuckle. "I wouldn't worry too much. God's a big boy. He takes care of himself. If He doesn't want you to lie, you'll be the first to know."

CHAPTER 24

As it turned out, Lily never had time that night to worry about God. When she got home, there were five messages on her answering machine: two from Tom, one from Gregarian, one from Officer Thompkins in Wharton, and one from Bishop Spencer—a version of the same message he left her every few months: As it turned out, the diocese had a great urban parish in the South End, desperately in need of an interim priest. Spencer thought she was just the woman for the job.

Despite herself, she smiled. Spencer didn't want to lose Lily to her work at the center. He'd made that clear for years. But Lily grew less interested in parish work as the years passed. It was a tug-of-war they'd probably play for many years to come.

The rest of the messages just said to call right away. Lily chose to phone Thompkins first. She wasn't sure why, except the woman officer had sounded calmest on the tape.

Once Lily identified herself, Thompkins didn't waste any time. "Look, I shouldn't be telling you any of this, so I'd appreciate it if you didn't know this from me."

"Okay," said Lily. "That's fine."

"Captain Miller busted Andy Hatcher today on an OUI. They impounded his van, inventoried it, and found a lot of money—I don't know the exact amount. Then Miller got a warrant—I'm not sure how—to search Hatcher's house and the shed out behind Anna Banieka's place, where he found a gun and a bottle of whiskey."

"What's going to happen?" asked Lily. She could feel her heart speed up as she talked; it was hard to get a deep breath.

"Miller seems to think that Andy stole the money from Professor Banieka. She doesn't have a bank account. People say she keeps a lot of money in that cabin."

"A lot of money—from what? She was a professor at Wharton. Where was all this money supposed to come from?"

"Around here, it doesn't have to be much. She was a single woman, she lived pretty simply, she'd been drawing a decent salary for twenty years or so. She could have put away quite a bit. I'm not saying she did. But that's the rumor."

"Do you think the money's from Anna's house?" asked Lily.

"I have no idea."

"Do you think Andy killed her?"

Thompkins didn't answer right away. "We don't know she's dead," she finally said.

Lily heard voices in the background, as if a couple of men had come into the room where Thompkins was talking. She could tell Thompkins had covered the mouthpiece with her hand. She heard Thompkins's voice—it sounded more like a bark than an appeal for quiet—and the other voices stopped.

"Look," said Thompkins. "After a certain amount of time, it's always hard to believe the person's still alive. That isn't necessarily true, though."

"Right," said Lily. She could tell Thompkins was being nice, and she couldn't bear to push that any farther.

"Do *you* have any thoughts about what might have happened to her, specifically?"

"No," said Lily.

"Or who might have been involved?"

"Not exactly."

"Do you think it's Hatcher?" asked Thompkins.

"No."

"Me neither," said Thompkins. "We need to find out. Father McPherson's helping the Hatchers get a decent lawyer. But if Miller finds the body around here, he'll charge Andy, if he can." Then as if she realized what she'd said, she added, "I know Professor Banieka was a friend of yours. I'm sorry."

"Thanks," said Lily. "I am, too."

Lily called the monastery and left a message for Charlie. She didn't bother to try to reach him on the emergency number. Nothing new had happened. He would be glad they'd arrested Andy Hatcher, and Lily didn't want to hear the gladness in his voice—or the irritation and disbelief when she explained that she knew Anna was dead and felt sure Andy Hatcher didn't do it. She could talk to him the next day.

She put the kettle on to boil, then washed the pile of dishes in the sink while she waited. Along with her prayer life, she had been ignoring other details of survival the last two weeks. Her apartment was her haven, so when the dishes piled up and the laundry piled up and her desk disappeared under stacks of bills and letters, she felt anxious and guilty, as if she had been neglecting a sick relative.

She made herself a mug of tea and wandered back into the living room. For a while she sat in the viewing chair, listening to Barbara Hendricks's recording of Mozart's sacred arias. Then she put the mug down on the floor, got up, and replaced the Mozart with Trisha Yearwood's *Hearts In Armor.* Finally she stopped the music and took a tape out of the cardboard box on the floor by the bookshelves—one of Anna's tapes, dated March, exactly two years ago.

Anna's voice began in the middle of a sentence. ". . . to be honored. I'm not certain of the language I'm supposed to use here, but I do plan to write this all down as well, so there won't be any questions, I hope."

Lily felt so caught off guard by the sound of Anna's voice, she could barely decipher the words. She went to sit in her chair and knocked over the mug of tea; she should get a paper towel, she thought. She wanted to get a dishcloth instead, but she didn't have any dishcloths because she didn't like to put the dishtowels in the laundry with her clothes—and she hadn't done laundry all week anyway—so they lay in a mildewing pile in the corner of the kitchen. She watched as the tea spread across the hardwood floor toward the handwoven rug.

Anna had been more than a friend. She had been Lily's hero and adviser, the woman Lily wanted to be when she grew up. And now, when Lily had to make decisions about her future with Tom, which included her future in the church, which meant her whole idea of who she was and what she did, Anna had disappeared. Her thoughts struck her as appallingly selfish. But grief was selfish. The tea soaked into the rug.

Anna's voice continued in the background; she wasn't telling a story, as she had on all the other tapes. This sounded more like instructions—"I'm also asking him to keep the dogs together, to take care of them. I hope he will use the money for his education or to start a business—"

Lily stood and pushed Rewind, then grabbed a wad of paper towels and mopped up the tea. When the tape hit the beginning, she pushed Play. After a few seconds of white sound, Anna's voice began again. "This is a recorded version of my Last Will and Testament," she said. "The written version is under the floorboard, in the small cupboard beside my work table—the same cupboard in which I store my tapes. I won't bother to read the entire document verbatim. In brief, I leave all my worldly possessions—including the house, the dogs, and the money in the envelope containing the will—to Andrew Hatcher. He has been a great help to me over the years, and I have come to love him like a son."

Lily rewound the tape to the beginning a third time. It said the same thing. Anna left everything to Andy Hatcher, in the hopes he'd move into her house and take care of her dogs. She thanked all her friends—including Lily and Charlie, Jeffrey Tatum, Frank Leslie, and a few names Lily didn't recognize—for their love and support over the years. She also mentioned Stephan, her younger brother, the one who had died with her at Auschwitz. "I wish I could have helped him," she said. "I wish I could have saved him." Then Anna said she had begun to appreciate the simpler images of her faith. She had begun to think she would be rejoining her family in heaven. She hoped that was the case.

Lily sat in the chair long after the recording ended. She listened to the white blur of silence until the machine clicked off. If Anna had left Andy Hatcher her money, then he had all the more motive for killing her—that is, if he knew it. On the other hand, if he knew she left him her money, he wouldn't have any motive for stealing it, not if he also knew she was dead. Not if he'd killed her.

She couldn't keep her thoughts in place. They kept slipping out from under each other, the first contradicting the second, and on and on. But she knew one thing—until she could see how this was going to affect Andy Hatcher's case, she would keep it to herself.

When the phone rang, she answered it out of a sense of desperation. Maybe the person on the other end could tell her what to do. But instead of a kind voice, there was only silence. Lily said hello a few times. She was about to hang up when she heard a sigh, or someone catching his breath, trying to speak—maybe a young man.

Then the crying began, slowly at first, then faster, becoming a kind of sobbing. Between the sobs Lily could hear the words "I can't," repeated over and over. She knew this sound. When she had listened to the messages on Anna's tape machine, in the cabin in western Massachusetts, she had heard this sound—the same person, the same desperate cry.

CHAPTER 25

Lily couldn't sleep more than twenty or thirty minutes at a time; she kept dreaming—in her half-waking state—of the person who had called her and cried. He took a few different forms—one was a child in an empty room, another a man looking through a window, sometimes a stained-glass window, sometimes her own bedroom window, and she would wake with a gasp. Finally she got up and turned on the light, found a pencil and pad, and wrote a list of all the people it might have been.

Around five o'clock in the afternoon the following day, she met with Barbara, Tom, and Charlie in the office at the Women's Center. She skimmed over the talk with Betty Carl, saying only that the woman had seemed to know about Anna's disappearance. Lily had to be more certain, herself, of what had happened there before she told anyone. She also left out the story of hearing Anna's will on the tape, because she worried it would do Andy Hatcher more harm than good.

She reported her visit to both farms; explained the news from Officer Thompkins about Andy Hatcher; and, finally, described the phone call. "I started a list of people it could have been."

"Who have you got so far?" asked Barbara.

"Let's see," said Lily. "McPherson."

"The priest?" asked Charlie. "I don't think so."

"I just wrote down everyone I've met these past two weeks, everyone who could possibly have gotten my number or even figured out who I am."

"What do you mean, who you are?" asked Barbara.

"I don't know," said Lily.

"Go on," said Barbara. She sat at her desk, back straight, coffee cup at her elbow. She wore her gray flannel trousers again, this time with a sky-blue twin set and pearls.

Lily noticed she wrote on a legal pad while they talked. "What are you doing?"

"I'm making my own notes. That way, when I think about this at home in the evening, I can keep everything straight."

"You think about this at home in the evening?" asked Lily.

Barbara shook her head and looked over the top of her reading glasses at Lily. "You really believe you're the only one who wants to find Anna?"

"Sorry," said Lily. "I just forget—"

"That you're not alone?" asked Tom.

Everyone turned to him. He blushed and looked out the tall window across the room.

"Go on," said Charlie.

"The people at the Becket Center."

"But you only met two of them, right?" asked Charlie.

"Only two," said Lily. "And someone walked in on me in the chapel, but I never saw who it was."

"Was that before or after you stole their Bible?" asked Barbara.

"You stole their Bible?" asked Charlie.

"Yes," said Lily. "Speaking of which, do you still have that Bible we found in the cathedral?"

"No," said Charlie. "I'm pretty sure Anna took all that

stuff. She put it in the back of the station wagon that night, and then I think she took it home with her."

"Why?" asked Lily.

"I don't know," said Charlie. "But if Jeffrey's right, if she did plan to visit the Followers on her way to Wharton, maybe she wanted to show it to them, to kind of confront them."

"She stopped by the Becket Center?" asked Barbara.

"She had told Jeffrey she was going to," said Charlie. "So he called them right away, as soon as he heard about Anna. They said she never turned up. They hadn't seen her."

"You met them—what do you think?" Barbara asked Lily. "Would they lie about this?"

Lily remembered the man and woman on the hill, the lavish chapel, the eerie silence of the place. "I don't know," she said. "They're secretive, or at least private."

"But anyone would be, with that history," said Charlie. "And they did invite you to take a walk, to use their woods. If they were hiding Anna, I doubt they'd ask people to tour the facilities."

"What about the guy at the other farm?" asked Tom. "The guy who used to be associated with them."

"That's a harder call," said Lily. "I sort of liked him." Another thought, an image, had begun to distract her.

"But—?" asked Barbara.

"But after I left, I—" The image from Miss Betty came back to her—a hill, with buildings and people below. That was the view from behind the Followers' main house, and probably from behind the other man's—Steve's—main house as well. But it was also the view from the lookout point at the top of Anna's road in Wharton.

"You what?" said Charlie.

"It was weird," said Lily, pulling herself back into the present. "Because he gave me the impression that the farm-house was all there was, that it was a really small place with just a few people. But when I drove back past it and saw the other buildings—identical to the layout at the Followers'—I got this sort of chill. It was as if he had lied to me, but indirectly."

"Who else is on the list?" asked Tom.

Lily studied the sheet of paper in front of her. Hatcher came next, but she skipped it. "There's the Boston group, Anna's friends around here, the people we called that first day."

"What about the Hatchers?" asked Charlie.

"That just seems so unlikely," said Lily. "You really think one of them would call me and cry?"

"I have no idea what the Hatchers would do. But Andy Hatcher was just found with a bunch of money in his van and a gun hidden in the woodshed—a gun we should have reported, by the way."

"What does that have to do with this?" asked Lily.

"That's what we're trying to figure out, right?" asked Charlie. His voice had grown a little louder; he sat forward in his chair.

"So what do you think?" Barbara asked him, her voice calm and smooth. "I mean what do you think actually happened?"

Charlie stood and put his hands in his pockets. He wore his off-duty uniform—a pair of black jeans and a white oxford cloth shirt. Lily noticed the dark circles under his eyes and knew that he, too, had been awake a lot the past few nights. Maybe Andy Hatcher seemed like a good idea to him because Charlie didn't believe Hatcher would hurt Anna, and because he was a known entity, not a shapeless fear.

Charlie walked to the nearest window and stared down at the street. When he turned around, he looked defeated. "Maybe Hatcher found some money she had hidden, and then when she got home, she discovered it missing and—"

"And he killed her?" Barbara asked.

"No—maybe. I don't know. Maybe they're keeping her in their house."

"But Miller searched their house," said Lily. She tried to make her voice gentle. Charlie didn't answer. Lily and Barbara exchanged glances. Tom drew on a note pad. He had been quiet, which he always was, but quieter than usual. That was her fault, Lily knew, but she still didn't know what to do about it.

"Yes," said Charlie. "But there must be a million places around there where they could keep her hidden."

"Do you think they're keeping her hidden somewhere?" asked Barbara.

"I don't know. I don't know. I don't know." Charlie's voice got louder with each repetition, so by the end he was almost yelling.

"Charlie," Lily began.

"No," he said. "I'm sorry. I can tell what you want me to say, but I'm not going to give up until I have to."

"That's fair," said Tom. "And it's always good to have someone covering each of the bases."

"What do you mean?" asked Charlie.

"It's good you're holding out for Anna being alive," said Tom. "Because she might be, and if we forget that, we might miss something."

"Fine," said Charlie. "I'll make that my job."

CHAPTER 26

Tom waited around until Lily locked up the offices, then they walked out into the spring evening. The city had a kind of sheen to it, a pale wash of warm air and fading light. Lily felt distanced from the pleasures she would normally feel on a night like this—as if the feelings were lingering off to the side somewhere, waiting for her to join them. Tom linked his arm through hers. She wasn't sure if she liked that or not, but then she noticed it felt good, at least for the moment.

"You want to eat?" he asked.

"Sure," she said. "Where?"

"Italian?"

"Excellent choice," she said. So they walked around the corner to the trattoria. As they reached the restaurant window, Lily remembered looking in at Tom two weeks before—back when she thought she had a crush on Gregarian. She felt the blood rise to her cheeks; what must Gregarian think of her now, she wondered.

"Are you blushing?" asked Tom.

"No," said Lily.

"What were you thinking about?"

"I have no idea. But I'm pretty sure I wasn't blushing."

When they walked into the front room, the bartender

saw them and smiled. The bar was almost full of an older but still hip crowd of editors and Newbury Street store owners and the stray renegade lawyer. From her many years in and around the parishes of Boston, Lily recognized a few people, but she wasn't in the mood to chat.

"Let's eat in the back," she said.

She led Tom into the second, darker, quieter room. The space felt to her like a haven—cool, almost empty, with white tablecloths and bright blue stucco walls. Across the back was a shelf holding a row of Chianti bottles, interspersed with large, sepia-tinted photographs of Rome and Venice and Ravenna. She could remember getting up from the table one night, not long ago, probably last fall, during a dinner with Tom, to study each photograph because she was interested. That woman seemed like a stranger, innocent and a little foolish, with time to spend contemplating pictures of Italy. They found a corner table and sat down.

"I'm not sure I'm going to be very good company," said Lily.

"That's okay," said Tom. "I'm feeling pretty sullen myself. We can sulk together."

The waitress came up and asked if they'd like anything to drink. Yes, thought Lily. I'd like a couple of those fiascoes of Chianti on the wall over there, and I'll chase that with some Armagnac and a little champagne. But she ordered a table bottle of mineral water. Tom asked if she minded if he had a drink.

"No," she said. "Someone might as well feel better."

"Would you rather I didn't?" he asked.

"No," she said. "I'd rather you did."

"That's not such a great sign," he said. "Is it?"

"What do you mean?"

"I mean, if you're thinking about what I'm going to drink, isn't that—"

"Could you just order?" she asked him, glancing up at the waitress. "Whatever you want."

The problem with getting to know someone well, she thought, was that then they got to know you well, and you couldn't keep any secrets. Tom knew the details of her old drinking days, and the decision she'd made to stop drinking, and her failure to stick to that decision. He knew she'd walked into a couple of AA meetings and walked out; he knew she needed help and wouldn't get it; he seemed to feel it was up to him to talk her into it. Sometimes when she was with him, she wanted to wrap a cloak around herself, like that magic one in the children's story that made the wearer disappear.

Tom ordered a glass of pinot grigio and the appetizers—grilled calamari and grilled artichokes, their usual. They would figure out the entrees when the waitress brought the drinks. Lily wished he'd ordered grappa—she wanted that vicarious rush she'd gotten the last time she'd seen him drinking it. No one knew better than she did that all this thinking about alcohol was a bad sign, but she was not going to bring it up now, not when she felt so vulnerable already.

"So how've you been?" he asked.

"Weird. All I can focus on is finding Anna, but the rest of my life seems to expect me to be in it, too."

"You mean like me?" asked Tom.

"Actually, I meant like Barbara and work and my laundry. But, yeah, you, too."

"I'm glad I made the cut."

"You really are sullen."

"I haven't even seen you for a week. You're off on expeditions to cult sites. I know you don't want me to worry about you, but I do. It's not so unusual for people to worry about people they love."

She got that constricted feeling again, as if she were in her tiny, windowless study carrel in the seminary library.

"You're right," she said. "It's not. But what am I supposed to do? You want to worry about me. I don't want you to worry about me. You want to live together. I—"

"You what?"

"I'm not sure. Look, I love you, you know that. And I'm not trying to string you along because it gives me some kind of cruel thrill. I'd much rather say, yes, yes, fine, let's do what you want, so I can make you happy and stop feeling guilty. But if I make the decision that way, if I say, let's move in together, for emotional efficiency's sake, it's going to blow up all over both of us."

"Nice image," he said. The waitress set down the glasses and the bottle of mineral water. They ordered their dinners—pasta bolognese for Tom, risotto with mushrooms for Lily. Then Tom poured her a glass of the water and added some to his wine.

"You're so funny," she said.

"Oh, yeah? How's that?"

"You're so careful. I love the way you always water down your wine."

"That way I don't get dehydrated," he said.

"Yeah, I know. It just wouldn't occur to me. Anyway, I have a plan. Listen to this."

"I'm all ears."

"Nice image."

He smiled for the first time, grudgingly. She could always get him to smile, because he was at heart a good-natured person, unlike her, at heart a superstitious pessimist.

"Okay," she said. "Here's the plan. Let's have dinner together regularly, like this, a couple of times a week, because this is fun and I miss you when I don't see you. Until we find Anna, or find out what happened to Anna. Then once that's settled, once I know where she is, let's try—I emphasize try—to work out the details of living together. Or, I should say, to try living together."

"That's a lot of trying. Why don't we just do it?"

"Because I can't just—"

Tom put up his hands, to stop her. "Just kidding. That's fine. Are you sure?"

Lily could see the waitress approaching with the appetizers. She had just done what she said she wouldn't do—made a decision for the sake of emotional efficiency. But she wanted peace, she wanted to finish this part so they could eat, so Tom could make her feel better, the way he always did.

"Yes, I'm sure."

CHAPTER 27

Lily lay in bed staring out through one of the tall windows in her bedroom. She'd placed the curtain rods halfway down the window frames, so the white sheers touched the floor while the top panes remained uncovered. The sky had begun to turn from dark blue to light blue. A pale star faded as she watched.

Tom lay beside her, snoring quietly. She liked his snoring; it sounded gentle and rhythmic and reminded her of the ocean. She liked having him there next to her; she had missed him. But when she thought about having him there next to her every morning, the thing with the shallow breathing started again. She placed her hand on her heart and made herself take a few deep breaths.

On and off throughout the evening she had considered telling him about Miss Betty, about her own certainty that Anna was dead and Andy Hatcher was innocent. But she hadn't told him. And then during the night, during one of her short bouts of sleep—she'd dreamed she stood on a hill with the woman from the Followers. The nun had swept her arm out across the land below them and everything—the grass, the trees, the square, the white buildings—had started to sparkle, as if lit by a giant disco ball. Then the woman pointed toward the vernal pond. When Lily bent over to look, she could see something white and glowing under the surface of the water. The woman became Jeffrey Tatum, or maybe Frank Leslie, because in the dream Lily worried he might collapse and hit his head on something. He desperately wanted her to see, so she leaned down farther and found herself face-to-face with Steve, the man at the second farm—his eyes open, his skin stretched tight over the bones, his hair matted with pine needles. Then she lost her balance and fell toward the water, toward the hideous stretched skin of the dead man.

Awake now, she watched the star fade and began to make some plans. She needed to talk with Miss Betty one more time, to get as many details as she could about the hill Miss Betty had described. Then she would go back out to Lester and Ahearn, visit both farms, and get into those other buildings.

For a while she thought about Tom and her, about how Tom worried, about waking up next to him. She knew what he wanted; she wasn't sure what she wanted; she was afraid they weren't the same thing. Then she must have fallen asleep again because when she woke next, daylight filled the room and Tom sat on the edge of the bed, using his phone. He held his pants in one hand, resting against his knee, his cell phone in the other.

Mostly, Tom grunted single word replies—"Yeah," "Nope," "Okay"—as if listening to a long story. He put his pants next to him on the bed, but didn't turn around. In fact, it seemed to Lily he tried to keep her from hearing what he and the other person said. She caught the words *Hatcher* and *body.*

They had moved to the couch in the living room. Lily sat curled up, wrapped in the blue comforter off her bed. Tom had made tea and cut up part of a cantaloupe, which he'd eaten, but she'd only sipped the tea and set it down on the wooden chest that served as her coffee table. As it turned out, Gregarian had called Tom to give him the news: Andy Hatcher had led the police in Wharton to Anna's body.

"The thing is," she said, "that I knew she was dead. So it's not really a surprise. But hearing it out loud, learning where the body is, that makes her death so specific, so physical."

"What do you mean you knew she was dead?"

"I just did," she said. Again she had an urge to tell him, and again she decided against it. Too late, too complicated, and she felt too distracted by what she was thinking of as *the wall*—the solid screen that had come down between her mind and her feelings. "I just knew, after so much time had passed. So I'm not surprised about her being dead. It's just that now her death has been confirmed, so it's almost as if I'm finding out for the first time, even though I'm not. Even though I knew."

Tom nodded. One of the great things about him was his solid presence, in space, in time. For instance, even though he was late for work, Lily noticed that he didn't glance at his watch or try to hurry her. He sat on the couch like a man who had no place else to be.

"Look," she said. "I know you're late—"

He waved it off. "I'll call in a minute," he said. "Don't worry about it."

Lily picked up her mug of tea and put it back down without drinking any. "So Hatcher says he found the body last week?"

Tom nodded.

"And then he moved it. But why?" It was as if her mind grasped at the facts—what made sense, what didn't, and why—in order to distract herself from the larger, simpler truth.

"Gregarian doesn't know. I'm not sure anyone knows, except maybe Hatcher."

"And where did Gregarian get all this information?"

"From Miller, the chief of police over in Wharton. He called Gregarian first thing this morning."

"I don't get it, though," she said.

"Which part?" he asked.

"All of it. To repeat, why would he move the body? And why didn't he tell someone when it happened? And if he hasn't told anyone yet, why would he tell Miller, and why now? Why wouldn't he tell his lawyer or Father McPherson?"

"I don't know that, either," said Tom. "I do have the impression that no one much likes Miller, but it doesn't sound as if anyone's accusing him of wrongdoing."

Lily picked up her mug again. This time she wrapped both her hands around it and held it close to her body. "Has Gregarian told anyone else?"

"Like who?"

"Did he call Charlie?"

"I don't think so," said Tom. "I think he called me so I could tell you first. He probably figured you'd tell Charlie."

"I ought to go over to the monastery to tell him. And then I guess he and I need to go out to Wharton. I don't even know who's in charge of the funeral. She doesn't have any family. Someone's got to make arrangements for her house, and the dogs." She remembered the face of one of the small yellow dogs, the one who had come into the room and cocked its head to listen when Lily had played the tape of Anna's voice. Sadness threatened to break through.

She set down her mug and reached for a paper napkin from a pile Tom had placed on the table. He put his arm around her. She could tell he thought she was about to cry, and that was enough to bring her back to the land of logic. She leaned against him for a minute or two, because she could tell he expected it, then straightened her back, blew her nose, and pulled her hair away from her face. "So," she began. "I ought to get to the monastery."

"You want a ride?" asked Tom.

"No, thanks," she said. "I think I'll take the T. I could use a little time on my own before I tell Charlie. Or I might walk, depending on the weather."

"Are you sure?"

"Yeah, I'm sure. Thanks." She stood, gathering the comforter behind her. "I've got to call Barbara, and—"

"And what?"

"I was thinking of some friends of Anna's who should know—Jeffrey, Frank, Bishop Spencer. But that will wait. I'm not really sure what to tell them at this point."

She got halfway to the door then turned to him. "Andy Hatcher may have found Anna's body. And he may have moved the body. And he may have kept the whole thing a secret. But he didn't kill Anna."

"How do you know?"

"I just do," she said. "I know that sounds really stupid and pompous, and I'm sure it's frustrating to hear, but I do."

"I believe you," said Tom.

"Yeah," said Lily. "I know you do. But nobody else will."

CHAPTER 28

Lily opened the outside door to the monastery chapel and slipped in quietly. She'd planned to spend a few minutes alone, to light a candle for Anna and pray about what to say to Charlie, how to tell him, and how to help him after she told him. But once her eyes adjusted to the light, she noticed that the altar was bare, the crucifix gone. Then she remembered—Good Friday.

So Charlie couldn't drive her to Wharton. He would have to stay here with his community for Easter weekend. Lily had planned to go to church with Barbara on Sunday, but everything had changed. Barbara would understand—Lily would leave a message at the office. She didn't much want to talk with Barbara in person, because Barbara would probably have a more practical approach than to drive over to Wharton with so little information and no real plan, and Lily didn't want to hear a more practical approach.

The chapel was empty; dim light filtered through the stained-glass windows and three or four votive candles flickered around the base of the statue of Mary in the narthex. Lily walked over and knelt before the statue, a blue-robed Madonna holding a placid baby Jesus in her left arm, her right arm raised in benediction. Lily lit a candle, said a prayer for Anna, and waited to feel comforted, but nothing happened. Once again, it felt to her as if these simple rituals of faith had disappeared behind a thick veil of loss and disappointment and hours of seminary arguments. Miss Betty had called it pride, and maybe she had been right. Lily had grown too smart to believe in anything anymore.

Someone opened the door from the hallway that led to the refectory. When he bowed to the altar, Lily could see it was Charlie. He knelt at the rail and crossed himself. After a moment, his shoulders began to shake, and Lily could hear his sharp intakes of breath.

Half an hour later, the two of them sat on a stone bench in a protected corner of the guest house garden. A pale sun shone through a high, thin layer of clouds, but strong enough to warm the air and the bench and Lily's hands and face. It turned out that Charlie had called Lily earlier—right after she'd left to come find him—to check in, since he knew he'd be out of circulation all weekend. When he couldn't get her at home or at the office, he'd called Gregarian and heard the news.

His face looked red and tender from crying. Lily held one of his hands and they sat in silence for a few minutes, until he asked, "So what do you think we should do?"

"What do you want to do?"

"I can't do much of anything at this point—I've got to be here. And Gregarian said the body would be at the morgue for a while, because of the autopsy. I guess they'll figure out the stuff about the dogs and the house. Maybe we should just plan to go next week."

Lily released his hand and shifted on the bench. "I'd rather get over there today. And I'm fine going by myself. I want to talk with Thompkins, or maybe even Andy Hatcher, if they'll let me."

"Why?" he asked.

"Because—some of it doesn't make sense. And you know I'm always looking for a chance to miss Easter."

"How will you get there?"

"You think Father Mark would let me borrow the station wagon?"

"For how long?"

"The weekend, I guess. I could be back by Sunday evening, Monday morning at the latest. Our office is closed Monday anyway."

"That's probably okay. I'll check with him in a minute."

"No hurry," said Lily. In truth she felt impatient to get going. She couldn't tell Charlie, but—irrational as she knew it would sound—she worried that the longer it took her to get there, the more likely it was that Andy Hatcher would be accused of murder, tried, and sentenced.

CHAPTER 29

When Lily reached the police station in Wharton, around four that afternoon, the desk sergeant told her Thompkins was out on patrol duty. She would be back by five. Lily thought about asking to see Captain Miller, but based on what McPherson had said about him, she had a feeling that she wouldn't learn anything anyway. She thought she would spare herself the pleasure a while longer. She crossed the street to a coffee shop, Brown & Brew, which turned out to be more of a coffeehouse—old armchairs and sofas, long wooden tables, a small stage, four or five kinds of coffee, and a sense of innocuous grime over everything—an establishment that could exist only in a college town. She ordered a chicken salad sandwich on seven grain bread and tea with milk. The young man behind the counter had a wispy goatee that made him look like the youngest brother of the Billy Goat's Gruff; he seemed confused by the tea order.

She found a table in one of the bay windows, where she could sit and watch the entrance to the police station. On the sound system, a woman sang about the ups and downs of bisexuality. Two tables away a young couple sat, both reading what looked like college textbooks. The woman had short red hair, straight and lank across her forehead; the man had a huge, curly bush of blonde hair. His sandals lay on the floor beside him, and every once in a while he would rub his foot up and down the woman's shin.

Lily ate and watched the building across the street. Not much happened—Thompkins didn't arrive, and Lily didn't recognize anyone coming or going. Then she saw an old red Ford truck drive past and park. In a few minutes, Father McPherson climbed the steps to the police station. She bused her own table, putting the china in a bin near the counter, and left.

She opened the station door to find McPherson at the front desk, arguing loudly with the sergeant.

"Let me guess—Miller's not here and you don't know when he'll be back, right?"

The sergeant, a small, pale man with a long face and a comb-over, nodded. He continued to stare down at his desk; he appeared to be checking off items on a list, or at least he pretended to be checking off items on a list.

"I want to talk with Andy."

"Mr. Hatcher is currently not receiving visitors," said the sergeant.

"What the hell does that mean?" asked McPherson.

"You can't see him."

"Says who?"

"You know, Father, I don't want to argue with you. And I don't make the rules around here. But let me offer this piece of wisdom: If I were you, I'd cultivate a more amiable relationship with the captain. Because then he might let you in on some of this shit from time to time. As it stands now, you might as well get used to knowing nothing."

"Thanks, Sergeant," said McPherson. "I'll keep all that in mind. Meanwhile, you might consider what it means, professionally and personally, as a Christian man, to carry out the orders of a power-hungry asshole who is dangerously close to violating his prisoner's rights." McPherson turned and walked straight past Lily without speaking. She reached out and touched his arm. For a moment, his face remained blank and angry, then he recognized her. His expression changed, his cheeks got red, and tears welled up in his eyes.

McPherson insisted Lily stay with him while she was in Wharton. She got in the station wagon and followed his truck to a small brick house on a short street near the campus, lined with maples and oaks. The house stood back from the street, facing south, the long front yard tucked between two larger houses on either side. The garden appeared to be a couple of weeks farther into spring than the rest of the countryside; Lily could see crocuses, daffodils about to open, the green sprouts of tulips and irises, even the first shoots of perennials. Roses—not yet in bloom—twined around the split rail fence.

She parked on the street, grabbed her backpack, and they walked together up the path to the house.

"I'm sorry about my greeting," he said as he opened the door. The tears had never materialized, but it had taken him a few seconds to pull himself together. "I've been so caught up in the Hatcher thing, I haven't really let myself think about her being gone. For some reason, seeing you made it real."

"I get it," said Lily. "It doesn't seem real to me yet, either." She thought but didn't add, ". . . and I've known about it for days." Once again, she had an urge to tell someone the whole story—of Miss Betty, of Lily's own suspicions about the Followers, of what she had learned about Anna's will—but she would wait and see.

Inside, the house looked like a stylish country cottage, with bleached wood floors, throw rugs, a stone fireplace, and a large open kitchen to the right of the front door. He showed her to her room, a guest room and study on the first floor, with a single bed, an old-fashioned schoolteacher's desk, and two walls lined with books. Vines grew around both the windows; the shadows of the leaves made the room feel like a bower. She left her belongings by the bed and followed McPherson into the kitchen.

"You want anything to eat, drink, whatever?" he asked her.

"No, thanks. I had a sandwich at that place across the street from the police station."

"Brown & Brew? Our local throwback, run by a couple who graduated in the sixties and just couldn't tear themselves away. They come to church sometimes still. They're pretty nice people—but not too clean." He stood by the kitchen table for a few seconds looking uncomfortable, as if waiting for something. "I've got to get ready for the Good Friday service in half an hour, or I'd tell you the whole story now. But I kind of hate to get into it and not be able to finish. As soon as I'm done, we'll go back to the station and find Thompkins. Maybe the three of us can figure out what to do next."

"Can you give me a thumbnail sketch before you go?" Lily asked.

"Sure," he said, but he didn't move. "Look, normally I wouldn't suggest this, but it's been a tough few days." He reached into a cupboard over the refrigerator and brought down a bottle of Glenlivet, the scotch Lily used to drink. "Want a drink?"

"No, thanks," she said again. She could taste the scotch on her tongue, feel the burn down her throat, into her stomach, feel the way her muscles would start to relax.

He poured himself a shot—a normal-sized shot, Lily noticed, just covering the bottom of the glass. After he'd had a swallow, he sat at the kitchen table and offered her a chair.

"In brief—" he began, then took another swallow. "Miller busted Hatcher and searched his van. He found money, over seven thousand dollars. Not that much in the real world, but a lot around here."

"A lot for Andy Hatcher," said Lily.

"Yeah." He seemed at ease now. "Then they searched the shed at Anna's, where they found a gun, some liquor—I'm not sure what all they found."

"What about the body?" she asked.

"That's where I got left out of the loop," he said. "All I know is that for some reason—maybe Andy figured he'd be better off telling the truth, maybe Miller offered him some kind of deal, although if he did, Andy's lawyer doesn't know about it—anyway, Andy decided to tell Miller about finding her body and burying it in the woods, near some lookout spot she used to visit."

"Up behind her house?" asked Lily.

McPherson nodded.

She remembered the German shepherd lying in the clearing, growling, as if protecting something precious. "I may know it. I think the dogs took me up there when we stayed at Anna's—when was that? The weekend before last. Seems like years ago."

He finished the scotch. "But why Andy moved her body and never reported it—I have no idea."

"You're pretty sure Andy didn't do it, right?" asked Lily. "Didn't kill her?"

"I know he didn't. He's a pain in the neck, but he's not a murderer. He'd been working for Anna for years. She was the closest thing he had to family, since he can't stand his grandfather."

"I wonder what that's about," she said.

"Tradition, the generation gap, the usual," said McPherson. "They've always fought. Anna was more than just an employer, that's for sure. And he was more like—I don't know." He looked at his watch, a large face with a black leather band. "I've got to get going." He stood and returned the bottle to the cupboard, then put the glass in the sink.

"Why don't you come to the service with me? We'll go to the station from there."

"I'm not—okay, sure," she said. The last thing she wanted to do was attend a Good Friday service on a college campus with a drunk priest. Be fair, she thought. He had one drink.

On the other hand, she didn't feel any better about being left alone in a strange house with a mind full of questions and a bottle of Glenlivet.

Lily had imagined a small, desultory crowd in a lackluster space—filled with handsewn banners proclaiming a season unto everything and the need to house the homeless—but she'd been wrong on both counts. Students and faculty filled the room—Lily sat in the next to the back row and had to move over a couple of times for latecomers. The chapel was modern but pleasant, with large, leaded windows, comfortable chairs, and a beautiful rose window. The evening sun shone through the stained glass, casting a soft glow on the space behind the empty altar.

McPherson turned out to be a skilled liturgist and an equally good preacher. He and two assistants entered silently from the back, but the silence seemed meditative rather than dramatic. Instead of the traditional Passion of John, McPherson provided an edited, shortened version—"the Jews" had become "the people," "the high priests" had become "the officials," and no one yelled out "crucify him," much to Lily's relief. In his sermon, McPherson focused on the compassion of Jesus, from the moment the soldiers appear in the garden, when Jesus asks that his disciples be spared—"I told you that I am he; if you seek me, let these men go"—to his final moments on the cross when he entrusts his own mother and his favorite disciple to one another's care—"Behold your mother." McPherson reflected on the remarkable presence of mind and spirit it had taken for Jesus to continue to act on his compassion for those around him, on the kind of faith it takes to go to your death with such awareness intact. "This is why he remains my teacher and my lord," said McPherson.

Lily had a new respect for McPherson. She didn't participate in the veneration of the cross and she couldn't participate in the Eucharist, since she wasn't Roman Catholic anymore. She sat in the back and let the slow rhythms of the long service wash over her. And whether it was because a dear friend had just died or because she hadn't slept well for the past two weeks or because the power of the Catholic ritual had worked its magic on her or all of the above, she didn't know—but the resistance she had admitted to this morning, in front of the statue of Mary, began to weaken.

Again, she had read so much and thought so much about text and history and interpretation that the story of Jesus' life had become a kind of metaphor—a finger pointing at the moon. But what if the story were true?—McPherson clearly thought it was, and he turned out to be a pretty smart guy. What if this man Jesus had been whipped and forced to carry a cross up a hill, a crown of thorns digging into his forehead, blood dripping into his eyes? She had believed that years ago. She could remember her feelings when, as a child, she kneeled to kiss the cross at Good Friday service.

She waited in her chair while the chapel emptied. The light had faded outside; lamps and candles had been extinguished. By now she could barely see the altar. She heard a mockingbird singing loudly nearby, his ridiculous medley of imitations. Then he stopped, suddenly, and the dark silence of Good Friday surrounded her.

CHAPTER 30

When Lily and McPherson entered the police station, they found Thompkins at a desk in the back of the room. She spotted them, closed a file folder, and came up front to meet them.

"Let's go somewhere else to talk," she said quietly.

"My house?" asked McPherson.

"No," she said. "I can't be gone long. How about across the street? No one from here can stand the place, so nobody'll see us."

McPherson turned to Lily. "Think you can handle two visits to the B&B in one day?"

"Sure," said Lily. "I like it. I get a sort of time traveler feeling."

"I'll meet you in a couple of minutes," said Thompkins.

Lily and McPherson left the station and crossed the street.

"Don't order food," said McPherson. "I've got some beautiful salmon at home, and plenty of stuff to go with it."

"That's fine with me. I can't say my chicken salad sandwich was worthy of an encore."

"You wouldn't catch me ordering chicken salad in here—or anything with mayonnaise, for that matter. But

I'm a little persnickety. I got salmonella poisoning once when I was a kid—it almost killed me."

"Literally?" she asked.

"No—but I sure thought I was dying. That's when I made my deal with God. You know, save my life and I'll dedicate it to you."

"That's why you became a priest?"

"Not really. I sort of knew I was going to do it. But the intention came in handy as a bargaining chip."

"And it obviously worked," she said. "Here you are, alive and well and wearing a collar."

They ordered—tea for Lily, coffee for McPherson—then found a table at the back, near the counter. The place was almost full now—mostly college-age kids in jeans and sweatshirts, nothing too outlandish. Lily spotted a couple of colorful dye jobs and more facial piercings than she'd ever seen together in one place. The littlest Billy Goat Gruff had been replaced by two young women, one tall and skinny with chopped-off black hair, the other small and beautiful, with thick, curly brown hair and violet eyes. Lily caught herself staring at the smaller woman, the sort of girl Lily had envied in her younger years—delicate, appealing, probably a potter or weaver or harpist, something calm and sexy.

"She's a beauty, huh?" asked McPherson.

"Yeah. My nemesis."

"Really? I thought she looked a little like you."

"Are you kidding? She's about half my size, eyes like an angel—"

"Oh, her. Not my type. I meant the tall one."

Lily glanced at him sideways.

"What?" he asked.

"As naive as this sounds," she said, "I guess I don't think of Catholic priests as having types."

"Everybody's got a type. Just because you've got a type,

doesn't mean you do anything about it. You think I lost my libido when I donned my collar?"

"No—but you did take a vow of celibacy."

"Look—I've been a priest a long time, and I know a couple of things. And the one thing I know for sure is that if I don't accept my own, well, defects—if I'm not willing to see them clearly as part of me—I sure as hell can't accept anyone else's."

"I'm not sure I get that. By accept, do you mean, 'Oh well, that's what I'm like, what can I do about it?'" She gave an exaggerated shrug to illustrate.

He shot her a look of ironic disbelief. "Is that what you think I mean?"

"I don't—"

But Thompkins came in, walked straight to their table, and immediately got down to business. "Have you been in touch with Devereaux?" she asked McPherson.

"Who's Devereaux?" asked Lily.

"Andy's lawyer, and a friend of mine, a parishioner," said McPherson. "He's gone for the weekend. Easter's kind of a big—"

"What about that woman, his probation officer?"

"Mrs. Creeley?—Mrs. Creeley cannot be reached until Tuesday. Her nasty colleague, Mr. Hampshire, informed me of her weekend plans early this morning."

"You need to talk with somebody before then," said Thompkins. "They've booked Andy on murder—no bail. They'll arraign him on Monday and then send him down to county jail in Pittsfield."

"Did something happen? Is there new evidence?" asked Lily.

"There might be, but it's not in Miller's favor," said Thompkins.

"What do you mean?" asked McPherson.

Thompkins hesitated, then glanced around at the crowd. "I feel like I'm in some kind of stupid spy movie," she said.

"I shouldn't be telling you guys any of this, and most days I want to keep my job. You know?"

McPherson sat back in his chair, then leaned forward, close to Thompkins. "You just do as much as you can," he said. "We've got resources—we can work this thing out on our own. Anything you feel comfortable telling us will help—you decide."

Magic, thought Lily. Leave it up to a good person's conscience—and Thompkins was clearly a good person.

She nodded, as if she'd just settled a war inside her head. "The word is that the *Boston Globe* ran the story and got a call from someone who'd been on the bus—the one Professor Banieka supposedly took. A Korean woman."

"Mr. Hatcher saw a Korean woman in the bus station when he went to look for Anna," said Lily.

"Evidently," said Thompkins, "from what I can make out, Professor Banieka gave this woman her ticket."

"What do you mean?" asked Lily.

"Professor Banieka never got on the bus," said Thompkins. "The bus was sold out. So Banieka gave this woman her ticket so she could ride with her children. The woman picked up the rest of the ticket for Albany here, in Wharton."

"Then how did Anna's body get into the woods behind her house?" asked McPherson.

"I have no idea," said Thompkins.

"Have you seen the autopsy report?" asked McPherson.

"It's not in. And I didn't see the body myself. But the word in the station is that there were no bullet wounds, no wounds of any kind, and no marks of strangulation."

"So how can they book Andy Hatcher on murder?" asked Lily. "They found his gun, but Anna wasn't shot. They found her body, but she never came home."

"It's a long story. After Miller busted him, they did an inventory on the van—it's a protective thing, so some drunk doesn't wake up Sunday morning screaming about how his Rolex is missing from the glove compartment of his impounded Mercedes. Anyway, they found the money in baggies, taped to the bottom of the seats."

"I guess it would make you wonder," said McPherson.

"According to Miller, Andy told them the money came from Professor Banieka's house—he said he took it after she'd been gone for a couple of days, that she owed it to him for back pay."

"What's he been doing for her, dental work?" asked McPherson.

"On the strength of that, Miller got a search warrant for Hatcher's house, Anna's house, and the shed out behind there, where they found the gun and the liquor. Andy's on probation, so he's already in deep shit at this point. Then—and I don't know what happened here—Andy told them about finding the body. He told them he'd found it and moved it."

"What the—can anybody get this kid to shut up?" asked McPherson.

"That's why I asked if you could find Devereaux. Andy won't see anyone else—he's basically only talking to Miller. Somebody's got to point out to him the error of his ways."

"What do you think really happened?" asked Lily.

Thompkins shook her head. "Just a guess—I think Andy found the body, moved it, and took the money."

"So he didn't report it because of the money," said McPherson. "He wanted to get that out first."

"But what if—" said Lily.

"What if what?" asked McPherson.

"What if she really did owe him the money and had given him permission somehow to take what he needed? Or, let's just say, for instance, that was his money somehow, his already, before he took it."

Thompkins and McPherson both looked at her, then McPherson said, "What are you talking about?"

"I don't know," said Lily. "Forget it. I'm just thinking out loud. Never mind."

McPherson turned to Thompkins. "I'll try to find Devereaux and figure out what happens next. If I can't—Do you think it's worth trying to talk to Miller? So we can at least know where Andy stands at this point, what they have on him, what they're charging him with."

"I don't think it's worth *you* trying to talk to Miller," she said. She looked at Lily. "Maybe you could. He doesn't know you, and he's a little better with women than men. Do you have your thing with you?" She pointed to her own neck, and then to McPherson's clerical collar.

"No," said Lily. "I hardly ever wear it anymore. What would I be talking to him about?"

"Here's what I'd do," said Thompkins. "You tell him you're an old friend of Professor Banieka's—which is true. That you want to figure out what happened here—also true. Then he's pretty likely to tell you the whole story of how he single-handedly apprehended the murderer. Most of which won't be true, but some of it will, and at least we'll know his version."

"That's fine," said Lily. "Do you think he'd let me talk to Andy?"

"You'd have to think of a reason," said Thompkins.

"Like what?" Lily asked.

"Like, maybe, since you're a priest you'd like to have a crack at getting him to confess," said Thompkins.

"Not very priestly," said Lily.

A young man with a ponytail and a woman in a long printed skirt had begun to set up on the small stage—two wooden chairs, two guitars, not an elaborate procedure.

"Why don't you just ask him?" said McPherson.

"Ask him what?"

"Ask Miller if you can talk to Andy. He won't let me, and he claims Andy doesn't want to talk to me. I don't know why that would be. Actually, he claims Andy doesn't want to talk with anyone, except him."

"Okay," said Lily. "I'll ask. Should I go over there now?"

"No," said McPherson. "I'm starving. I've got to eat."

"He's not there anyway," said Thompkins. "He's generally a nine-to-five guy. But he's been around a lot more these last few days. He thinks this case is going to make his career, whatever that means. I think he plans to run for president soon."

"Either that or King of the World," said McPherson. "Let's get out of here before they start singing 'Blowin' in the Wind.'"

CHAPTER 31

The next morning Lily sat in Jonah Miller's office, at the back of the Wharton police station. The open windows overlooked a small tributary of the Hoosic River; as she waited for Miller to arrive, she could hear the water rushing along outside. The sky was clear blue and cloudless, the temperature had climbed into the eighties, and the whole world appeared to have gotten a new paint job.

Lily felt sleepy but relaxed. The night before, McPherson had made her a magnificent salmon dinner, with grilled vegetables and wild rice and green salad. He'd opened a bottle of pinot grigio and drunk half of it, then put the rest back in the refrigerator, where Lily had seen it every time she'd gone to get milk or water or anything, for that matter.

They had spent a lot of time talking about Anna—not about her disappearance or her body, but about her, the woman they had known and loved. Lily described the contents of Anna's tapes, and as she spoke she discovered an idea that had been slowly forming over the past week—to transcribe and shape the material on the tapes, to write the book Anna had planned, the story of Anna's life. Before she had time to think the idea through, she presented it to McPherson. To her surprise, he had shifted in his chair and avoided looking at her.

"Do you mean about her childhood?" he'd asked, serving himself some salad.

"Yeah. Mostly. That's the material on the tapes—at least the ones I've heard so far. I'll probably do some research here to write the later parts, about her life in the States."

"How much do you know about that?" he'd asked then. "About her life here, when she first arrived?"

"Not a lot. She started to tell Charlie and me more about it the last night I saw her, when we all went out to dinner. And I found a book on O'Riordan and that whole group. But I haven't found anything on the tapes. Maybe she hadn't gotten to that part yet."

"Maybe," he'd said and changed the subject to how long Lily could stay. He'd convinced her to stick around for the vigil on Saturday night.

At the time, Lily had thought McPherson might be worried she wasn't up to the task. Or maybe he'd even had the same idea. But as she sat in Miller's office, reflecting on the conversation, that didn't seem right. McPherson hadn't been worried about her abilities as a writer; he'd been worried about what she might turn up.

She heard a loud voice in the next room, then she heard her name mentioned. She stood and faced the door and found herself staring down at a small, older man, at least three or four inches shorter than her, in the brown and tan uniform of the chief of police, without the hat. He had sparse white hair and an abundant white mustache, brown eyes, tan skin—leathered from exposure to sun and wind—and a small white scar from the corner of his right eye to the hairline directly above. Something about that short white line gave him a slightly comic look, a look of perpetual surprise.

"How do you do?" he asked. His voice was deep, his manner formal. Lily thought she might have detected the beginnings of a bow from the waist.

"Fine," she said. "I'm Lily Connor—"

"Yes, they informed me at the desk. You were a friend of Miss Banieka's?"

"Yes."

"Let me begin by expressing my heartfelt condolences. I myself was not a friend, but we had known one another for many years. I'm very sorry for your loss."

"Thank you," said Lily.

"Sit down, sit down," he said and pointed to the chair. "I'm just going to see to a few things. I'll return in no time."

He disappeared into the outer room. Lily could hear his voice—gravelly and impatient—but not most of the words. She did make out "god damn" and "coffee." After that he must have gone into another part of the building. He stayed away for at least ten minutes, then came back, cup in hand.

"Did you get coffee?" he asked. "May I offer you some?" he added, when he saw her hands were empty.

"No, thanks. I just—"

"I thought when we got some women on the force, the coffee would get better, or at least get made. That doesn't appear to have had the desired effect. I suspect you would like some information about Miss Banieka's murder." He sat behind his desk and suddenly seemed taller, as if the chair were especially high.

"Was she murdered?" asked Lily.

"I believe that's a safe assumption. We have the murder suspect in custody at this point in time—Andrew Hatcher, a neighbor and employee of Miss Banieka."

"And what makes you think he killed her?"

"Well, we found a large sum of money in his vehicle, to begin with, money he admits to taking from her home. In addition, he led us to the body."

"But why would he do that? I mean, why would he lead you to the body if he killed her? Wouldn't he pretend not to know where it was?"

He leaned back in the chair and sipped his coffee, keeping his eyes on Lily. Then he leaned forward and said, "I'm not sure how much you know about criminals, Miss Connor, but what might seem logical to you or I would not necessarily seem logical to them."

"Hmm," said Lily, nodding at him. If she wanted to find out anything, she needed him to like her, but it was getting harder all the time. "So he didn't admit to the murder?"

"No," said Miller. "No. That's quite rare, as you might imagine. He claims to have found the body in a shallow grave on Miss Banieka's property and to have moved it without reporting the death. At the very least, we have him on tampering with evidence, robbery, concealment of death," he paused. "Ahh, and possession of a firearm with an altered serial number—all of these, of course, constitute violations of probation."

"That's quite a list," said Lily.

"Indeed," said Miller and sipped his coffee. This time his white mustache came up stained brown. He took a folded handkerchief from his back pocket and patted his mouth. "Are you an academic yourself?"

"No, I'm a priest in the Episcopal church—and I run a women's center in Boston."

He widened his eyes comically. "A priest? I wouldn't have guessed that—no, not a priest."

Lily again reminded herself of why she'd come and what she hoped to accomplish, and stayed quiet.

Finally Miller leaned forward and asked, "How else can I help you?"

"Do they know how long she'd been dead?"

He did the thing with his eyes again. "You seem more than unusually interested in the details of this death. Why is that?"

"She was one of my best friends. I want to know what happened."

Miller had another sip of coffee, set down the cup, and

took out a file folder from the top right hand drawer. He made a show of reading slowly through the first few pages.

"The official autopsy is not in yet, you understand? The medical officer's best approximation is that the body was no more than twelve days old upon the time of examination—probably closer to ten days. That would imply that death had occurred approximately ten to twelve days earlier."

"But probably not more than ten days?" asked Lily. "She went missing two and a half, almost three, weeks ago. That means she could have been alive for a week before she died. Where did Andy Hatcher keep her all that time?"

"I'm sure the details will unfold as Mr. Hatcher understands the importance of telling us all he knows."

"It seems to me he's told you an awful lot already. Why is that, do you think?"

"That you would have to ask him."

"Okay," said Lily.

Miller replaced the file. "So," he said, leaning back in his chair. "If there's nothing else . . ."

"I'd like to ask him," said Lily.

"I beg your pardon?"

"You said I'd have to ask Mr. Hatcher. I'd like to do that. I'd like to ask him where he kept Anna all that time, what happened to her during that week."

Miller began to look through the neat pile of mail in the center of his desk. "That's not possible." He smiled to himself before throwing an envelope, unopened, into the trash.

"Why not?"

"Because he's requested no visitors."

"Not even his lawyer?" she asked, knowing she was blowing her cover but too fed up to care.

"That, as I understand it, is between his lawyer and him."

"Why would he do that?" Lily asked. Clearly, he wanted

her to leave, but she felt like a terrier with one end of a bone in her mouth—she couldn't let go.

He stood and walked to the door. "Why do people like Mr. Hatcher do any of the things they do? It's beyond the comprehension of most of us. And, I'll let you in on a professional secret—their reasons are never terribly interesting."

Lily stayed in her chair and didn't answer him. She'd lost all hope of getting in to see Andy Hatcher, but now she felt anger rising from its own dark source. "And I, in turn, will let you in on a professional secret," she said. She stood and faced him. "I'm one of those old-fashioned Christians who believe God comprehends everything and finds it all interesting."

She walked past him and out the front door of the building. When she got to the station wagon, she unlocked the driver's door and paused. What the hell did that mean? she wondered.

CHAPTER 32

"I know what you meant," said McPherson. She had found him in his office on campus, a bright, airy room with large windows. He was replacing books on the wall of shelves across from his desk.

Lily sat in a small armchair, in a corner by the window, and watched students enjoying one of the first truly warm days of the season, as only students can. "Yeah?" she asked. "What?"

"You meant that God knows what Miller's up to, even if we don't, even if Miller, on some level, doesn't, and that the guy's going to burn in hell."

"That sounds right," said Lily. "Except that I don't believe in hell. I'm not even sure I believe that God sees everything—or anything, for that matter."

"No," said McPherson. "Episcopalians mostly don't. The problem is that if you don't believe in hell, and the watchful eyes of God, and you see the Millers of the world getting away with all this, then where do you look for justice?"

"You remember Charlie?" she asked him.

"Yes," he said.

"Charlie firmly believes that the whole plan thing—the justice part, the balances—is bigger than what we can imagine, so it's not worth torturing ourselves with those questions. I used to believe that—part of me still does."

"But—?"

"If you buy that, then what do you do with the need for comfort? Believing in a plan beyond our comprehension is not the same as believing God sees everything, and cares for us. It doesn't have the same—what?—visceral effect."

"I agree completely," said McPherson. "Part of me also believes that God works on a much grander scale, that we can't always see divine justice. But that's pretty abstract, pretty adult. I need some childhood faith, too. I need to be able to pray and believe my prayers are heard. I need to be able to walk into church and feel safe and loved and cared for. And I do, most of the time. That's my childhood faith. And my childhood faith also tells me that Miller's going to burn in hell."

Lily laughed. "But don't you feel sort of duped if you go with the childhood faith, the images and symbols?"

"Duped?" he asked. "Why?"

"Because they're not true. God isn't up there with his giant Palm Pilot checking out that we're all getting what we deserve. Mary's not standing by his side saying things like, 'Oh, and, by the way, Father McPherson has been saying *lots* of prayers for Andy Hatcher. I sure hope you'll grant some of them.'"

Now McPherson laughed. "How do you know?" he asked.

Lily looked at him blankly. Then she smiled and shrugged. "It's just not how things work. You don't really believe that, do you?"

"Yes and no. There's some way in which I believe both things are true—the big abstraction and the comforting specifics."

"Like what?" she asked.

"Like God watching over Andy Hatcher, for instance. I couldn't do the work I do, with these kids, if I didn't on some level put each of them in God's hands every day. I may not know exactly what I mean by that—put them in God's hands—but I need those images sometimes. I use them when I need them. And I also use the language and images of Buddhism, and fundamental Christianity, and Orthodox Judaism, and all kinds of mysticism."

Lily watched a couple, younger, maybe freshmen, a girl with short blonde curls and a guy with thick curly black hair. They lay next to each other on the grass, talking, laughing. He took a blade of grass and ran it up her arm. Lily could almost feel the the tickling, teasing sensation. She turned back to look at McPherson. "So you think you pray to God and your prayers get answered?"

"I pray," he said. "And things happen. And then I get to make of them what I can. Sometimes it takes so long I don't notice the answer, and sometimes the answer is no, and sometimes I get exactly what I asked for and forget to notice it. And sometimes I don't see any connection at all."

"Yes," said Lily. "I have an either-or kind of mind. It's good to be reminded of the both-and school of thought."

"Dichotomy is the logic of the spiritual realm."

"I know," said Lily. "I know. So pray us out of this one. How are we going to get in to see Andy Hatcher?"

"Officer Thompkins called while you were at the station. She came up with a Plan B, just in case. She's on duty tomorrow night, midnight to eight, and she thinks she'll be virtually on her own some of the time—her fellow officer on duty in the station tends to fall asleep after a couple of sneaky beers in the back room. She thinks she can get us in to see Andy. Or at least she's willing to try."

"Why do you think she's doing this, risking her job?"

"Because she knows Andy's innocent, and she knows Miller's out to make this his big case, and she's sick of the town-gown split that's been going on here for years—especially since Miller's taken the side of the gown."

"And she's a good person," said Lily.

"And she's a good person," said McPherson.

"But that's not God answering our prayers, that's Thompkins."

"How do you think God works?" he asked her. "By showing us Jesus' face in a pizza? God works through people a lot of the time. Most of the time, in my experience. So in this case, it's God and Thompkins."

"Okay," said Lily. The couple outside had progressed from arm-tickling to back-rubbing. "If someone else is there with her, what will she say about me?"

"It probably won't work if there are too many people around. But she can say you're a family member of Hatcher's, if the question comes up."

"What about the ones who saw me today?" Lilly asked.

"What did you tell them?"

"I said I was a close friend of Anna's, and that I was trying to get some information about what happened."

"Okay. I'll tell Thompkins. She can say you're both—a member of the family and a close friend of Anna's. Or maybe none of the same people will be there. How many people did you actually talk with over there?"

"Just the guy at the desk."

"Ah, my old friend Sergeant Grimes. I doubt he'll be working Easter Sunday. He's a fiery Baptist. Anyone else?"

"Just Miller."

"Then that shouldn't be so hard," he said. "Let's call her and let her know what happened. Meanwhile, you might as well come to the vigil service tonight. You want to assist?"

"That's not legal, is it? An Anglican woman priest assisting at a Roman Catholic service?"

"No, but then neither is the Passion I used yesterday, or the communion open to all baptized Christians, or a lot of other things I do. You may not have heard this, but straight white guys—or, actually, any guys—aren't exactly beating down the doors to Catholic seminaries. Eventually, they'll figure out what I'm doing, and then we'll see. I look at it this way—my days are numbered, so I make each one of them count. You want to assist? If I can get one more person, we can have two communion stations—more efficient."

"Sure," said Lily, surprised not only by her response, but by the eagerness with which she made it.

CHAPTER 33

After an early supper, salmon salad, wild rice salad, and a mix of vegetables and greens from the night before—some of the best leftovers Lily had ever eaten—the two of them drove over to campus in McPherson's truck.

"We're going to get there early, so I'll walk you through the basics. Have you celebrated at a vigil—Anglican, I mean?" he asked.

"Yes, a couple of times, but the last one was a few years ago, a parish out in Lexington where I was serving as interim."

"You just hang with me. You don't actually have to do anything until communion. But that'll be a big help. We get a good crowd for this service."

"Is college in session? Don't students go home for Easter?"

"Our spring break was in March. Some of the students go home, but lots of them stay, and plenty of the faculty—the Catholic faculty, of which there aren't that many—tend to show up for the vigil. We also get town families—the Wharton church is conservative."

"Did Anna come to services here?"

"Oh yeah," said McPherson. "Regularly. I haven't told

anyone—about the body. Tonight's not the right time. I'll save it for—I don't know—later."

"What do you think happened, really?" asked Lily.

"I really don't know," he said. "I suspect it's pretty close to what Andy said. He found the body, moved it, and took the money."

"But how did the body get there in the first place?"

He pulled the truck into his parking place in the lot behind the chapel.

"You have a hunch, don't you?" he asked.

"What makes you say that?"

"You're definitely not talking about something," he said. "And I figure it's connected to Anna's death. So you must have an idea you're keeping to yourself. Am I right?"

"Yes," said Lily. "And you've got an idea you're keeping to yourself, too, don't you?"

He looked surprised. "What?"

"Something to do with Anna's past."

He stared out through the windshield. They'd parked across from the building, facing toward the town and the fields beyond. The spring dusk, a pale blue sky with pink clouds lit from beneath, gave the scene an odd intensity, as if the colors of the buildings and cars and budding trees and new grass vibrated slightly.

"What I have wouldn't qualify as an idea," he said. "I'd call it a bunch of fears. And I can't tell you about them because of how I know, if you see what I mean. It was confession material." He put his hand on the door, then turned to her. "Just be careful."

The vigil service didn't start until ten P.M. Around eleven, Lily felt baffled by what she could possibly be doing sitting in a chair behind the altar, listening to McPherson preach about the reality of the resurrection. He said that one reason he believed the story in Matthew to be true was that the writer claimed the women had known first. No one would have made that up, said McPherson. If the person recording the Book of Matthew in the first century A.D. had wanted to make this story up, he (probably) would have written that the disciples—the men—first knew of the resurrection. No one in the year 90 would have thought to invent a story in which an angel rolled back the sephulcre stone and sat on it (a nice, quirky little detail on its own, he claimed), then spoke to Mary Magdalene and "the other Mary" about Jesus' having risen from the dead.

Lily felt interested that McPherson even addressed the question of the historical accuracy of the story. Lily couldn't remember having heard any other Catholic priest do that—partly because when she was growing up, Catholic priests didn't talk about the Bible all that much anyway, and partly because when they did talk about it, the assumption was that every word was true—"Sacred Scripture is the speech of God as it is put down in writing under the breath of the Holy Spirit."

She had no idea where that quotation came from, but she had learned it as a child somewhere along the line. McPherson then spoke about the point of believing the resurrection truly happened. According to him, among the many obvious realities that Jesus' death and resurrection reveal, an important one is the reality of the spirit, the reality of our bodies as a brief resting place for that part of us connected to all things forever. In revealing that truth, the resurrection helps us to understand and even accept death, our own death and the death of people we love.

"Of course, the cross shows us the reality of sacrifice, the reality of a God that suffers with us here on earth, the reality of evil. But today what I'm finding in this story in Matthew is the hope of resurrection.

"Many of us have lost dear friends and family members this year," said McPherson. He took off his glasses and raised his head, staring out into the congregation. "Nothing replaces those loved ones, and no talk about God's plan for them cheers me up one little bit. No talk about accepting God's will or praying them into heaven has any effect on me whatsoever." He paused and looked down at the lectern, then back out into the chapel. "But do I feel soothed by the knowledge that their souls continue, that I may even, in some form or another, see them again?—I do. And on the most personal, unsophisticated level, that's what the story of Jesus' death and resurrection does for me tonight. It proves to me there is a life beyond this life, an opportunity to rest in God's love, united with God, after our deaths.

"So that when I die, I join my friends and Jesus in some place eternal. And they are there with him, maybe, now, and if so, I know they are all right. I know they aren't tormented anymore by the failures of their lives on earth, that they are safe with God and Jesus 'always, to the close of the age.'"

For just a moment, when he turned to walk down the steps from the lectern, Lily thought McPherson had a glow around him. Then she realized it was from the bank of candles behind him. But she didn't care. He had done something she hadn't thought possible—he had, for a moment, made her believe in Easter.

The rest of the service went smoothly, and if the line for communion was longer at the other station, the station at which Lily wasn't administering the wine, so be it. She was a stranger and a woman and you couldn't expect two miracles in one service.

The traditional feast after the Vigil had been laid in the room next door, a table of salads and meats and two loaves of braided bread with red-dyed eggs woven into the braid in the Greek tradition. She saw, too, grape leaves and hummus and falafel, and on a second smaller table, a huge pink frosted cake and baklava and a green Jell-O mold with pineapple—a little of everything.

Lily hadn't attended an Easter vigil dinner in years, since her stint at the church in Lexington, and that had been, after all, Lexington—chicken and salad and bread. This felt like a real party. She saw two bowls of punch and a couple of bottles of wine and a bottle of retsina.

A group of bearded men and long-haired women and a few children set up in the corner with a couple of acoustic guitars, a stand-up bass, spoons, and triangles. During dessert, a trio—two men and one of the women—began an a cappella version of "Tenderly, Tenderly." They followed that with "Oh Happy Day," which had everyone clapping and faking what they didn't know. Then two more women joined them, and the group sang the hymn "Come, Ye Disconsolate." Lily hadn't heard it in years, but when they got to the line, "Here speaks the Comforter, tenderly saying, 'Earth has no sorrow that heaven cannot cure,'" her throat closed up and tears filled her eyes. She turned and took a big sip of water from a glass on the table—she had no idea whose it was.

After the food had been cleared, square-dancing started. Lily sat at a table with McPherson and a group of students. One of the tallest students, a dark-skinned young man with a Caribbean accent, asked Lily to dance. But McPherson said, "Sorry, Nestadley, she's promised the first one to me."

Only a few people understood the calls, so the dancing felt to Lily more like directing traffic. She was surprised by how much she remembered from her childhood square dancing days, the camp competitions and Fourth of July barbecues. After half an hour she and McPherson returned to the table, tired and hot. McPherson went to get something to drink. He brought two cups of punch, and when she tasted it, she knew it had liquor in it.

"What kind of punch is this?" she asked.

"A kind of sangria sort of thing," he said, over the music. "They've got some without wine. You want me to get you that?"

"No, thanks," said Lily. "This is fine." Thoughts raced past her awareness but she couldn't slow them down enough to understand them. How could she feel so good, be so happy, when Anna had just died? Where was the sadness? She hadn't had this good a time in months, since long before Anna's disappearance. Could one cup of punch really do any harm? No one here knew she didn't drink.

"You ready for another round?" McPherson asked.

"Of dancing?"

"No," he said, shaking his head. "I'm still sweating. I meant another cup of punch."

"Sure," she said. "That would be great."

CHAPTER 34

Lily finished the second cup of wine punch, danced with Nestadley, then had a glass of white wine. After over a year of not drinking alcohol, even that amount hit her pretty hard. She began to speak very carefully, and she sat out the next few rounds of dancing. It wouldn't do for a visiting woman priest to fall down in the middle of the floor. At first, the light-headedness felt good, familiar, comforting, but once she lost her sense of control, she lost her sense of pleasure. She held her eyes open very wide in order to look alert, and nodded in agreement with anything anyone said to her. By the time McPherson suggested they leave, she'd stopped enjoying herself completely.

Around one o'clock, they pulled into McPherson's driveway in the old Ford truck.

"You want a nightcap?" McPherson asked, once they were inside.

"No, thanks," she said, though she did. "What time do we need to be over at the jail tomorrow, to see Hatcher?"

"I'm not going," said McPherson. He took the bottle of Glenlivet from the cupboard, poured himself a shot, and returned the bottle. "I've got two services—a nine o'clock and an eleven. And I could use the sleep. Holy Week wears me out. Anyway, Thompkins said it wouldn't be a good idea for me to show up with you. Everybody knows I'm not welcome. We might blow it if we go together."

"So what time do I have to be there?" asked Lily. She felt disappointed and annoyed, but didn't say anything.

"Around six-thirty, maybe a little earlier. There's hardly anyone around then, she said, especially on Easter. The shift changes at eight—so you need to be long gone. You want an alarm clock?"

"Yeah, thanks. That would be great," she said. What she thought was, how the hell am I going to get up at six-thirty?

"I'll get it for you." He rinsed his glass and set it in the sink. "I'm glad you came. Anna's been at most of the vigils, and the parties. Having you there—it made me feel less lonely."

He left the room. Lily wanted to tell him about her experience at the service tonight. She wanted to tell him he'd given her back something she'd lost, but she didn't know how to do it without sounding drunk and maudlin.

"Here," he said and handed her a small, white travel clock. "Just set the alarm thing with this one, and then pull out the little knob. You got everything you need?"

"Yep," she said. "And thanks—for everything."

"No problem." He patted her shoulder. "You've probably had enough church for one weekend. If not, you can come to the eleven. So I'll see you there or back here around, say, two. I've got a few invitations to Easter dinner. You're welcome to join me. But we can figure that out tomorrow. Sleep well."

"Good night," she said, without turning around. "And thanks again—for everything."

He stopped at the foot of the stairs. "Are you okay?"

"Yep," she said. "Just tired. See you tomorrow. And thanks."

The tiny, glow-in-the-dark hands of McPherson's travel clock showed her it was almost four. She'd fallen asleep maybe five times and woken up soon afterward, always with vivid, Technicolor dreams. In the latest one, she and Andy Hatcher waited at the edge of a cold forest for someone. This person wore a uniform—all black—and carried something, a body. But before the person appeared, Andy ran out, into the danger. Lily had tried to grab him, to hold him back, but she woke up reaching for his sleeve, missing it, not able to keep him safe. Her legs ached, her mouth felt dry and cottony, her forehead tight and constricted.

She got up to refill her water glass and decided this time she'd get some ice. She moved slowly toward the kitchen in the dark. She opened the freezer, filled the glass with ice, and then, in a single gesture, opened the cupboard above the refrigerator and took out the bottle of scotch. It couldn't hurt. She'd already had three drinks. And she had to get some sleep or she'd never be able to make sense of her talk with Hatcher.

She meant to pour just a swallow, but ended with more than that—the glass was almost one-quarter full. She returned the bottle to the cupboard and sat at the kitchen table. The first sip burned her throat and brought tears to her eyes. She thought of a day in February, years ago, in seminary—snowy, the small courtyard below them covered in snow, two feet thick in spots, snow in heavy drifts against the colonnade—when she and a fellow student, Sarah, drank scotch in their third-floor room and listened to *Grievous Angel* over and over again, singing Emmylou Harris's harmonies. She thought about how much she had loved God back then, how clearly she'd felt a vocation to the priesthood. All gone now, she thought. Maybe the whole thing had been alcohol induced, the whole delusion.

Sarah had given her Anna's first book to read. Then Lily had given the book to Charlie. Anna had inspired them all and had fueled Lily's idea of becoming a priest in order to set the church straight, make it own up to its part in the sufferings of the past, the Crusades, pogroms, witch-hunts, blood libels, and the Holocaust. She must have seen herself as a lonely voice of truth in the ecclesiastical wilderness. The idea embarrassed her now, at the kitchen table in the dark, stealing somebody's scotch.

What's left of vocation when the romance is over? It's like a marriage, someone had told her, Charlie, probably. You need to move on to the next level. That's what she couldn't seem to do. She couldn't move on to the next level. Maybe there wouldn't be one for her, a more mature form of vocation.

Tonight in church, though, something had shifted, even if it had felt like going backwards to earlier beliefs, childhood beliefs. She imagined faith as a kind of spiral, a circling in which we pass through the same spots, but at a different level of awareness, so the old rituals return, but with new depth—or something like that.

She started to hear the sounds of the country night—the wind, a creaking limb, a barn owl, a truck starting up somewhere. She would like to live alone in the country, the way Anna had lived, teaching, writing, on her own. She imagined waking up every morning and looking out the little window in Anna's bedroom, seeing the mown field, the line of pines.

By the time she'd finished the glass, she felt sleepy. She ran a tiny bit of water into the bottle and shook it up. She couldn't remember how full it had been when she started, but this would have to do.

Bright light filtered through the vines around the windows. Lily had no idea where she was. Then she saw the traveling clock she'd borrowed the night before. A little after nine. The house felt empty. She'd missed something, but she didn't know what.

The next time she looked at the clock, it read a little after ten. Her eyes felt hot, her forehead tight. Thompkins had planned to meet her around six-thirty at the police station.

Shame washed through her. Automatically, her mind began to react—she tried to figure out a version of the story in which none of it was her fault. McPherson was supposed to wake me up. But the idea of blaming someone who'd been so good to her seemed especially heinous. The alarm hadn't gone off. Maybe it hadn't. She remembered pulling out the little knob on the back last night. She checked the clock—the knob had been pushed in. She must have woken up enough to turn it off and then gone back to sleep.

An almost painful thirst made her get out of bed. She reached for the water glass on the nightstand, but when she brought it to her lips, she smelled scotch, and felt her stomach heave. In the bathroom she rinsed out the glass and drank some water.

She saw a note on the kitchen table but ignored it. Then she put water on to boil and a piece of bread in the toaster. She stood at the counter and ate the first piece of toast, put two more slices of bread in, got out some butter and jam, found the tea bags and milk, and made a large mug with two bags. By then the next two pieces of toast had popped up, so she spread them with butter and jam, found a plate, and sat down.

Finally, she looked at the note. "I guess you needed the sleep, too," it read. "I should be back between 1 and 2—See you then, Paul."

She wouldn't have minded impatience, even anger, but the restrained niceness made her feel worse than ever. She put the note on the table, face down, and drank her tea. She certainly didn't want to be there when he got back. She'd already told him she had to leave today; she would be gone when he returned And she would leave a note, too, a nice, slightly apologetic note.

Suddenly she remembered reaching out for Andy Hatcher's sleeve, in her dream. She thought of him sitting in a jail cell in Wharton, with Captain Miller as his only company. And she thought, too, of Thompkins, waiting at the station, watching the clock, until it was too late. Had Thompkins called, woken McPherson up? Had they talked about how irresponsible she'd been? Had McPherson noticed the scotch missing in the bottle, or the smell of scotch in the guest bedroom?

She needed to think of what to do next, how to make it up to everyone, especially Andy Hatcher. But she couldn't think; her head ached and the shame seemed to grow—she flashed on the exam slept through in seminary, the time she'd showed up late for a baptism at the Lexington parish, her graduation dinner, during which she'd had too much to drink and started crying, inconsolably. Then, underneath the shame, a murky thought started to form—she had to find out what had happened to Anna. She owed them all that much.

CHAPTER 35

Once she had dressed and packed, Lily called the police station, but Thompkins had been gone for a while. She left a message and included her home phone number. Then she wrote McPherson a note on the back of his note to her:

"I'm sorry I slept through the alarm. If you talk with Officer Thompkins, please pass on my apologies. I have an idea, and if it works, it might answer some of our questions, and might—I hope—help Andy. As soon as I know anything, I'll call.

"Thank you for all your kindness—"

She loaded the car and drove away, with a last glance in her rearview mirror at the blossoming garden. At a station across from the campus entrance, she stopped and got gas and a Coke. She knew she should go find McPherson and say good-bye—she wanted to see him before she left—but she felt too sick and too embarrassed, so she drove to the highway.

Lily's eyes still burned, but her headache had stopped. For the first hour or so, she couldn't focus well enough to do anything but go the speed limit and keep the car on the road. As she drove out of the Berkshires, the sky grew overcast, and the air became warm and muggy. It looked as if her emotional state had been projected onto the rest of the world. But the thought that had started to form earlier, when she'd been sitting at McPherson's table, slowly became a sort of plan.

At Lester she stopped at the gas station she'd visited on her first trip to the Followers' farm, only last week. She parked near a pay phone on the corner of the lot and walked to the glassed-in office. The older man with the ginger whiskers, the one who'd been watching the mechanic work when Lily had visited before, leaned against the desk. He stood staring at a small TV on a shelf above the Coke machine. He glanced at her, then looked back up at the TV, where a baseball game was in progress.

"Can I help you?" he asked, keeping his eyes on the screen.

"I was looking for the other guy who works here, you know, the one whose mother used to visit the Followers?"

"The Followers?" he repeated, still watching the television.

Lily remembered the Red Sox were playing Cleveland today—a makeup game from a rain-out a few weeks ago. "Who's winning?" she asked.

"Nobody," he said, looking over at her. "O and O. Bottom of the fifth. It's a pitcher's game—you know what I mean?"

"I do," said Lily. "Good we've got Pedro."

"No kidding," he said. "What'd you say you wanted?"

"I'm on my way to the Followers—"

"Weren't you here last week?" he asked.

"I was," she said. "I told the other guy—the Catholic guy—I'd stop back by if I was over this way again. Is he coming in today?"

"Yeah, later. He's got about fourteen hours of church to go to first. He's supposed to be here this evening. Why he's stayed open, I don't know. And what I'm doing here, I don't know either. But here I am."

A muffled roar from the TV crowd drew his attention. "Shit. Second time they've loaded the bases."

"Just tell him I came by, would you? Tell him I'm going back to the farm in Lester. And maybe to the other farm, the one over in Ahearn. I thought I'd let him know. Would you do that?"

She waited, but his eyes never left the screen.

"In fact," she added. "I'm just going to leave my name and number for him, okay?"

"Sure," said the man. He finally turned to her. "Look, I know it's none of my business. But he's got a wife and kids, you know? Well, kid—a baby girl."

"No problem," said Lily. She picked up a pen lying on the counter and wrote her name and number on the back of a smudged receipt. "Strictly business."

At the car, she got out her address book and long-distance card and looked up Betty Carl's number. Then she went to the pay phone. The woman answered on the second ring.

"Where have you been?" Miss Betty asked her. "I've been calling—your office and your home. Of course, Barbara won't tell me anything. I came home early from Easter service thinking you might call. Are you all right?"

"Yes," said Lily. She felt annoyed by the questions and the rush of concern. "I'm fine. Why?"

"You just sound a little—you're not sick, are you?"

"No," said Lily. "I'm not sick. Just tired. Why have you been looking for me?"

"The hill. Since we visited, I've had three more images of that hill—"

"I wanted to check with you about that," said Lily. "I think maybe I know the hill. They found Anna's body late last week."

Miss Betty made a noise, like a sigh or a whisper.

"What?" asked Lily.

"You always hope you're wrong, even when you know better. I'm sorry—I'm so sorry about your friend."

Lily didn't want to hear anyone's sympathy right now. Her feelings about Anna still lurked at a safe distance, and she wanted to keep it that way. "Thanks," she said. "She was buried at the top of a bluff, with a view of the valley down below."

"No," said Miss Betty, then she paused. Her voice sounded, for the first time, uncertain. "Not—was she alive when they brought her there?"

"I don't know," said Lily. "A young man's been charged with her murder, but he claims he found the body and moved it up there."

"Do you believe him?" asked Miss Betty.

"I think so."

"Then that's not it. She was alive on this hill, the one I'm seeing. Because I saw it through her eyes. She was alive and not frightened. She became frightened later, but on the hill—I'll tell you what I thought of—I thought of Levittown. You remember Levittown?"

"You mean the housing development, in the fifties, after the war?"

"Yes," said Miss Betty, a note of triumph in her voice. "Just that one. Have you ever seen a picture of that place?"

"No," said Lily. "I don't think so. Wasn't it laid out around themes, like types of tree or something?"

"I don't know about that," said Miss Betty. "But I do know the houses in each section looked identical. That's when people used to make jokes about a white man driving up to the wrong house after work, eating dinner, making love to his wife, and never knowing the difference. You wouldn't remember that. But that's what I thought of when I saw the view from this hill. Levittown."

"Okay," said Lily.

"Does that help?"

"I have no idea."

Neither of them spoke for a couple of seconds, then Miss Betty said, "Once you figure this out, then call the police. There's something I can't see—or I can't understand what I'm seeing, and that's not good. Now, where will you be?"

"It's complicated," said Lily. "If you don't hear from me tomorrow morning, call Barbara and tell her I've gone to the Followers. She'll know."

"The Followers," said Miss Betty. Lily could tell she was writing it down. "That's fine." She paused and added, "The part I can't understand . . ."

"Yeah—what?" said Lily.

"You don't have asthma, do you?"

Lily laughed. "No, not that I know of."

"Okay," she said, sounding relieved. "Maybe it's just extra information, from somewhere else. That happens. Anyway, watch your step, do you hear me? Trust your instincts. And keep God with you every inch of the way."

"I hear you," said Lily, feeling a surge of gratitude. She hadn't gotten such good advice in a long time.

CHAPTER 36

Lily took a wrong turn and ended up one road over from the Followers'. After she figured that out, she retraced her route, almost back to the gas station. The second time she found the road, drove to the gate, and stopped.

The spot looked different. Cars lined the driveway and the area in front of the barn. A few people had parked along the side of the road. Lily stayed on the road and drove past the last car, kept going another fifty yards, then pulled in under a huge horse chestnut tree, its long candle-like blossoms just starting to bud. She opened her backpack, took out her Swiss army knife, and stowed the pack under the passenger seat.

After she locked the car, she stuck her keys in a back pocket with the knife and walked to a split-rail fence that ran along the edge of the field. From there, she could see the house and the beginning of the long slope down to the buildings below; the buildings themselves were hidden by the thick woods surrounding that part of the farm. She started up the road toward the main house.

Probably, she thought, they were having an Easter dinner after Mass. Judging from the number of cars, there had to be at least thirty or forty people there, maybe more.

Maybe enough to get lost in, or maybe enough to provide a distraction while she looked around.

Her head and eyes felt better, but she was aware of a kind of gulping, demanding hunger she rarely experienced. Too bad, she thought. That can wait.

She needed to figure out where she wanted to look first. And what she was looking for. Originally, she'd hoped to find a dummy dressed in the striped clothes of the camps or a Nazi flag—something to connect this group with the vandalism in the cathedral. Which would connect them with Anna in the recent past. Which would connect them, possibly, with her death.

But now Lily knew that Anna had been alive for a whole week after she'd disappeared. So she had to have been kept somewhere. And Miss Betty said Anna had stood on a hill. Lily had no way of knowing if this was the right hill, but it was the only place she could think to look—here and the farm in Ahearn. She'd started here because it scared her less.

After she'd walked about twenty yards, she saw a path that led across the field and into the woods bordering the Followers' property. Since she didn't have any better ideas, she took the path. The air felt muggy and still; tiny gnats rose out of the long grass and swarmed around her head.

Once she reached the woods, the air seemed cooler but heavier. The growth was thick—black pines, maples, oaks—the forest floor covered with pine needles in spots. Seedlings dotted the few areas that got any direct light. She felt thirsty as well as hungry, and exhausted. But behind the exhaustion, a mix of fear and anticipation created a kind of persistent hum.

The path became harder to follow. She kept on in what she guessed was the direction of the four buildings at the foot of the hill. After a few minutes, she heard something over the sounds of the forest, a murmur that became human voices. Without thinking, she stepped between two pines, in among the low branches.

She saw them at a distance—a man and a woman, the woman wearing the same black habit Lily had seen on her first visit, but this didn't look like the same woman. She looked smaller and older. The man, medium height, dumpy, wore a black suit and possibly a clerical collar. Something about him looked familiar, but Lily couldn't see him well enough to be sure. She realized she probably wouldn't blend with this Easter crowd, dressed in her jeans, Asleep at the Wheel T-shirt, and cowboy boots. She would have to get into the buildings without being seen.

After the couple passed, she waited until she couldn't hear their voices anymore. Then she started off in the direction from which they'd come. Eventually, she saw a glimmer between the trees that turned out to be a vernal pond—it looked like the same one she'd found on her first visit. She approached it and her dream of the pond came back to her hazily—the men, the falling, the fear.

She walked more quietly. The trees began to thin, and she reached the edge of the forest. She stepped back, near the spot from which she'd watched the week before—could it have been last week? Time had changed shape and weight since Anna's disappearance; the last week had seemed large and heavy, filled with unbearable events packed tightly together.

She heard a new set of sounds—someone calling out, the hum of a group of people talking and laughing, the clatter of plates and cutlery—but she couldn't see anyone. They must be having lunch outside, in the courtyard formed by the four buildings. She'd had vague expectations of weird rituals, something suited to the ornate chapel with its jewel-like patches of light. This sounded more like a country club luncheon.

The forest ringed the field. From where she stood, it looked as if the building farthest from the chapel, facing it across the courtyard, bordered the wooded area. She retreated into the trees a few yards and then followed the curve of the woods toward the buildings. At least she could get a glimpse into one of them.

After a minute, the sounds grew louder. Through a gap between the two nearest buildings, she could see the crowd. They sat at tables with white tablecloths. Many of the people looked older, in their sixties, some of the women dressed in habits and some in floral print Easter dresses, the men in clerical black or dress suits. So not everyone there was a member of the community.

The line of trees curved sharply toward the buildings now. The noises grew louder; she could even make out individual voices. A few yards on, she caught sight of the group again—she could see the table in the next gap between the buildings. She was much closer than she'd been the first time, so she stepped farther back into the trees.

Jeffrey Tatum sat at the table, talking with a woman on his right. Lily knew he stayed in touch with the group—he'd told them that, Charlie and her, at dinner—but for whatever reason it shook Lily to find him there today. No one else looked familiar.

She had reached the corner of the building on the edge of the woods. Because of the raised foundation, the first-floor windows started just at eye level. Standing on tiptoe she should be able to see inside. She left the cover of the trees, flattened herself against the house, next to the first window, and waited. She heard a door close inside the building, then footsteps on the stairs, then children's voices. The children's voices seemed out of place—it felt dangerous for them to be there, but she didn't know why. Then she remembered the tape recording of the crying, the incoherent words of misery. It sounded as if these children were reciting something in a sort of singsong chorus.

Until now, the hum of adrenaline had kept her alert and hopeful. But as she waited, her heart sank. She'd never be able to look inside, much less to get inside. Too many people. All this stupid lurking around for nothing, she thought. But if she discovered nothing, then Andy Hatcher would be charged with Anna's murder. And no one would ever know what really happened.

She edged to the corner of the building. From there she could see Jeffrey's table, but not Jeffrey. She *could* see the man sitting to Jeffrey's left. It was Steve, the man from the farm in Ahearn.

Before she had time to take that in—Steve had said he didn't know Jeffrey, and Jeffrey had never mentioned him, never mentioned that farm as a place to look for Anna—she had a new thought. If he was here, the farm in Ahearn might be empty. She needed to go there.

Then she heard a new sound—voices from behind her, in the woods, coming closer. Lily stepped away from the corner of the building and into the trees. The man in the black suit and the woman in the habit, the pair she had seen earlier, walked by a few yards from where she stood. The man was Frank Leslie.

CHAPTER 37

The three men from her dream, Frank Leslie, Jeffrey, and Steve, together at the farm. Again she stood perfectly still while the couple passed. She waited as long as she could—until their voices faded—then found the path they'd been on and followed it back toward the center of the woods, and to the road. Now that she knew what to do, she felt an urgent need to do it.

The clouds had thinned. A watery sunshine filled the woods and the air felt warmer. Gnats swarmed in clumps. She could hear a woodpecker nearby, mourning doves, the small high songs of sparrows and finches and chickadees. At one point, a chipmunk rattled some low bushes by the path and Lily startled. Her heart thudded and her throat felt dry. She knew she needed something to eat, and a gallon of water, but Steve would return to his farm soon. She had to have time enough to look around before that happened.

She drove beyond the entrance to the Ahearn farm without slowing down and parked farther up the road, just over the crest of the hill. She locked the car, put the keys in the pocket with her knife, and walked toward the house.

Since the road climbed above the property, she could

see the house, about one hundred yards away, and the valley below, where the four buildings stood, identical in size and arrangement to those on the Followers' property. Levittown, she thought. She watched for a couple of minutes. No signs of human life—no voices, no slamming doors, no car engines starting up.

She felt light-headed with hunger and thirst and adrenaline. She walked down the road toward the house. At the porch steps, she hesitated, but no one had bothered her so far, so she climbed the stoop and knocked on the metal frame of the storm door.

She waited, knocked again, then tried the handle, but it was locked. The windows on either side of the door still had the storm panes, shut tight. She cupped her hands and peered inside. The furniture in the front room looked a lot like what she remembered from the other farmhouse—love seat, rocking chair, even a doily on the table. And in the hallway beyond, a row of doors.

She walked around the house, edging in between yew bushes to try the first-floor windows—all with storms, all closed. At the back she came to a screen porch. The door was latched, but the screen on the bottom hung loose across the middle of the frame. She reached her hand through and knocked the hook out of the eye-screw, then grabbed the handle from inside and tugged—something clicked, and gave, and the door opened.

The back door and windows echoed the arrangement at the front, except that the door seemed narrower than the front door, and the windows a bit wider. At one end of the porch stood at least half a cord of ricked wood—meticulously stacked. She peered inside through the window on the left. The kitchen looked as if it hadn't been touched in sixty years—green tile counters, green linoleum floors. But it looked, too, as if it belonged to an abandoned house. Nothing on the counters—no cookbooks, no canisters, not even a dish drainer. No calendar on the wall, no notes stuck to the refrigerator, no wall phone, nothing to indicate anyone had ever cooked there, or eaten there, or even opened a box of cereal.

Through the other window she saw a second empty room—what would have been a dining room—long and narrow, with a row of doors to the left, matching the row in the hallway. Closets?—then why the double set of doors? Bathrooms?—too small. Five small cubicles in a row with doors accessing both sides—confessionals.

A chill passed through her, something about this row of confessionals in a rural farmhouse seemed off, a little crazy. For the first time she thought she should turn around and go home. Then she remembered Andy Hatcher. She tried the door and two windows, tugging so hard on the second window that she strained her shoulders and back.

She thought about trying to break the glass on the door, but it was thick, and she didn't have anything to use. Except the wood. She picked up a piece, weighed it in her hand, then put it back. She didn't know how much time she had, and she needed to try to get into the four buildings behind the house. If Steve came home and found the door shattered, the first thing he'd do would be to check the grounds.

She returned the wood, left the porch, then reached her hand back through the screen and replaced the hook. She couldn't figure out how to lock the handle again—there was probably a button to push, but she'd forgotten to look—so she left it.

The four buildings at the base of the hill were in fact identical, at least from the outside, to the ones on the Followers' property—two-story prefab set on raised foundations. The only difference seemed to be that the windows of these buildings had been taped over, from the inside, with black fabric. Everything was locked, the doors made of light-weight wood with night latches in all the knobs.

Except for the building farthest from the road and house—on that one, the door had a keyhole for a dead bolt above the knob. She listened for a moment to be sure she heard no one inside, or nearby, or even a car approaching on the road by the main house. She walked around the building twice, then climbed the concrete stoop to the front door. She counted to ten and threw herself against the door, wedging her right shoulder into the frame.

Nothing happened except that her shoulder, already sore from tugging at the porch windows, flared with pain. Then she stood back as far as she could and kicked at the wood near the lock. It gave a fraction of an inch. She kicked again, this time getting her full weight into the heel of her cowboy boot. She heard the wood give. Two more kicks and the door swung open crazily, banging against the wall behind it.

CHAPTER 38

She took a deep breath and stepped inside—dark and close, hot, too little air, and a smell of something moldering, like dirty clothes left in a pile. She felt for a light switch, but then realized someone might be able to see the light through the fabric. She should shut the door, too, she knew, but it would be too claustrophobic for her in there. She pushed it almost closed, leaving a thin slice of light and air.

For a moment she couldn't see anything in the partial darkness. She closed her eyes, allowing them to adjust. When she opened them, she could make out shapes of furniture against the walls. Not furniture. Big shapes, cartons, draped with canvas or sheets.

Her eyes adjusted. She touched the cloth—canvas—then pulled it off one of the boxes. She found her knife and cut through the packaging tape. She pulled out a handful of booklets and almost laughed out loud—she'd expected machine guns or serpents or dead bodies.

She stepped closer to the light from the door. The top booklet looked impressive, serious, the title printed in dark gray on heavy cream-colored stock—HISTORY AND MYTH—and below it, the subtitle—*The History of Jewish Crimes, The Myth of Holocaust.* She turned to the first page, on which she found the entire title once again, and, below it, a quotation: "Whether or not the Holocaust, as such, happened, is not a fruitful debate; the evidence certainly points to the existence of camps, ghettos, and deportations. As to the nature of these camps—their exact purposes and conditions—healthy and honorable debate must continue. As to the guilt of the people there interred, there can be no debate." Beneath it she read the name Sebastian O'Riordan, S.J. And at the bottom of the page she found the seven stars and seven torches encircling the name Philadelphia Press.

Lily opened three more boxes. In the second she found additional copies of the original booklet. In the third she discovered something different, a bibliography of publications printed by Philadelphia Press. The titles included, "The Holocaust: Divine Justice in Action," also by Sebastian O'Riordan, and a range of other titles by a variety of authors, from "Who Killed Christ?" to "A Myth Exploded: A Technical Review of the Alleged Execution Chambers at Auschwitz."

She jammed a copy of each, the booklet and the bibliography, in the two back pockets of her jeans. Then she walked through the downstairs rooms, musty and deserted. A cheap table—laminated wood with metal legs—stood in what might have, at one time, been the dining room. The kitchen consisted of a row of cabinets, a sink, and a refrigerator. The refrigerator held a loaf of bread, a jar of peanut butter, grape jelly, butter, a pack of assorted small cereal boxes—Cap'n Crunch, Trix, Frosted Cheerios—and milk. The date on the milk was two days away. A child must live here.

Through the kitchen, opposite the back door, she found yet another door, locked, and the stairs to the second floor. She climbed slowly, not knowing what to expect. The upstairs windows had been taped as well, though why someone would bother to cover them, she couldn't guess. The fabric let dim light through; her eyes had grown accustomed it.

There were three tiny bedrooms—this must be what Goldilocks felt like, she thought. In each of the first two she found a full-sized canvas cot, a table and chair, and a large crucifix with a white cross and a blond, pale-skinned Jesus bleeding profusely—miniatures of the crucifix in the Followers' chapel. A small bathroom stood at the end of the hall.

The third room looked lived-in. Along with the cot and the table she found a wooden desk with a black laptop, a printer, a cordless phone, and a fax machine. They looked ludicrous and out of place. In the closet, she discovered a small set of shelves filled with clothes—a pair of pants, two turtlenecks, a sweater, two pairs of socks—all black. On the floor were two pairs of shoes, also black, dress wing tips and Nikes with a white swoosh, but large shoes, not a child's size. The cot in this room also had a pillow, a sheet, and a small quilt, folded neatly at the foot of it.

As long as she kept moving, adrenaline and curiosity had fueled her. But when she paused to try to sort through the information she'd gotten so far, she realized she felt weak and sick to her stomach. The combination of the heat in the house, the hangover, and not enough to eat and drink had finally hit her. She sat in the chair by the darkened window and put her head down between her knees.

After a moment, she went into the small bathroom and turned on the cold water tap. She drank from her cupped hands for a long time, used the toilet, then splashed water on her face. She looked up and saw herself in the mirror—her skin wet and pale, her lips bloodless, dark blue circles under her eyes—and felt her stomach heave again, but this time with self-loathing. She remembered the moment of waking up that morning, knowing she was supposed to be at the jail, knowing she'd let everyone down. She turned to go, but as she did, she thought she heard something below her, a kind of scraping sound directly underneath, in the kitchen.

She stood and listened. After a few seconds, she realized she had stopped breathing. She took a deep breath and focused again on the rooms downstairs. Someone was there. She knew that, even though she couldn't hear anything else.

She didn't dare move, because the hard soles of her cowboy boots on the bare floor would give her away. She sat on the closed lid of the toilet and pulled off her boots. She still hadn't heard anything else. Then, just as she decided to try making her way to the head of the stairs, she heard it again.

She lost track of time, waiting in the dark. Eventually, she realized she hadn't heard a noise in what seemed like a long while. As quietly as possible, she stood, boots in her hand, and walked to the head of the stairs. Still nothing. It occurred to her then that if the sound had come from the kitchen, it could have been a mouse. The house was out in the country. There had been food in the refrigerator. There might be crumbs lying around.

At the top of the stairs, she listened again and heard nothing. If it was a mouse, she should quit this foolishness and get on with looking in the other buildings. And if someone was down there, what would she do, anyway? She had nowhere to go. It seemed useless to stand terrified at the top of the stairs with her boots in her hand.

She sat down on the top stair and put her boots back on. She might as well look dignified if she were going to be caught trespassing, she thought. But something in her knew better than to make light of this.

She didn't see or hear anything on her way down. But when her foot touched the ground floor, she knew she'd been wrong not to trust her first instinct. Someone stood behind her, a couple of feet away, then suddenly at her right elbow. She first reached for her knife, but the pamphlet in her pocket made the knife too hard to find. She wheeled and raised her right arm—the person grabbed her hand and twisted it behind her back, facing her outward, away from him. A bolt of pain shot through her shoulder. Then she could see, out of the corner of her eye, something swinging down toward her head, fast. As the floor rushed toward her, she thought, it wasn't a mouse.

CHAPTER 39

She woke from a dream of a huge dormitory, somewhere in the desert. Children cried all around her, and she wanted to help them, but she didn't know how. In fact, she wanted to help them in order to shut them up, so she could get back to sleep. Also, she needed to know what that smell was—sweet and noxious. But when she tried to raise her head, she thought she must still be asleep, because she couldn't quite move, at least on one side.

Later she wanted to take off her clothes. Inexplicably, she had fallen asleep in her jeans and boots so of course she was sweating all over. And she needed that glass of water by her bed, the one her father had just given her. They must have been out riding all day, and he'd put her to bed in her clothes. The water didn't taste good, but she needed more, because of her mouth being so dry. But she didn't reach out for the glass, because she remembered the pain on the right side of her body. The part of her who knew it was true—not just a dream, and that she couldn't use her right hand—started to cry.

Pitch black and hot, the air bone-dry from the heat. She didn't want to sleep anymore. She didn't want to keep waking up miserable and confused. She tried rolling onto her side so she could sit up, but when she did that, her stomach heaved from the pain. She lay still. The concrete floor under her face felt cool compared to the air around her.

After she got her breath and stopped feeling as if she might throw up, she rolled slowly, tentatively onto her left side. That felt okay. But she couldn't use her right arm to push herself up. She freed her left arm and maneuvered herself into a sitting position.

Sitting up, she discovered she also couldn't concentrate. When she thought about where she was or how she'd gotten there, her mind began to spin, slowly, like a kind of lazy Susan, filled with a variety of images, one of them an image of the lazy Susan. She got stuck there for a while. Her boots were gone, but she'd had them last time she woke up—at least she remembered having them. She'd taken them off, sitting on a toilet seat. Then she'd put them back on and walked down some stairs.

She couldn't see either, but there was nothing wrong with her eyes, because when she closed them she saw a different kind of darkness, not the same as when they were open. But the space around her was without light. Slowly, she began to feel for a wall to lean against. She must be in a room with no windows. Her throat constricted, but she took a deep breath and continued to breathe normally.

She half-crawled, half-dragged herself a few inches to her left, and bumped into something smooth and hard. She ran her good hand over the shape—a pedestal that curved sharply up from the floor and ended in a bowl with a lip—a toilet.

She almost cried out. Something about the toilet—what was it? If there was a toilet, that meant this room had been planned; someone had built it like this, no windows, no light.

She dragged herself to the wall behind the toilet and leaned against it. The wood felt new, smooth, not old and splintery. So this place had been built recently, within the last few years.

A sharp noise on the other side of the wall made her sit up straighter. If someone was coming, maybe she should pretend to be unconscious, at least until she could figure out where she was. But then the noise turned into a sort of chugging machine sound, and finally became a steady hum.

Heat seeped through the wall—a furnace. The space got hotter. She had forgotten about her thirst and hunger, but the thirst came back full force. She couldn't move her tongue; it stuck to the roof of her mouth.

There might be water in the toilet beside her, but she wouldn't be able to tell if it was clean. She wasn't that desperate, yet.

The heat continued. The machine hummed on behind her. She felt heavy and lopsided. Finally she lay down again on her left side; the concrete felt cool on her skin. She stretched out her whole body on the floor.

CHAPTER 40

Someone sat her up. She opened her eyes then shut them again quickly because the light hurt. She had dreamed the whole thing, she thought, and relief washed through her. She sat on a cot, propped against a wall, in a room with light. She felt a kind of buoyant joy.

She raised her right hand to shield her eyes and the pain returned. She raised her left hand and opened her eyes. She could see the wall across from her—two-by-fours of bare wood, and a crucifix, a miniature of the one in the Followers' chapel. She hadn't dreamed the whole thing. She had seen a crucifix just like that sometime earlier—in a bedroom.

The person who had helped her up was doing something in a corner to her right. Lily turned her whole body—she couldn't move her neck. A man in black jeans and a black turtleneck had his back to her. The room was tiny, more like a box. His head brushed the ceiling.

Her throat ached. She tried to wet her lips, but the muscles in her face didn't seem to be working, especially on the right side.

At the instant she thought that, the man turned and handed her a glass of water. He didn't speak to her. It was Steve, the man who owned the farm in Ahearn. She had last seen him having lunch in the Followers' courtyard. Then she had come here, to his farm. She'd broken into one of the buildings. All the windows were taped with black fabric, but light got through. Not as in this room, where there were no windows.

She took the water and tried to drink, but it hurt to swallow. She had trouble propping herself up and holding the glass at the same time. She could feel herself start to sag to the right. She remained as erect as she could and held the water in her mouth, letting it trickle down her throat, a little at a time. It tasted bitter, but she didn't know if the taste came from the water or from the dry film on her tongue.

She decided not to speak. Actually, she wasn't sure if she could speak, but she thought it might be better if she seemed less aware than she felt—if that was possible. She took another sip of water and held it in her mouth. She didn't look at him or at the walls, which seemed to be getting closer the more awake she became. She kept her eyes on the glass of water in front of her—a plain glass, cheap, with a little bump near the top, like the ones you find in a diner. If she squeezed it hard enough she could break it in her hand. But she might cut herself. And, besides, she had no idea what she'd do with the broken pieces after that. She didn't think she was up to overpowering anyone at the moment.

He stood in front of her, waiting for her to hand him the glass. She realized that part of her mind was searching around for something to say, as if this were a social situation, as if someone she was visiting—Paul McPherson, for example—had just brought her a glass of water.

When she thought the words, "for example," tears came to her eyes. That was the way people thought in the real world—they used phrases like "for example." But she wasn't in the real world anymore.

She wondered if the man would speak. She didn't think of him as Steve, because that, too—a proper name—seemed like something left behind. Also, if she didn't use his name, even to herself, she didn't feel such a need to say something, to be congenial. He waited until she finished the water—it took a long time, holding it like that in her mouth, swallowing it in little trickles. But he didn't move or make a sound.

When she finished, he took the glass from her. She watched him, keeping her head down, just looking out of the corner of her eyes. His back was to her again. She studied the space—concrete floor, wooden walls, wooden ceiling with a single light fixture like a glass ball inside a cage. The whole space about ten feet by ten feet—the shape of a large box. She saw the toilet, but she couldn't find a door.

Her breath began to get shallow; her heart sped up. She kept thinking about no windows and no door. She heard the click beyond the wall that meant the heater had switched on. She imagined the heat rising in the box, filling up the box, leaving no air for her to breathe.

She glanced over at him, her head still lowered, and the light above went out. She didn't think he had touched anything—a light switch, a pull cord. She heard him walk across the room and turn the keys in a lock. Then she felt a rush of cooler air and saw a gray darkness beyond, lighter than the darkness of the room. The door closed, and she heard the sound of the lock again.

For a moment it felt as if her heart were expanding to fill her whole chest, rising up toward her neck, into her throat. But, ironically, the darkness helped, because she couldn't see the confines of the room. She imagined a regular room at night, with windows to the outside. She imagined the guest room at Paul McPherson's, the windows framed in vines that cast shadows on the floors and walls in the morning. She imagined she was there. And her heart began to slow; her breathing steadied.

She told herself it wouldn't do to try to think about too much at once. She said the Lord's Prayer, the Serenity Prayer, and began the Twenty-Third Psalm. When she got to, "Yea though I walk through the valley of the shadow of death," she began to feel calmer. Is that what she feared, that she was going to die? But before she could answer her own question, the blackness from outside crept inside her. She turned over onto her stomach, her forehead touching the metal frame of the cot, cool and real and somehow reassuring.

CHAPTER 41

She must have fallen asleep against the frame of the cot. As she shifted onto her back and rubbed her forehead with her left hand, she found she could think better than before. The man had given her water that tasted bitter, and she had gone back to sleep, or passed out again.

Her right arm and shoulder ached, but she was able to locate the pain—the shoulder joint and the muscles around it felt stiff and swollen. So she'd pulled something, or fallen; she couldn't be sure. And her lip felt swollen; maybe the whole right side of her face felt swollen. The pain seemed muffled, somehow, not sharp, almost as if someone else were in pain.

Her brain felt muffled, too, not as bad as it had been, but her thoughts came slowly, each one struggling out of a kind of cloud. He must have given her something, sedatives or painkillers—the bitterness in the water. And she'd been asleep a long time; she remembered waking endlessly, over and over again.

She pulled herself up and leaned against the wall. The skin in the crook of her left arm, inside the elbow, seemed tender and a little swollen. She had all her clothes, except for her boots. Her pockets were empty; he'd found the keys and the knife.

Friends look for people like me, she thought. But friends had looked for Anna. For the first time she understood she might be in the same room where Anna had been kept, maybe the same room where Anna had died. But Lily didn't think she was going to die, not yet.

Because he didn't speak, she hadn't spoken, and something told her to keep it that way. The less he knew about her the better, and she would be bound to reveal herself if she opened her mouth. Also, if he pictured her as cowering and helpless, she would have the advantage of surprise later, when she knew what to do.

Somewhere in the distant past Lily had told Miss Betty to call Barbara on Monday morning and to tell Barbara to look at the Followers' farm. And she had left her name and number for the gas station owner. He knew she'd asked directions to this farm, the one in Ahearn.

Now she needed to think about what she should do, how she could find out how long she'd been there, maybe even where she was. But first she needed to go to the bathroom. This presented a few problems. To begin with, she had to find the toilet.

Also, it occurred to her that she shouldn't drink the water he gave her, not if it tasted bitter. She didn't want to stay sedated and confused. She hadn't seen a sink in the room, but there might be one. If not, she needed to test the water in the toilet. If the water seemed clean, she should drink a little of it before she used it.

She thought she remembered where she had seen the toilet, but she also thought it would be a good thing to explore the room carefully, to find the door and anything else useful. She climbed down onto the floor and began to crawl along the perimeter of the space. She moved slowly, feeling her way in the black darkness. Every few seconds, she stopped, sat back, and ran her left hand over the wall next to her—her right arm still felt almost useless, and the crawling was painful enough. The boards had been closely fitted, the cracks between them caulked, and a baseboard sealed the space between the wall and the floor.

She came to a corner, turned, followed the length of the wall without bumping into anything, came to a second corner, turned again. When she reached the spot where she thought the door might be—if she remembered right—she became more thorough, pushing against the wall, feeling the surface carefully, running her fingers along the seam where the wood met the concrete floor. But she couldn't detect any differences in the structure.

Then she felt a crack, a seam. She followed it down to the floor; there was no baseboard, and she could feel a slight change in air temperature. She lay flat on the floor, turning her head to try to see under the door. She thought there might be a gray strip of light, minuscule.

Fatigue disoriented her. She wanted to get back to the cot and lie down with her head against the cool metal frame. Instead she crawled forward, searching for the other side of the door.

She ran her hand along the bottom of the door until she found the beginning of the baseboard in the next section of the wall. At the corner, where the new board started, she felt something loose, something small and hard wedged between the wood and the concrete floor. It felt like plastic, the edge of a plastic case or box.

Using her fingernails, she began to work the object out from under the baseboard. But it had been shoved there with some force, and she had a hard time getting a grip on the smooth surface. Just as she was about to give up, the object came free. In a few more seconds, she held it in her hand. It was a rectangle with two holes through it—a miniature tape cassette.

The cassette—its size and shape—seemed familiar; it was about the same size and shape as the tape in an answering machine. She thought of the one in Anna's machine, the one with the crying on it, that she had given Gregarian.

She heard a noise beyond the wall. She assumed it was the furnace clicking on again, but the sounds seemed farther away—she discerned a scraping of metal on metal, then a door opening and closing, then footsteps on wooden stairs. The shoes had soft soles, but the wood of the stairs creaked. He was coming back. She slipped the tape into her hip pocket.

Lily wanted to get back to the bed. For some reason it seemed important to her that he not know she'd been up on her own, exploring the room. She realized she hadn't walked yet; she'd been crawling around like an animal. Her legs felt weak, and she couldn't see where she was going, but she forced herself to stand. Her head banged against the ceiling. She found her footing and followed the perimeter of the room back to the bed. She leaned heavily against the wall, half of her senses trained on the small space around her body, the other half listening to the noises beyond.

She bumped into the toilet, then a small table. The table didn't move when she hit it. He must have been standing at the table when she watched him, last time. So the bed would be against the next wall, to the left.

She found the metal frame of the cot at the same time she heard a key in the lock. She understood now that the cot, like the table, was fixed to the floor. She sat on the edge of the cot, then lay down and pretended to be asleep.

The light clicked on before the door opened. Lily tried to watch through squinted eyes as he came in, but her eyes had to adjust. She could see a blur of a man carrying a tray—shiny, metal. She smelled something different, food, maybe chicken broth, and she started to salivate. She hadn't known how hungry she'd gotten.

Her eyes slowly adjusted. She saw the toilet and the table, no sink. She tried to focus on every moment as it passed. In the back of her mind, she said the Twenty-Third

Psalm again; she said it a few times. It calmed her this time, too, and that helped her to pay attention.

He stood at the table, then he walked toward her, grabbed her right arm, and jerked her into a sitting position. Her head slammed against the wooden wall behind her. Her shoulder burned with pain; as she sat with her eyes barely opened, the pain became a dull, pernicious ache that extended from her fingertips to her forehead. She felt a surge of fear and anger.

He turned toward the table, then came back again with a thick green bowl and a large spoon. He fed her without speaking; her hunger gave her no choice but to swallow what he gave her. She kept her eyes on the spoon so he couldn't see her anger, so she couldn't see the windowless box of a room.

This time something else happened when he stood in front of her—she felt naked, as if he could see through not her clothes but her skin, into her brain, into her thoughts. She had experienced something similar with Miss Betty, only then she wasn't so much afraid as annoyed and suspicious. Now she wanted to pull a blanket over herself, over her soul.

The chicken broth tasted normal, no bitterness—as far as she could tell. Not that it would have mattered; she would have eaten it anyway. Then she lay back down, her face to the wall. That way he couldn't make her drink any more water. He took the bowl away, then came back and sat on the edge of the cot. Her body wanted to recoil from him, but she tried to stay still.

He leaned down and put his hand on her right shoulder, pressing hard. She let out a sound, like a yelp. He spoke directly into her ear. "I can see you're getting stronger, and that's good. I look forward to talking to you next time. Perhaps we can get some of this confusion straightened out."

She didn't move or make a sound, but for a moment something shifted inside her. "Confusion" implied mistake, which meant something could be solved, or fixed. Which meant he might let her go.

"I'm sorry about your shoulder and your face." My face, she thought—it must be bad. "I wouldn't have hurt you if I'd known," he continued. "I didn't know who you were, of course. I feel bad this happened this way, not an auspicious beginning. So I would like you to hear my side. Because I think you might find it quite persuasive."

He patted her shoulder, like an old friend. She winced. The lights went out. Lily watched as he opened the door, but her eyes hadn't quite adjusted to the darkness yet. She could feel the air as it entered the room and see the gray light beyond, but nothing else.

CHAPTER 42

She dreamed about Miss Betty—Miss Betty and a boy, one of the boys whose picture had been on Miss Betty's wall, the boy who had been shot delivering pizza. The woman and the boy climbed a tall hill. Then they looked down at the buildings below, four buildings forming a square.

The buildings were made of LEGOs, or Lincoln Logs. Miss Betty lifted the roof on one of the buildings. Inside, termites covered every square inch, crawling on top of each other, a huge mass of bugs or slugs. They chewed through the wood that held the house together, so the structure began to fall apart—a miniature wall collapsing here, a window falling out there. Finally, when the building crumbled and lay in pieces, Miss Betty swept the remains aside and there was Lily, on a tiny bed in a tiny room underneath the house.

"Take up your bed and walk," said Miss Betty. "Knock and the door shall be opened unto you."

"What do you mean?" Lily asked her.

"Get up and slam him in the head," said the boy. Beside him, Miss Betty nodded in solemn agreement.

He must have brought in a chair because he sat by her bed. The light was on. He pulled her up again, leaning her against the wall. She concentrated on not looking at him and not looking at the room. Instead, she looked at her hands—white, freckled with faint sun spots, long-fingered—they looked familiar; they made her feel sorry for herself.

But that didn't last. She still felt Miss Betty's presence. She didn't actually have a plan, but at least she knew what to do. She knew where she was—in the basement of one of the buildings at his farm—and she knew she would be getting out of here soon.

"This doesn't really seem fair," he began. "Because I know a lot more about you than you know about me—at least, I think I do." He reached into his back pocket—head still lowered, she watched his hands—and took out a small card. He held it toward her, in her line of vision; her own face stared back at her. He had her driver's license, which meant he'd found the station wagon and gone through her pack. Which meant he'd probably moved the station wagon. Which meant no one would find it on the road.

"I moved the car into the barn. It isn't registered to you. It's registered to the Society of Saint Peter on Brattle Street in Cambridge. I know the Society of Saint Peter, and I don't think somebody driving their car would actually be interested in doing a retreat here—or at the Followers, for that matter." He stuck her license back in his pocket. "Does that seem like a fair assumption?"

Lily almost nodded. But she didn't. She watched her hands; she had made two circles with her thumbs and index fingers and linked the circles.

Suddenly he reached over and pulled her hands apart. His hands were like ice. She jerked her head up and caught his eye. His face looked white and blank, with small lines and wrinkles, like a piece of crumpled paper.

"You had better listen," he said. "That way there won't be any more confusion."

He doesn't like confusion. And he has on jeans and hiking boots and a turtleneck and a sweater; and it's about eighty-five degrees in here. And his hands are like ice.

"I found these on you," he said and showed her the two booklets he must have taken from her pockets. He lay them on the cot. "I don't actually think this is your kind of reading material, is it? I suspect you'd be more interested in Primo Levi, Elie Wiesel, Raul Hilberg. You know the group of whom I speak."

His voice sounded casual, as if they were chatting over tea. "That's my parents' milieu. But I, as you can see," he said, tapping one of the booklets, "have followed a different route."

She half-listened, although some of what he said sounded weirdly logical. "Here's the thing," he said. "If you're a member of a group like ours, you see, you admire Hitler, and Mussolini, and Pinochet, and, of course, the South African government before de Klerk. You admire their policies and their regimes, of which you are, essentially, a follower. . . .

The heater clicked on. Soon the air in the box would start to heat up, and she'd be trapped here listening to him talk. Because he sounded as if he might go on forever, until someone found her.

"On the other hand, you can't afford to have the Holocaust myth alive and flourishing, because it has become a kind of mainstay of the Jewish economy. So, you're in a bind. What Father Sebastian was able to do—brilliantly, I think—was own that the Holocaust happened, in a benign form. That is to say, the entire set of events—not the cosmic drama the Jews have cooked up; something a good deal milder—happened for a reason. They happened as a punishment for the Jews' role in history, not only the killing of Christ, but the centuries of blood libel, of well-poisoning, moneylending, raping of Christian women and children, torture and rape of young Christian children . . ."

The heat rose, and he never stopped talking. She kept

her hands still, because she didn't want him to touch her again. She felt the walls closing in, the box getting smaller. She couldn't fill her lungs.

"Punishment is a necessary ingredient of justice, and justice is a necessary ingredient of faith. Where I was raised, punishment was taken to an art form, I'd say. Especially with the children—a process of the formation of souls."

Suddenly his voice stopped. Lily heard the furnace chugging away, and behind that, another sound, faint, irritating—the sound of crows, a bunch of crows fighting in their horrible raucous voices. And she remembered the world beyond this room. She closed her eyes and pictured the crows on the ground by a basement window, fighting over something they'd found, their stupid beaks opening and closing. Not long, she thought, not long. He had started talking again.

"I had many people here with me at one time. We had a very robust organization—the printing press, training sessions, classes. When I became ill, the numbers dwindled. And now I'm alone."

She pictured them fighting over a bunch of grapes; she saw them attacking, hopping sideways, their wings flapping. Wasn't there a fable about a crow and a bunch of grapes? The fox and the crow.

"Our last act was the murder in the cathedral. That's what I called it, of course. It wasn't a reference familiar to most of the members, not the ones left by then. They're all gone now, unfortunately." He stood up from the cot. "But they'll return, once I've got my health back. You might be interested in knowing more about our work, when you're better. I can see that you're getting tired."

She had kept her eyes closed. She listened, carefully. He walked to the table—she guessed it was to the table—then returned to the cot.

"Perhaps before I go," he said, leaning toward her, "I'll

just take a look at that shoulder." She felt him lean close to her and pull back the collar of her T-shirt. She felt his icy fingers on the skin around her collarbone. Then he ran his hand to her shoulder and squeezed, once, hard. Pain shot through her. She fought back tears, but they filled her eyes and fell down her cheeks.

His head was next to hers, only an inch or two away. *Slam him in the head.* She kept her eyes closed and didn't move. She couldn't do it. She heard him walk away from her, carrying the chair toward the table, then toward the door. The light in the room went out; she could tell with her eyes closed. When she heard the key in the lock and felt the air, she opened her eyes. This time she could see perfectly. The door opened to the right, the hinges on the left.

CHAPTER 43

This time she didn't drift off. She waited until she heard him climb the stairs and close the second door; she didn't hear him use keys on that door, the second door. In the silence that followed, she pushed herself off the cot and stood next to the wall. She walked slowly forward, keeping her head bent so she didn't hit the ceiling. She found the door and stood just to the left of it.

She turned and imagined waiting to hear him come down the stairs again, to hear him take out the keys for the door to the box. Then she imagined what she would do next. After a moment, she followed the wall back to her cot. She lay down and could feel her heart pounding with the effort and the fear.

She lay on the cot until her heart slowed down. She could close her eyes, but only for a minute, because she needed to stay awake. Sweat poured off her, from the heat and the exertion and the fear. But she couldn't rest long. She had to know when he was coming.

She jerked awake, terrified. She had missed him. But the room was dark and a little cooler. Her skin felt clammy, filmed with dirt and sweat, and she couldn't hear anything, not even the crows. The thought of the crows cheered her. When she'd become fully awake, she repeated the whole exercise—the walk to the door, the wait behind the door, the return to the cot.

But this time she lay still for only a few minutes before trying again. Her legs felt tired but steadier. She needed to take advantage of the cooler air before the heater clicked back on and made thinking and moving impossible. In fact, she thought as she walked along beside the wall, as soon as the heater came on, she would go back and wait beside the door. Then the heat couldn't lull her to sleep.

When she got back to the cot this time, she sat up straight and meditated. She focused on each part of her body, her feet, her calves, her stomach, her chest, the pain in her right shoulder. She stayed there for a while. It's only pain, she thought. I'll be fine eventually.

When she reached the collarbone, she remembered the feel of his fingers. She panicked. He would touch her again if her plan didn't work. She forced herself to breathe.

She focused on her face, her swollen lip, the soreness along her jaw. She didn't think she'd been disfigured. She'd just been hit. People got hit every day and survived. He might hit her there again, though.

She said every prayer she could remember, starting with the Lord's Prayer, going through the prayers of the rosary, the prayers of her childhood, the prayers of her adult faith.

He ascended into heaven, and sitteth on the right hand of God the Father almighty. From thence he shall come to judge the quick and the dead. Her mind wandered to the image of Father McPherson coming down from the pulpit with the glow of the candles behind him. He had taught her something about Jesus, though she couldn't remember what it was, not right at that moment.

O My Jesus, forgive us our sins, save us from the fires of

Hell, lead all souls to Heaven, especially those most in need of your mercy. Most Episcopalians don't believe in hell, he had said. She hadn't believed in hell, or heaven, or the picture of Jesus leading souls anywhere. But these prayers comforted her now in a way her own thinking could not comfort her.

Hail, holy Queen, Mother of mercy, our life. . . . To Thee do we send up our sighs, mourning and weeping in this valley of tears. Miss Betty said she passed her pain on to heaven, all the pain she couldn't bear here on earth. But what did that mean, Lily wondered. How did you do that? *Turn then, most gracious Advocate, Thine eyes of mercy towards us. . . .* Maybe it just means this, what she was doing right now.

She needed help to get out of here. She couldn't do it alone. Through her thoughts she heard the heater click on nearby. She pushed herself up and began her walk to the door, which seemed miles away, in another land. She felt as if she traveled along the wall forever. Then she felt the crack, the smooth wood, and the next crack. She stood for a moment, then slid down the wall, sinking to her knees. *And after this, our exile, show unto us the blessed Fruit of Thy womb, Jesus. O clement, O loving, O sweet Virgin Mary.*

She knelt beside the door until she heard a noise on the stairs outside. Then she stood and waited.

CHAPTER 44

She took deep breaths and listened. Sweat trickled down her face, her ribs. She heard him reach the bottom of the stairs and take out the keys. She closed her eyes and prayed for help, from anyone, with anything. Anna's face came to her, awake this time, serene, so clear it startled Lily into opening her eyes. The light in the room had come on; it blinded her. She closed her eyes again.

The key turned in the lock. The door opened. Eyes still closed, she waited until she heard him move forward, over the threshold, then slammed her body into the door.

He grunted and stumbled against the door frame—a crash of dishes and metal followed. She slammed the door again and heard it hit something hard—she thought it must have been his head, because she heard him fall this time, the keys hitting the floor. She jerked the door back, walked through, and opened her eyes, shielding them with her hand. The room beyond was dim, a basement with a small, blacked-out window in the corner near the stairs. She could make out his shape, seated on the floor, just to her left. He lifted his head.

She kicked something, the tray. She picked it up and turned toward him, then slammed the tray down on him twice. She didn't aim, but she made contact. He collapsed onto the floor, his hands raised over his head.

She saw the keys on the floor next to him. If she reached for them, he could grab her. But if she didn't, she might not be able to get out. She might need them for the outside doors—she couldn't remember. And she might need them to lock him in.

This time she looked straight at him. She raised the tray and felt something tear in her shoulder, but she couldn't feel the pain, even though she knew it was there.

He looked up at her and she slammed the tray flat against his face. He moaned and fell back. She dropped the tray, grabbed the keys, and got halfway up the stairs before she heard him.

He wept like a child, crying and gasping and saying, "I can't. Oh, please. I can't." Something happened to her then. She fought the desire to go back to him, to comfort him.

The door at the top had a dead bolt with a knob. She turned it and pushed the door open. She found herself in a dark hallway, across from the back door of the building she'd broken into.

She heard him weeping, but softly. She slammed the door behind her. On this side the lock took a key. A Yale lock, with a regular-size keyhole.

She searched through the keys in her hand, but there were seven, six of them similar—standard-size brass keys. She began to try them one by one. She had to lock him in, to buy herself time to get away. The first two fit, but neither one turned. She tried the third—the same. She couldn't hear anything from the basement. The weeping had stopped.

She glanced at the back door. A dead bolt with a knob. She could get out. She reached the door and turned the lock, but the door still didn't open. Then she saw a second bolt higher up with a keyhole.

She ran to the front door, the one she had kicked in. As she reached it, the pounding started. She didn't know where it came from. She thought it must be him, coming toward her. But that was wrong. Someone stood outside, pounding on the front door and calling a word she couldn't recognize—it sounded like *gryphon.*

He hadn't fixed the front door, the one she'd broken, just piled two of the book cartons against it. She could see where the wood had splintered around the dead bolt by the doorknob. She shoved the top carton off onto the floor. Then she began to drag the second carton out of the way.

As soon as she moved the box, the door opened a crack and the person on the other side began to push. A shoulder appeared, then a body. A man forced his way into the room, then turned to her.

She reached out her left hand, and Frank Leslie took it.

"Where is he?" he asked her.

"In the basement," she said. She could talk, but she also needed to cry at the same time. "But I couldn't lock it. I have the keys." She held them up. "But I couldn't get it to lock."

"Okay," he said. "That's okay. That's not a problem." He led her out through the half-opened door into the clean darkness of the night. "Can you stay here, for a minute?" he asked her.

"No," she said. "I can't stay here. We have to go. We have to get out of here." She kept crying, but she didn't mind.

"Okay," he repeated. "That's okay." He walked her down the steps to the paved courtyard, surrounded by the four buildings. "Can you walk?"

"Yes," she said. She nodded her head and wiped the tears off her cheeks. "I can walk."

He put his arm around her waist, and they turned toward the hill that led to the farmhouse.

"I got up here by myself," she said. "I had to hurt him to get here, though. He's hurt, but I think he's all right."

Frank stopped. "Badly hurt?"

"I don't know," said Lily. "I don't think so. I hit him with a tray." She spoke through her tears.

"But he seemed all right afterward?" Frank asked.

Lily looked at him. "I'm not—" she said. "I couldn't— He kept me in the basement, in a box."

"I know," said Frank. "I know."

CHAPTER 45

Lily lay on the back seat of Frank's car, a small, two-door sedan, staring up through the rear windshield at the stars in the night sky. They had not spoken much. He had insisted she lie down in the back and made sure she was comfortable, that she didn't need an ambulance; he'd assured her he would take her to a hospital. She didn't think she needed a hospital either, but she didn't trust her judgment.

She watched Orion's belt, one of the few constellations she could recognize. From time to time, she felt tears on her cheeks. Unbelievably, she found herself worrying about the man in the basement, about how badly she had hurt him. Then she remembered that Frank had been worried, too. And Frank had said, "I know," when she told him about the box. But she felt too disoriented to make sense of it.

"What time is it?" she asked.

"About two A.M.," he said.

"What day?"

"What day?" he repeated. "Technically, Tuesday morning. Two A.M., Tuesday morning."

"Is it the Tuesday after Easter?" she asked.

"Yes," he said. After a few moments he added, "How long were you there?"

"I'm trying to think," she said. "Since Sunday, sometime Sunday afternoon. I came from the Followers' place in Lester." She watched the sky through the windows change as the road curved. "I saw you there, at lunch, on Easter."

"Saw me where?" he asked.

"At the Followers' farm. You were taking a walk in the woods with a woman—one of the members of the order out there. A woman in a habit."

Lily shifted, to keep from bumping the right side of her face on the back of the seat. "Why were you there?" she asked.

"What do you mean?"

"Were you there to visit a friend?"

"At the farm?" asked Frank. "In part."

She couldn't find the rest of Orion, only his belt. She thought she might have spotted one of the Dippers—Big, Little, she wasn't sure. The stars had never much mattered to her before, but it was as if she were seeing them for the first time. Some clusters were so faint they looked like powdered sugar scattered across the blackness.

"What's the other part?" she asked him.

"The other part of what?"

"You said you were at the Followers' farm in part to visit a friend. What's the other part of the reason you were there?"

He didn't answer.

"So you were involved with them, too. Did you know Anna and Jeffrey back then?"

He hesitated again. "Yes," he said. "I knew them."

She moved farther down on the seat, so she didn't have to twist her neck to avoid the armrest under the window. She just wanted to ride along in the car at night, like a child whose parents were taking her on a road trip. But she couldn't ignore her thirst, or the throbbing pain on her right side, or the questions that wouldn't leave her alone, a sense that things weren't right, not yet.

"Do you have any water?" she asked him.

"No, unfortunately I don't. Would you like me to stop at a gas station and get you something?"

She started to cry, again. When she was able to speak, she said, "Would you mind?"

"Not at all."

The stars seemed to be getting brighter, rather than dimmer. But if they were driving toward Boston, the stars would be getting harder to see. And she had asked for something to drink, a while ago. Maybe everything was closed this time of night.

"Aren't any of the filling stations open?" she asked him.

"I beg your pardon," said Frank.

"I thought you were going to stop to get me something to drink—and maybe something to eat, too, if you don't mind."

"Not at all," he said again.

She lay on the back seat, waiting for Frank to slow down or pull over, but he didn't. "What time is it now?"

"Let's see," he said. "Around two-forty-five."

"Are we near Boston?" she asked.

"Everything appears to be closed," he said. "All the gas stations and diners are closed. Why don't I just keep an eye out for vending machines?"

"Anything's fine," she said. She thought she felt pressure in her ears, as if the road was climbing into the foothills. She raised up onto her elbow and stared out the side window into darkness—not the outskirts of Boston. Then, as she watched, she saw the headlights shine on a road sign that read Route 2 West; they were headed into the mountains.

"Frank?" she said.

He didn't answer.

"How did you know where I was?" she asked him.

He remained silent.

"Frank," she repeated. "On Sunday I left messages with two different people. They know about the Followers; they know about Steve's farm. It's only a matter of time before they go there looking for me. The coincidence would be too great—Anna and me both disappearing. Think about it."

The car took a sharp curve, and she lost her balance for a moment. Then she heard something like a deep sigh, a sudden intake of breath. After a few moments, the car slowed. Then Frank pulled the car onto the shoulder of the road and turned off the engine.

She watched him over the back of the seat. He put his arms on the steering wheel and leaned his head against his hands.

He stayed that way, with his head resting against his hands, for a few minutes. Lily didn't want to interrupt whatever he was thinking, because it seemed to have to do with her, maybe even with her staying alive. She didn't know how she could be so sure of that—something like a shift in the air.

Then he opened the door and got out of the car. She raised up on her elbow again and saw that he'd parked on a gravel cut-in, some kind of scenic viewing spot, with a split-rail fence guarding the edge. Eventually, she gathered her energy, sat up, and clambered out on the passenger side. She didn't see him at first, sitting on the ground. She closed the door and sat down next to him.

She didn't want to look at him, and she didn't want him to look at her. She didn't know how bad her bruises were, and she didn't want to see her disfigured face reflected in Frank's eyes—not literally, but in the sympathy or surprise or maybe even disgust he might show. She felt too vulnerable.

But along with the raw dryness in her throat and the pulsing pain down the right side of her face and into her shoulder, she felt a strange peace—maybe it's a kind of dementia, she thought. Before, in the car, she could tell the whole thing wasn't over yet. Now, though Frank had said very little, she understood that she was safe, back in the world again, and about to learn the truth.

After a moment, she said, "So, you want to tell me what's happening?"

"You couldn't begin to understand," said Frank. His voice sounded different—exhausted.

"Where were you taking me?" she asked him.

"I don't even know. I thought I was going to—"

"To Anna's house?" she asked.

"No—well, yes," he said. "Probably. But I realized it didn't make any sense."

"Are you the one who took Anna there, who took her body there?"

"Yes," he said. "I'm the one."

"And how did you know where to find her?"

"I'd driven her to see him. She asked me to," he said, a note of defensiveness in his voice.

"But why?"

"To see Stephan," said Frank. He pronounced the name as if it were Eastern European, short vowels, accent on the first syllable—the name he'd been calling out as he pounded on the door. It sounded natural, even loving, on his tongue.

"Stephan?" she echoed.

"The young man who—the one who kept you in the building there."

He's not so young, she thought. "And how do you know him?" she asked. "From the Followers?"

"Yes," said Frank. Then he said, "No."

"Is that how Anna knew him?" she asked.

"Anna and I knew him the same way," he said. "He's our son."

CHAPTER 46

Frank answered a few more questions, his voice flat and tired. Stephan was born before the move to the farm. After the move, he was raised by O'Riordan and the Handmaidens—single women who lived in the children's dormitory. But after a little over a year on the farm, Anna had left. "She could see what was happening," said Frank. "The fighting among the groups—the people loyal to O'Riordan, the people loyal to the church, others with their own need for power—it had begun to tear the place apart. Anna said the hatred we'd put out in the world had come back on us. And then there were the issues with the children."

"What issues?" asked Lily.

Frank continued without answering her. "I think maybe if we'd left with her, if I'd taken Stephan away earlier, our lives might have turned out better. But by the time we joined her—he'd been part of the center since he was born, for almost eight years. It was as if he couldn't exist without them. He wouldn't eat, he wouldn't go to school. So I took him back. I stayed for a few more months myself, then I left."

"You mean you left for good? You left him there? Where was Anna?"

"Anna and I separated. I went to seminary on the West Coast. By the time I came back, Stephan was a young man, a teenager. He didn't want to know Anna and me. From then on, we all lived as if the past didn't exist. This last year, he'd begun to call me. Sometimes he'd be crying. He told me about the farm, how he was raised, how they treated him—" Frank's voice broke off.

Lily felt as if she were drifting in and out of Frank's story. She could hear the whole thing, but she couldn't stay with it enough to take it in. "But if you—"

"I can't talk about this anymore," he said and stood.

"Just—" said Lily.

"No," he said. "I'll take you to the hospital."

They got back in the car and didn't talk on the ride to Boston. She lay in the back seat, watching the stars fade, the sky go from dark blue, to pale blue, to pale pink. She couldn't think about what Frank had told her, except to think it must not be true. By the time they reached the emergency room entrance at Mass General Hospital, the sun was rising.

"I've got to put some things in order," he said, without turning around to look at her. "Can you do this on your own?"

He glanced in the rearview mirror. She nodded. She didn't feel sure she could do it alone, but she didn't want to ask him for help. It seemed perverse, backward.

He got out and pulled the seat forward for her. She made it through the car door without touching him.

As she turned toward the entrance, he reached for her arm and said, "I'm sorry."

"Yes," said Lily. "I can see that. But why didn't you do something about him before this?"

He shrugged his shoulders, lightly—a tough question, would the Sox make the playoffs? Then he looked at his feet. Lily saw him clearly for the first time that night—a dumpy, harmless guy in a frayed black suit with dandruff on the shoulders and a white spot on the lapel.

"I liked my life the way it was," he said.

"Is that why you didn't call the police when Anna died?"

"It wasn't his fault," said Frank. "She had a heart attack. But when he called me, and I saw the room in the basement, where he'd kept her—I knew they'd lock him up, which is what they'll do now. And that's probably right. But—"

"But what?"

"He asked me for help. I'd never done anything for him. He's my son."

She didn't answer. As she reached the sliding glass doors, she heard the car drive away. She wanted something else from him—she wanted him to take it back, the things he'd said. She wanted them not to be true, but she knew they were.

The attending doctor—a redhead with round glasses and freckles on every inch of his body, or every visible inch—looked about twenty-three and sounded as if his voice was still changing.

"Do you want to tell me—" he began, then cleared his throat and started again, his voice deeper. "Do you want to tell me who did this to you?"

"I have a friend who's a policeman. Can I call him? He'll bring someone with him, and I can tell the story to all of you at the same time."

Lily gave the nurse—a big white guy, with a black ponytail and a nose ring—all of Tom's phone numbers. She had trouble swallowing, and her head still pounded a regular rhythm on the right side, from the crown, down her neck, into her shoulder and back.

The doctor said he'd fix up an IV drip to hydrate her,

and asked her, his voice calmer now, if he could give her something for the pain. She smiled to herself. When she'd lain in the heat and the darkness on the cot, she'd wanted more than anything to clear her head so she could think. But she didn't want to think anymore.

"Sure," she said. "Whatever you've got."

Tom showed up about twenty minutes later. She lay on a gurney in a tiny cubicle defined by one wall and three white curtains, just off the emergency room, waiting to be taken for X rays.

When he saw her, his face showed exactly the mixture of sympathy and horror she'd been trying to avoid.

"I know," she said. "I'll tell you all about it. Hatcher didn't do it. He didn't kill Anna. Can you get that message to Thompkins, Miller, somebody, right away?"

He nodded but didn't say anything. He took her hand and looked away.

"Is it that bad?" she asked.

"No," he said. "I just didn't think I'd see you again."

He was crying, or trying not to, and she didn't want to upset the balance. Besides, the painkiller was kicking in. This one was a lot more pleasant than the ones in the basement. It would take a real addict to lie here comparing painkillers, she thought, given the situation. Then she thought for just an instant—all she could bear—of her pathetic showing at McPherson's house, the stolen scotch, the waking up sick and ashamed. Maybe it's time to do something about it—the drinking and the self-deception. In the gentle haze in which the pain began to drift away and settle a few feet off from her, it didn't seem so hard, the idea of stopping drinking, of asking someone for help, of giving up.

When she got back from X rays (which seemed to take hours, but she couldn't really tell, because of the slow-motion underwater quality of her drug-induced calm), Gregarian was there with Tom. They walked next to the gurney as a new nurse—a small, young woman, under thirty, with dark skin and cornrows with bright-colored beads on the ends—wheeled her into a larger room, an office.

"What's this?" Lily asked.

"Doctor Sheehan said you could use his office," said the young woman. "To talk to these guys. You must have impressed him."

"I'm pretty impressive. I look good, don't I?"

"You look okay," said the woman. "You look like you're alive—that's impressive."

"Good point," said Lily.

The woman left them. Gregarian leaned against the desk; Tom stood next to the gurney. "You want to tell us what happened?" he asked.

"Sure," she said, then she smiled at him. "Listen, if you're ever in pain, this stuff is great."

Tom patted her on the ankle.

"Oh, shit," she said.

"What?" asked Tom.

"He's got my boots."

"This is going to be one hell of a story," said Gregarian.

She told them almost everything. She didn't tell them who Stephan was; she didn't tell them about Anna. She said Anna had known about Stephan's group and had suspected them of the vandalism at the cathedral, so Frank had taken her out there and left her to talk with him. That Stephan had locked Anna up—just as he'd locked Lily up, but Anna's heart probably hadn't been able to take the heat and the closeness and the fear.

She said that Stephan had called Frank when Anna died, and Frank had tried to protect Stephan, because he'd known him as a child, in the Followers. Frank had taken Anna's body to her home in Wharton and buried it. He was probably on his way back there now, to Stephan's farm, to try to help Stephan, maybe even to help him escape.

As soon as he understood, Gregarian got on his cell phone and sent somebody out there to Ahearn. Six hours ago, all she would have wanted was for the man, Stephan, to have been caught and punished. Now, she almost didn't care. In fact, now she hoped they got away, Frank and Stephan, to someplace where Stephan couldn't hurt anyone anymore, where Frank could ease some of the guilt he felt about abandoning his son, where some of Anna's mistakes could be put right.

CHAPTER 47

Lily allowed herself to be waited on for two days. She lay on the couch in her living room and, uncharacteristically, even cheerfully, took tea and broth and meals and books and advice from Tom and Barbara and Charlie. Bishop Spencer came by and asked her a few questions. She told him what she'd told Gregarian. He seemed satisfied. Before he left, he told her he had a nice little parish out in Dedham that needed an interim priest—all aboveboard. Their former rector, a woman, had moved to Maryland.

She laughed. "Good try," she said.

"You need to be doing some parish work," he said as he left. "I won't give up."

"No," said Lily. "I wouldn't expect you to."

When she was alone, she tried not to think, but of course that proved impossible. She had started praying again, in earnest, in that hole in Stephan's basement, and she hadn't been able to stop. So the prayers came, almost unbidden, along with the thoughts.

She thought about Stephan Leslie, about his life and his inheritance, about what had been passed on through him, the hatred, the darkness of the soul. And about Frank Leslie and Sebastian O'Riordan and Jeffrey Tatum and Anna—all of whom had passed it on, helplessly. And about the other Anna, the one Lily had known and needed and admired, whose life she had coveted. She hadn't been able to put them together, those two versions, so for now she thought of them as separate, two women, only one of whom she knew. She prayed for all of them.

And she prayed for herself. She was down to a couple of painkillers a day, but she found herself looking forward to them. While she wasn't quite ready to admit what that meant, at least she was willing to notice it. She thought about Tom and her, about Gregarian, about the confusion she'd been feeling in her life over the past year. She felt tired of walking through her life in a haze. She wanted to act from the heart, to do things she cared about and believed in, not to keep secrets, not to lie. She wanted her life to be transparent, something clear and clean, water over rock.

At times, the feel of the sun shining through the tall windows on her face, or the shadows of the curtains against the yellow walls caused something deep inside her to stir—as if an unfamiliar emotion had begun to grow. When she noticed it, she classed it under the genus *gratitude,* but thought it might be a new species, or new to her, at least. It had something to do with being glad to be alive.

On the morning of the third day of her convalescence, the Thursday after Easter, Gregarian showed up at her building. She was on her own, in a pair of gray sweatpants and a Dixie Chicks T-shirt, her hair dirty—it was hard to wash it with a neck brace and her arm in a sling. When she heard his voice over the intercom, she tried to figure out how to improve her appearance, then immediately gave up. At least this way he won't think he missed out on anything, she thought.

She buzzed him in. Then she washed her face—delicately, the right side was still excruciatingly tender—and braided her dirty hair and met him at her front door.

"You look better," he said.

"Whoa," said Lily. "In that case, let's not think about what I looked like before. You want a cup of tea?"

"No, thanks," he said. Gregarian did not look better; he looked even tireder than usual—his eyes puffy, his curly hair uncombed. He wore a not entirely clean pair of khaki pants, a green knit shirt, a navy blue sport coat, and his work boots. Under his right arm he carried a blue plastic GAP bag. "I can't stay long. I just wanted to let you know what was happening. And ask a couple of questions—stuff I can't figure out. Is this an okay time?"

"Yeah," she said. "I'm on my own and starting to feel a little restless."

"How's the neck?" he asked, as she led him into the living room and sat in the viewing chair. "Great chair," he added.

"It was my dad's. I brought it up here from Texas. And the neck's fine, or will be. Nothing broken. No wired jaw. Just a lot of contusions—as they call them—a pulled ligament, some strained muscles. The doctor said the guy must have hit me a few times, or maybe kicked me after I fell."

"Nice," said Gregarian. He sat at one end of the couch, facing her. When he leaned back, the contents of the bag bumped against the arm of the sofa. "Oh," he said. "These are for you."

She took the bag and opened it. "My boots—excellent. Thanks."

"No problem. I also wanted to let you know we found Banieka's—Ms. Banieka's suitcase."

"Where?"

"In the basement, outside the room where you were—kept. We found the Bible from the cathedral in with her stuff and a tape recorder Charlie gave her. We had Charlie come down and go through it all."

"Oh, my God," said Lily.

"What?" he asked.

"Was it a little tape recorder, one of those miniature ones, with the tiny cassettes?"

"Yeah," he said. "But there wasn't anything in it."

"Oh, okay," she said. She'd just remembered the cassette she'd found between the floor and the wall of the box.

"Why?" he asked her.

"I don't know. Because I remember Charlie offering to give her one. It brought back the memory."

"Is there an awful lot you're not telling us?" he asked.

"No," said Lily. "Not an awful lot. And it doesn't—the facts of what happened are the same, regardless."

"If I wanted to," said Gregarian, "I could make you tell the whole story."

"You don't want to," said Lily. "And it may all come out, anyway. But if it does, I'd like the people involved to tell it themselves."

He studied her for a minute. "Is it about your friend, Ms. Banieka?"

"Yes," said Lily. "Partly."

Then he shifted his gaze to the window behind her and stared out for another few moments. "Okay," he said, at last. He looked back at her. "We know Frank Leslie is Stephan Leslie's father."

"How?"

"Frank told us. But what we don't know—"

"Won't hurt you," said Lily. "Trust me."

"Why should I?" he asked her. He looked straight into her eyes this time, and she knew he wasn't asking about the case.

"I owe you an apology," she said.

"For what?"

"For—I don't know. What do we call it these days? Leading you on."

"Good," he said.

"Good, what?"

"I'm glad you said that, because I had begun to think I was crazy, or really old, that I was going around imagining beautiful women coming on to me."

Lily blushed. "No. You may have imagined the beautiful part, but not the other. I did—I think you're really attractive, and we have a lot in common, but I've got this thing, with Tom."

"I know. He's a good guy, a friend. I wouldn't want to mess that up, for me, or for you."

"Thanks," she said. "I've been kind of confused lately, and I think maybe I let the confusion take over for a while."

"Well, if things don't work out with Tom, and you get confused again, let me know."

She smiled as much as she could without hurting herself. "Thanks. What's going to happen to them, to Frank and Stephan?"

"Hard to tell. Stephan's under psychiatric observation. Frank Leslie's out on bail. He seems like a decent enough guy."

"Yes," said Lily. "I think he is."

"He turned himself in and led us to his nutcase son. On the other hand, he covered up a possible homicide, and you seemed to think he planned to get rid of you—somehow."

"I may have been wrong about that," she said. "I was pretty disoriented by then."

"Think about it," he said. "It's important to be clear. It would make a difference."

"Okay," said Lily. "I will. Anything else?"

"No," he said and stood up to leave. "By the way, I saw the box—where he kept you."

"What did it look like?" she asked.

"Like something out of *The Collector,*" he said. "Like

hell. I have this little problem with closed spaces. I'm not sure I could have lasted. You did a good job getting away."

"I might not have gotten away if Frank hadn't shown up though."

"Oh," he said. "I suspect you'd have figured out something."

CHAPTER 48

As soon as the door shut behind Gregarian, Lily found the paper bag they'd sent home with her from the hospital. She unfolded her jeans and reached into the back pocket and felt the cassette. It seemed like something from the bottom of the ocean, from another world. But there it was in her hand.

The problem was, she didn't have one of those miniature tape players. She returned to the living room, tape in hand, and sat in the viewing chair. After a couple of minutes, she got up and popped the tape out of the answering machine. Then she inserted the cassette she had found and pushed Rewind. When it hit the beginning, she pushed Play Messages.

The ambient sounds almost overwhelmed the voice. Lily heard crowd noises, footsteps and rustling and low talk, and somewhere in the background an announcement over a loudspeaker. Lily couldn't adjust for quality, so she turned up the volume as loud as it would go and sat with her ear near the machine.

"The things I remember of Stephan," said Anna, "—at five, he spoke fluent English and Polish. He used to sing in Polish, and they would stop him. They made him speak English, always, so he came to connect Polish with me. And Polish was bad.

"They said the bruises on his knees were from playing, from falling down. Sometimes he couldn't walk. He was so light I would carry him piggyback. He was the smartest one, of all the children, and beautiful—those large eyes. He looked like my brother. He had my brother's name."

It didn't really sound like Anna—too hollow and tinny—but Lily recognized the accent and inflections.

"To be honest—and why not, finally. To be honest, I knew something was wrong. Not with Stephan—something was wrong between Father Sebastian and Stephan. Sebastian chose him as his prince, the next in line. And he passed on all the wisdom and all the hatred. But when Frank and I left him there, I felt nothing but relief, as if I'd been given my life—for a third time. And I felt as if I were owed a life. That Sebastian O'Riordan owed it to me, and the Germans owed it to me, and the world owed it to me."

A loudspeaker close to the recorder blasted out a second announcement—Lily heard the names Springfield and Pittsfield somewhere in the garbled noises. Anna stopped speaking until it finished.

"So now—I have been feeling ill for the past few weeks, and I am scared of this meeting, of seeing Stephan again. I don't know where this tape will end up, whether or not anyone will find it, or even if it's necessary. But I will record it and take it with me, all the same.

"I have left a will in my house, inside the small cupboard beside my writing table. Two wills—one on tape, one in print. The written document is under a floorboard in the cupboard, with the money. Over the years, I have sent Stephan most of what I made. The rest—the money that is left in the wall, and the house, and the dogs—it all goes to Andrew Hatcher.

"I expect Andrew to care for the dogs, and for his grandfather, and to live in the house. With the money, he can go back to school. Or start a business.

"He should do what he wants. He should know he was loved—"

Another announcement blasted through Anna's voice—Lily heard the names Hyannis and Cape Cod, then a click and a long white blur of silence.

In the scramble of the last eight days, Lily had forgotten about Anna's will. As soon as she heard the recording, she called Gregarian's office and left him a message.

He called back a half hour later.

"Start from the beginning," he said.

"Okay," said Lily. "You know I had a bunch of tapes from Anna's house, stuff I'd brought home with me to listen to, when she first went missing. I just put one of them on, and there it was, the will, on tape, and instructions about where to find the written document."

"Interesting timing," said Gregarian. "The guys at CPAC might want to listen to these tapes. I don't know."

"CPAC?" she asked.

"Crime Prevention—the DA's office."

"Can I get them back?" she asked him.

"Yeah, eventually," he said. "What made you listen to the tape?"

"I missed her," said Lily. And even though she was still lying about the tapes, about what she'd found, about Anna's past, the truth of what she had just said caught her off guard. She felt a sob rise up and, before she could stop it, she found herself crying loudly.

"Sorry," Gregarian mumbled.

"It's not your fault," she said through the tears. "I just—with everything going on, I'd forgotten that part. I'd forgotten how much I missed her."

CHAPTER 49

Two days later, Lily sat on the stoop of her apartment building waiting for Tom. They planned to drive together out to Wharton, to Anna's memorial service. Anna had asked that her ashes be scattered from the lookout point in the woods, into the valley below her house. A wake would follow at McPherson's; he had organized the whole thing, according to instructions in the will.

Outside for the first time since her return home from the hospital on Tuesday, she felt as if she'd been underground for a long time, much longer than thirty-six hours, more like twenty-six days, since Anna's disappearance, and in her absence the world had become this blowsy, frivolous character. The trees had leafed out fully and each leaf seemed to be a slightly different shade of green; the air had warmed up, so that the sunlight had a texture, a richness to it; crows and pigeons wrangled loudly in the gutter over a spilled box of popcorn.

Tom pulled up at eight A.M., on the dot. Lily had stopped taking the painkillers. Her face and head were still tender, her right arm still in a sling to keep the shoulder immobile, but at least her mind felt clear.

"Route 2 or the Mass. Pike?" he asked her when she got in beside him.

"Let's take Route 2. It's so beautiful, and we're not in any hurry." She didn't say out loud that she wanted to travel that road in daylight, in a car with someone she loved; maybe it could help to ease some of the memories from these past few weeks.

"You look better," he said.

"So I keep hearing," she said.

"Oh yeah? From who?"

"People," she said. "Gregarian."

"What?" he asked. "He came by?"

"He brought me my boots. I told you, remember?"

"Right," he said.

"Any news?" she asked him.

"Like what?"

"Like what's going to happen to Frank or Stephan—or Andy."

"Or us," said Tom.

"What do you mean?"

"Do you remember talking last week about making a plan? You think it's too soon to start trying to work out the details?"

"I think—" she began.

"What?"

"I think I've been really confused over the past couple of years, since my dad's death, and all that stuff at the parish, when I was interim. And because I met you when all of that was going on, you've gotten—or you and I as a couple, somehow—have gotten caught up in the confusion."

"But I'm not confused," said Tom.

"I don't mean that you're confused. I mean I've been confused about you and me."

"I don't think I want you to break up with me on the way to Anna's memorial service," said Tom. "So if that's what you're doing, let's hold off on this talk."

"That's not what I'm doing—at least, it's not what I

want to do. But I also—I don't think I can live with you. Because I don't think I can live with anyone. You know, I spent a lot of time longing for Anna's life, the solitude, the writing, the scholarship, then—"

"What?"

"Then I sort of rejected the whole thing, Anna and her life, for my own reasons. But I'm trying to be less all-or-nothing, and in this case I'm coming to think that what appealed to me most was her independence, and solitude. And I need time to see if that's true or not."

"You've been living alone your whole life," he said. They had reached the Fresh Pond rotary, and Tom stopped talking while he navigated the steady stream of spring day-trippers—families in Subaru station wagons, a young couple in an old MG convertible, a big Chrysler with two older couples, men in front, women in back. Once he was through, he said, "How long do you need?"

"Here's the thing," she said. "For a long time, my life made perfect sense to me. And then it stopped making sense. But I've just kept doing the things I was doing, without too much thought.

"And other people in my life have expected the same things from me they've always expected—with good reason. I'm not blaming them. You know, Bishop Spencer wants me to get on the stick and do parish work, and Barbara wants me to get on the stick and do my work at the center. And you want me to get on the stick and move in with you. But I'm not sure yet what I want to do, and until I know, I don't think I can make any decisions about the future. Does that make sense?"

"Well, I understand the part about your not wanting to live with me."

"But I don't want to lose you either. I want to be with you—like, forever. I just don't want to live with anyone. But I want to start working again, doing something, for real, the way I used to. And when I do work that way, I pour myself out, completely. You've seen me after a three-day workshop. And when I'm like that, I need someplace to come back and be totally quiet, totally within myself."

"But married people do that all the time. Everyone needs space and all that shit. I need it, too. Why can't we live together and try? I'm not going to hang around reciting love poetry while you try to meditate."

She laughed. "I know that. And I know other people do it. But I can't—or, I mean, I don't want to. I want you to be my guy forever, but I want to live by myself—at least for now. You might not want that, I might lose you, and I would hate that. But—I don't know what else to do. It's a risk I have to take."

Neither of them spoke for a few minutes. They were out on Route 2 now, driving toward Concord. The couple in the MG passed them, and Lily wondered about that life, the life of antique cars and convertibles, the pursuit of pleasure. She'd never actually tried it, but she decided it was too late to start now. I'm earnest, she thought, and plodding. So be it.

"I'm going to have to think about it," said Tom. "It's not exactly the future I had in mind."

"I know. Me either. But I realized the future I had in mind wasn't my future. It was somebody else's future. I want my own—with you." His hand rested on the gear shift. She reached for it and held it. "I'm not even saying this is true forever, necessarily. But it's true for now."

"If I get a place near you, and we stay together, will you stop flirting with my colleagues?"

"Oh, God. I'm so sorry about all that. I apologized to him—"

"So apologize to me."

"I just did."

"That's the best you can do?" he asked.

"Here's what I think happened," she said. "I think I didn't want to move in with you, but I didn't know it, or I couldn't admit it. So I entertained the notion of being with someone else, or maybe a lot of someone elses. When really I want to be with you, just not in the same house. So, I'm sorry. I am."

"That's it?"

She leaned over and kissed him—with the left side of her mouth—on the cheek, then on the ear, then on the hollow space below the ear.

"I can't kiss yet," she said. "The right side of my mouth is still sort of tender."

"It seemed fine to me," he said.

"Does this mean we're okay for now?" she asked.

"Yeah," he said and sighed. "I guess so."

"You don't sound very happy."

"I'm not very happy. But I'm a lot happier than I was when I thought we were falling apart for good. So I guess this will do."

Lily kept his hand in hers. Out the window she saw a Route 2 West sign. Soon they would be into the foothills, soon they would pass the spot where Frank Leslie had pulled the car over and told Lily the story of Anna and Frank and Stephan, a story Lily would carry around forever, on her own.

CHAPTER 50

Lily sat at McPherson's kitchen table and watched him cut a cantaloupe into thin slices and place them on a cobalt blue serving dish. She and Tom were the first to arrive, and McPherson had sent Tom out for ice and olive oil. On the counter stood a large bowl of chicken salad (with almonds and green grapes), another large bowl of potato salad (with black olives and scallions), two kinds of bread, and three kinds of cheese—and this just for lunch. At one point, he asked her to get the butter. When she opened the refrigerator door, she found a cold chicken, a ham, a huge fruit salad, and a bowl of cherry tomatoes with mozzarella and basil.

"Maybe you should think about doing a little catering business on the side," she said.

"This is what I do when I have a feeling. I cook."

"That's better than what most of us do," she said. "Like me, for instance."

He put down the paring knife and looked up at her. "What, you mean stealing people's scotch?"

She blushed and nodded. "Yeah, for instance that."

He picked up the knife and went back to cutting and peeling the melon. "Do you have a drinking problem?"

"Well, it depends on when you ask me. I go for a long

time without a drink—so if you asked me during one of those times, I'd say no."

"How about right now?"

"Right now I'd say yes."

"Let's keep it in the moment, then, shall we? Are you willing to get help?"

"I don't think I have much choice," she said. "Evidently, I can't do it on my own."

"Hah," he said. He stood and put the platter of melon next to the bread and cheese. "Nobody can. Don't you know that yet?"

"I'm learning."

"I know," he said, as he sat down next to her. "It's one we just keep getting taught over and over. And for people like us, it's hard. We think we're supposed to be helping everyone else. It never occurs to us to ask for help."

After a moment of silence, she said, "I'm sorry."

"For the scotch? Don't worry about it."

"That, and screwing up my chance to talk to Andy. What's going to happen there—do you have any idea?"

He stood and went to the refrigerator. "You want a glass of iced tea?—I mean real iced tea, Oklahoma iced tea, brewed Lipton's with lots of sugar and lemon and mint. I made it myself."

"I figured," she said. "Yeah, I'd love some. Are you not going to answer me about Andy?"

He got out the pitcher and the glasses and the ice. "Here's the thing," he said as he put the glass down in front of her. "Andy has a good chance of getting off altogether, because of Miller's tactics."

"Coercion?" asked Lily.

"Yeah, coercion." He poured them both tall glasses of tea and returned the pitcher to the refrigerator. "The problem is, the information Miller used to coerce Andy could get someone else in a lot of trouble."

"Who?" she asked.

"His grandfather."

"How?"

"How much do you want to know?" he asked her. "Because I'm not supposed to know most of this, so you're really not supposed to know it. Which means you couldn't tell anyone, not a soul."

"That's okay," said Lily. I can add that to the growing list, she thought. "I'd like to know."

"It appears that Mr. Hatcher—not his real name, of course—fought in World War II, on the wrong side, according to us. He doesn't have legal immigration papers; he probably couldn't have gotten them. Andy was born here, so he's a citizen. But Mr. Hatcher has been living here a long time with false papers."

"How did Miller find out?" She took a sip of tea and was transported to her childhood—the screen porch off the kitchen where they ate in good weather, the horse and leather smell on her father and the ranch hands, the tight feel of a sunburn across her nose and cheeks. "This is good," she said. "Thanks."

McPherson nodded and said, "I have no idea. I'm not sure anyone does. But he told Andy he'd have his grandfather deported—gone before Andy ever got out of jail. He'd never see him again. Unless Andy told him everything he knew about Anna's death."

"But if the lawyer presents that in court, then Mr. Hatcher will still be deported."

"We've got someone working on it, trying to start the process to get him legal papers. But it won't be easy. Once we know how likely that is, and how long it will take, then Devereaux can figure out what to do next. Meanwhile, with Andy cleared of murder, he's out on bail. And Miller's deep in the shit house—turns out the investigation wasn't entirely aboveboard in a lot of ways."

"So what was Andy's part? What did he do?"

"He did just what he said. The dogs dug up the body. He

found it and moved it to a safer place, someplace Anna would have liked, he said. Then he took some of the money from that cupboard—only some, about half."

"Money that was actually his," said Lily.

"Yes," said McPherson. "One of the many weird parts of this story."

Lily tipped her glass and drained the last of the tea. "People's lives are complicated, aren't they?"

"Yes, they are."

"How much do you know about Anna's life?" she asked him.

"A lot," he said.

"She told you?" asked Lily.

"She told me—most of her story, anyway. She told me about her life here in the States, when she first arrived. She told me about—those connections."

"Why didn't you say anything?" asked Lily. "Did it occur to you—"

"That it might have saved her life?" he asked. "Yeah, after it was all over. I thought about the Followers a few times, but I've been there with her before, and they're decent people, really, not the kidnapping type. I didn't think of—" He stood and took his glass to the sink.

"I know," said Lily.

"Know what?"

"I know about Stephan."

He sat back down. "How much?"

"I know he's her son."

"Who told you?"

"Frank."

"Did you tell anyone else?"

"No."

"Good," he said. "I'm glad you know."

"Why?" asked Lily.

"Because I hated being alone in the knowledge. She told me part of the story in confessional, part over the years, as friends. I don't even know what's what anymore, which information came from where. So I just had to keep my mouth shut. It's a great relief, believe me."

They sat together at the table, both of them very still. Then Lily shook her head, slightly, almost invisibly, and reached for the piece of mint at the bottom of her glass. "It's bound to come out, eventually."

"Probably," said McPherson. "I hope so. In general, I think it's better that the truth be known. But I'm not going to talk about it."

"Me neither," said Lily. She bit off a small piece of mint, the tip of a leaf. "I still don't understand how she could have been involved with something so—opposite to everything she believed."

"Everything she came to believe," he said.

"What do you mean?"

"When she first got here—I honestly don't think she'd reflected too much on what happened during the war. She was so young, and everything about it was so extreme. It's not like she had a clear sense of the political, religious realities. She was a kid when she saw her family slaughtered, was taken to an orphanage, and ended up in Auschwitz. My guess is that the experiences themselves didn't leave a lot of room for reflection and analysis. Plus, don't forget she grew up in Catholic Poland—about as anti-Semitic a culture as you could want."

"Yes," said Lily. "I remember now."

"She talked to you about it?"

"No, not exactly. But you know the tapes I mentioned, of Anna remembering the war years, her childhood, her time in the camp? She says something like that, in the tapes. She talks about being scared of the Jews. She thought they would kill her."

"That sounds about right," said McPherson. "She might even have blamed them for her parents' death, for the loss of her family and her world. So the Followers' brand of anti-Semitism, particularly about the war and the camps—this idea that it was all a just punishment for their sins—fit pretty well with Anna's own fears. And, then, too, I don't think the anti-Semitism was very prominent in the beginning. It was insinuated. But it got worse later on."

"When did her own thinking change?"

"After she left the Followers, and Stephan went back there, and she and Frank split up—the marriage was never legal, you know?"

"What do you mean?"

"They were married by someone at the Followers—not O'Riordan, someone O'Riordan had ordained, illegally, and they never got a marriage certificate. So the marriage wasn't legal in the outside world." He stood, opened the freezer, and filled his glass with ice. "After that she went to college again, to U Mass. She studied history and theology. I met her a few years later, and by then, she was pretty much the person you and I have always known or, at least, on the path to becoming that person." He poured more tea for himself. "Want some?"

"No, thanks," said Lily. "I'm having a hard time."

"With that?" he asked.

"With Anna, with trying to figure out who she is, was. I have this split in my mind, these two people; the first one is the one I thought I knew, the one I want her to be, and the second one is the one I've just discovered. I don't know what to do with this new information. I keep them separate, because when I try to join them, I feel like I've been abandoned by someone I love."

"Sometimes I think that's the human condition, feeling abandoned by someone we love. Maybe that's the source of religion, you know? This desire to reunite with the perfect other."

"I'm not talking anthropology here," said Lily. "I'm talking about Anna."

"No," said McPherson. "You're talking about you. Because Anna was exactly what she was, all along. But your ideas of her have had to change, will have to change. She wasn't this idealized old lady, living out here in the mountains, writing books and doing good."

"She was to me," said Lily. She could feel the tears rising.

"But you see, that's too bad. Because, finally, she's three-dimensional and flawed and failed and hugely marked by life—more than almost anyone I've ever known, she was marked by life. She had terrible things done to her and she made terrible mistakes, did terrible things to other people, but she kept going, trying to get it right. In the end, I think she did. She atoned for the greatest harm she'd done. She wasn't afraid—well, I think she probably was afraid. But she did it anyway."

Lily held her hands out in front of her, as if she were showing him something. "But what am I supposed to do with all these pieces of her?" She was crying as she talked.

"Look," he said. "You've only got one job here, and that's to accept her as she was. That will take time and prayer and talk with good people. You might need to tell someone else about Stephan, so you can get some help sorting it all out. Or you can call me, anytime." He took hold of one of her hands.

"Thanks," said Lily. "I think I will."

CHAPTER 51

The group of mourners moved together up the road toward the woods and the lookout point—Lily walked with Tom and Charlie, in the middle of the group, behind Barbara and Miss Betty, who had insisted on coming even though Barbara had tried to talk her out of it. Lily could see Thompkins's head above the crowd, near the back, walking with the Hatchers. Bishop Spencer led the group, along with McPherson.

Lily felt the warm sun on her hair and cheek, on her bruised arm and shoulder, but the air seemed heavy, and to the west a circle of clouds—high and white on top, dark and flat underneath—gathered on the horizon. She could smell the pines. In the distance, she heard a tractor start up, its steady chugging sound mixing with bird calls and the sporadic tapping of a woodpecker.

Tom had his arm around her waist and was half-guiding her, half-pushing her up the hill. This particular arrangement might have annoyed her a week ago, but at the moment she felt grateful. When they reached the steep path through the trees, he moved ahead and took Miss Betty's other arm. Lily dropped back and walked with Thompkins, the Hatchers, and the dogs.

They stood in a semicircle, facing McPherson. He stood holding the prayer book, his back to the valley, a small gray box beside him on the ground. The clouds covered the sky. Lily stood between Charlie and Barbara, at the edge of the drop. She could see the farmhouse she'd noticed during her first visit. No one came and went today. The valley seemed quiet.

McPherson began with the traditional "I am the Resurrection and the Life." Lily's mind wandered. They had decided to leave time during the service for people to speak about Anna. Lily didn't think she would say anything.

She heard the rain on the trees before she felt it—light and feathery. Umbrellas sprang up in the crowd. Luckily, Barbara had brought her giant golf umbrella. Miss Betty had a red collapsible one, and Jeffrey Tatum moved over next to McPherson, holding a large black umbrella over them both.

The air grew soft with dampness. McPherson's voice blended with the sound of the rain on the trees and umbrellas and the scent of damp pine needles. Then he invited others to speak. For a few moments, there was only the rain and soft air. Then Jeffrey stepped forward.

He talked about Anna as a young woman, about her resilience and brilliance and beauty; he described what she looked like the first day he met her—her short black hair and elegant red lipstick and nail polish. No one at Holy Cross had ever seen anyone quite like her, he said. She would argue with professors fearlessly, and often won. "She made mistakes," he said. "Just as we all have. But I consider her the bravest person I have ever known. And I will miss her."

Jeffrey knows, too, she thought. And it hasn't affected his feelings for Anna. A light breeze kicked up, and Lily noticed the rain had turned to mist. She couldn't hear it anymore, but she could feel it on her hands as it drifted down, angling beneath the trees and umbrellas.

McPherson cleared his throat and said that Anna had not been perfect, but she had been about as close as anyone he knew, at least in ways that mattered. Then he told a long story about a period at the college years ago in which Anna had made it her goal to get rid of fraternities and sororities on the Wharton campus. She had talked with hundreds of students—scholarship students, gay and lesbian students, students of color, and others—who'd had humiliating run-ins with the system. So she'd badgered the administration into calling a meeting on the subject.

At the meeting, in the chapel, tempers had flared, someone called someone else a name, then Anna had stood up in the middle of a sea of angry people, this little woman with a Polish accent, still, and red lipstick, still, and listed all the wars she knew of that were happening on the earth at that very moment—wars in the Middle East, and Eastern Europe, and Africa. Then she had listed all the places where people were starving—India, Dorchester, Bangladesh, Manhattan, Georgia, Wharton. He couldn't remember them all, but he remembered she ended with Wharton. Finally she had suggested that they keep this subject in perspective. McPherson said that the way he remembered it, nothing had been resolved that day. But at the moment, as they stood together on that hill, there were no fraternities or sororities at Wharton College.

The mist stopped and the breeze picked up. Charlie told a story about Anna's having been invited to read to the Diocesan Convention. She'd been supposed to read from her new book, the interviews with survivors, but instead she'd read a short letter she'd recently received from someone she'd gotten to know in Poland during the interviews, a woman who, like Anna herself, had been in the camps as a child. It was a letter about forgiveness, about how the woman had decided to make forgiveness the work of her life. At the end, Anna had said that this should be the work of all our—. Charlie couldn't finish the last sentence of the story, but Lily felt sure everyone knew what he'd intended to say.

Lily began to feel cold and damp. Two people from the college spoke, a young woman, maybe a recent student, and a woman Anna's age. Then another long silence fell. Just as McPherson seemed about to resume the service, Lily heard a voice from the back of the crowd, the voice of a young man. "I want to say thank you," the young man said. "I don't know what else to say. She treated me better than anyone ever had. I really appreciate it." Someone in the group shifted, and Lily saw Thompkins give Andy Hatcher a pat on the back.

McPherson took a ceramic jar out of the box beside him on the ground. He unscrewed the top, set it down in the box, and said, "Into your hands, O merciful Savior, we commend your servant, Anna, a sheep of your own fold, a lamb of your own flock, a sinner of your own redeeming. Receive her into the arms of your mercy, into the blessed rest of everlasting peace, and into the glorious company of the saints of heaven. Amen." Then he turned the jar over, and the ashes fell out in a clump, until the breeze caught them and spread them into a fine silver mist.

Together, they said the Our Father. McPherson said a prayer for the ones left behind, in mourning, and a benediction. Then silently, in twos and threes, people started down the hill. Lily didn't want to talk to anyone right now, or help anyone, or be helped. She just wanted a few minutes of silence on her own. She whispered to Tom she'd meet him at the car and stepped back into the trees.

The clearing emptied and Lily walked to the edge, where McPherson had emptied the ashes. She didn't have anything in mind, no special words or ritual. She just wanted to see it for the last time. So she could remember.

As she turned, she noticed some movement near the path. A man walked down the hill through the trees. He had gray hair and wore a black suit. Then he came out on the road below, and she saw it was Frank Leslie, alone.

CHAPTER 52

By the time Lily and Tom reached McPherson's house, the sky had cleared. Some of the guests had brought chairs into the front garden and were sitting, enjoying the fresh, rain-washed air. Charlie sat by himself, over to the side of the house, facing away from the crowd, toward the afternoon sun. He motioned to Lily, and she took the chair next to him.

"How are you?" he asked her.

"I don't know what to say," she said. "I'm all right, I guess. Given where we are and what we're doing."

"I have this weird feeling—" he began.

"What?"

"How come you didn't say anything?" he asked.

"I just—I've been feeling pretty sad, and I wasn't sure I could keep it together."

"You mean you were afraid you might cry, like I did?"

"Yes," she said and patted his arm. "Something like that."

"And how come everyone kept talking about her not being perfect, about making mistakes? Of course she made mistakes. I think we're all too hard on one another in this community. We take this saints of god thing way too literally."

Lily thought about all the secrets she'd been keeping. If anyone deserved to know who Anna really was, Charlie did. Charlie believed that all things worked to the good for those who believe in God, even if nobody really comprehends why. For him it wasn't a question of comprehension; it was a question of faith. And because of his faith, he would be able to accept the truth about Anna. He would be able to forgive.

"You're right," she said.

"I am?" asked Charlie. "You never agree with me so quickly."

"Yeah. But this time you're right."

She would tell him, but not now. For now, they would sit together in silence and miss their friend.

Afterward, Lily helped in the kitchen until she began to feel tired, then she lay down in the guest room, with the door shut. When she woke up, the light outside had faded, the room had grown dim and pink. Lily could hear a breeze rustling the vines around the windows. She decided to find Tom.

Almost everyone had left, except for a few people Lily didn't know, who lingered in the kitchen, washing dishes, talking, drinking scotch out of small juice glasses. Lily considered joining them and then thought better of it.

Through the window in the dining room she saw McPherson and Thompkins, Tom and Charlie, Barbara and Miss Betty, Bishop Spencer and Jeffrey Tatum, sitting together in the garden. It occurred to Lily that most of that group—she didn't know about Thompkins—believed some version of what Charlie believed, and they were all smart people, people she admired. And Anna had believed it, too; despite everything in her life, she had believed that the world is good. As Lily watched, she guessed McPherson was telling a long story, because she could see the looks on the faces around him—slightly numbed; appreciative, but numbed.

She walked out the front door and joined them. Tom brought her a white plastic lawn chair, and she settled in between him and Thompkins. McPherson started again—something to do with Anna and him, some escapade of theirs involving the college administration and an all-night, candlelight vigil.

The setting sun cast long shadows across the lawn. Lily thought she could smell the damp earth and a faint scent of hyacinth. She listened to a pair of mourning doves nearby. In the fading pink light, the faces of the people around her looked a little younger, a little less sad and worried. She closed her eyes, leaned her head back, and listened to the end of McPherson's long story.

ACKNOWLEDGMENTS

Many people contributed to this book. For their generosity, time, and expertise, I thank Linda Bamber, Linda Macmillan, Linda Mizell, and Shelley Evans, for her great sense of story; from the Boston Police Department, Sergeant Margot Hill, Bruce Blake, Lieutenant Rachel Keefe, and Officer Ted Lewis, truly an officer and a gentleman; from the Williamstown Police Department, Chief Parker, who bears no resemblance to Chief Miller in this book and who seems to be, in fact, his opposite—that is, a man of integrity and dedication; John Traficonte; Neal Lerner; David Siegenthaller; as ever, my agent, Gail Hochman, and my editor, Martha Bushko, two of the best; my father-in-law, Herschel McFarland; my father, Thomas Walter Blake; my sister, Tessa Blake; my children, Katharine and Sam; and my husband, Dennis McFarland, a partner in every good sense of the word.